RACHEL GIBSON

"DELIGHTFULLY WACKY . . .
[GIBSON'S] A WINNER."
Detroit Free Press

"WITH HUMOR AND ELOQUENT PROSE,
GIBSON BRINGS SUBSTANCE AND DEPTH TO . . .
MODERN ROMANCE."
Publishers Weekly (★Starred Review★)

"A PERFECT 10."
Romance Reviews Today

"EDGY, SEXY, FAST-PACED ROMANCE."
Jayne Ann Krentz

"SEXUAL TENSION SO HOT
YOUR PALMS WILL SWEAT."
Booklist

D0028238

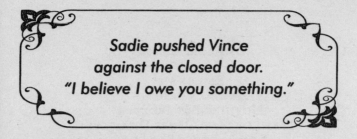

Sadie pushed Vince against the closed door. "I believe I owe you something."

She slid her hands up his chest. "When we were in the bride's room, I ran out and didn't say thank you." She pressed into him and kissed the side of his neck. "I was raised with better manners." She pulled at the bottom of his shirt. "You smell good. Thank you."

"My pleasure."

"In charm school I was told to always make people feel welcome. It was pretty much a number-one rule." Her fingers lightly raked his stomach and chest as she pushed the shirt up. He sucked in a breath.

"Do you feel welcome, Vince?"

By Rachel Gibson

ATTENTION: ORGANIZATIONS AND CORPORATIONS
Most Avon Books paperbacks are available at special quantity discounts for bulk purchases for sales promotions, premiums, or fund raising. For information, please call or write:

Special Markets Department, HarperCollins Publishers, 10 East 53rd Street, New York, New York 10022-5299. Telephone: (212) 207-7528.   Fax: (212) 207-7222.

RACHEL GIBSON

RESCUE ME

AVON

An Imprint of HarperCollinsPublishers

AVON BOOKS
An Imprint of HarperCollins*Publishers*
10 East 53rd Street
New York, New York 10022-5299

Copyright © 2012 by Rachel Gibson
ISBN 978-0-06-206912-2
www.avonromance.com

First Avon Books mass market printing: June 2012
First Avon Books mass market special printing: January 2012

Avon Trademark Reg. U.S. Pat. Off. and in Other Countries, Marca Registrada, Hecho en U.S.A.
HarperCollins® is a registered trademark of HarperCollins Publishers.

Printed in the U.S.A.

10 9 8 7 6 5 4 3 2 1

RESCUE ME

Chapter One

On December third, 1996, Mercedes Johanna Hollowell committed fashion suicide. For years, Sadie had teetered on the brink—mixing patterns and plaids while wearing white sandals after Labor Day. But the final nail in her fashion coffin, worse than the faux pas of white sandals, happened the night she showed up at the Texas Star Christmas Cotillion with hair as flat as roadkill.

Everyone knew the higher the hair, the closer to God. If God had intended women to have flat hair, He wouldn't have inspired man to invent styling mousse, teasing combs, and Aqua Net Extra Super Hold. Just as everyone knew that flat hair was a fashion abomination, they also knew it was practically a sin. Like drinking before Sunday service or hating football.

Sadie had always been a little . . . off. Different. Not bat-shit crazy different. Not like Mrs. London who collected cats and magazines and cut her grass with scissors. Sadie was more notional. Like the time she got the notion in her six-year-old head that if she dug deep enough, she'd strike gold. As if her family needed the money. Or when she'd dyed her blond hair a shocking pink and wore black lipstick. That was about the time she'd quit volleyball, too. Everyone knew that if a family was blessed with a male child, he naturally played football. Girls played volleyball. It was a rule. Like an eleventh commandment: Female child shalt play volleyball or face Texas scorn.

Then there was the time she decided that the uniforms for the Lovett High dance team were somehow sexist and petitioned the school to lower the fringe on the Beaverettes' unitards. As if short fringe was a bigger scandal than flat hair.

But if Sadie was notional and contrary, no one could really blame her. She'd been a "late-in-life baby." Born to a hard-nosed rancher, Clive, and his sweetheart of a wife, Johanna Mae. Johanna Mae had been a Southern lady. Kind and giving, and when she'd set her cap for Clive, her family, as well as the town of Lovett, had been a little shocked. Clive was five years older than she and as stubborn as an old mule. He was from an old, respected family, but truth be told, he'd been born cantankerous and his manners were a bit rough. Not like Johanna Mae. Johanna Mae had been a beauty queen, winning everything from Little Miss Peanut to Miss Texas. She'd come in second place in the Miss America pageant the year she'd competed. She would have won if judge number three hadn't been a feminist sympathizer.

But Johanna Mae had been as shrewd as she'd been pretty. She believed it didn't matter if your man didn't know the difference between a soup bowl and a finger bowl. A good woman could always teach a man the difference. It just mattered that he could afford to buy both, and Clive Hollowell certainly had the money to keep her in Wedgwood and Waterford.

After her wedding, Johanna Mae had settled into the big house at the JH Ranch to await the arrival of children, but after fifteen years of trying everything from the rhythm method to in vitro fertilization, Johanna Mae was unable to conceive. The two resigned themselves to their childless marriage, and Johanna Mae threw herself into her volunteer work. Everyone agreed that she was practically a saint, and finally at the age of forty, she was rewarded with her "miracle" baby. The baby had been born a month early because, as her mother always put it, "Sadie couldn't wait to spring from the womb and boss people around."

Johanna Mae indulged her only child's every whim. She entered Sadie into her first beauty pageant at six months, and for the next five years, Sadie racked up a pile of crowns and sashes. But due to Sadie's propensity to spin a little too much, sing a little too loud, and fall off the stage at the end of a step ball change, she never quite fulfilled her mother's dream of an overall grand supreme title. At forty-five, Johanna Mae died of unexpected heart failure, and her beauty queen dreams for her baby died with her. Sadie's care was left to Clive, who was much more comfortable around Herefords and ranch hands than a little girl who had rhinestones on her boots rather than cow dung.

Clive had done the best he could to raise Sadie up a lady. He'd sent her to Ms. Naomi's Charm School to learn the things he didn't have the time or ability to teach her, but charm school could not take the place of a woman in the home. While other girls went home and practiced their etiquette lessons, Sadie shucked her dress and ran wild. As a result of her mashed education, Sadie knew how to waltz, set a table, and converse with governors. She could also swear like a cowboy and spit like a ranch hand.

Shortly after graduating from Lovett High, she'd packed up her Chevy and headed out for some fancy university in California, leaving her father and soiled cotillion gloves far behind. No one saw much of Sadie after that. Not even her poor daddy, and as far as anyone knew, she'd never married. Which was just plain sad and incomprehensible because really, how hard was it to get a man? Even Sarah Louise Baynard-Conseco, who had the misfortune to be born built like her daddy, Big Buddy Baynard, had managed to find a husband. Of course, Sarah Louise had met her man through prisoner.com. Mr. Conseco currently resided fourteen hundred miles away in San Quentin, but Sarah Louise was convinced he was totally innocent of the offenses for which he'd been unjustly incarcerated, and planned to start her family with him after his hoped-for parole in ten years.

•

Bless her heart.

Sure, sometimes in a small town it was slim pickings, but that's why a girl went away to college. Everyone knew that a single girl's number one reason for college wasn't higher education, although that was important, too. Knowing how to calculate the price of great-grandmother's silver on any given day was always crucial, but a single gal's first priority was to find herself a husband.

And Tally Lynn Cooper, Sadie Jo's twenty-year-old cousin on her mama's side, had done just that. Tally Lynn had met her intended at Texas A&M and was set to walk down the aisle in a few short days. Tally Lynn's mama had insisted that Sadie Jo be a bridesmaid, which in hindsight turned out to be a mistake. More than the choice of Tally Lynn's gown, or the size of her diamond, or whether Uncle Frasier would lay off the sauce and behave himself, the burning question on everyone's mind was if Sadie Jo had managed to snag herself a man yet because really, how hard could it be? Even for a contrary and notional girl with flat hair?

* * *

Sadie Hollowell hit the button on the door panel of her Saab and the window slid down an inch. Warm air whistled through the crack, and she pushed the button again and lowered the window a bit more. The breeze caught several strands of her straight blond hair and blew them about her face.

"Check that Scottsdale listing for me." She spoke into the BlackBerry pressed to her cheek. "The San Salvador three-bedroom." As her assistant, Renee, looked up the property, Sadie glanced out the window at the flat plains of the Texas panhandle. "Is it listed as pending yet?" Sometimes a broker waited a few days to list a pending sale with the hopes another agent would show a property and get a bit more. Sneaky bastards.

"It is."

She let out a breath. "Good." In the current market, every sale counted. Even the small commissions. "I'll call you tomorrow." She hung up and tossed the phone in the cup holder.

Outside the window, smears of brown, brown, and more brown slid past, broken only by rows of wind turbines in the distance, their propellers slowly turning in the warm Texas winds. Childhood memories and old emotions slid through her head one languid spin at a time. She felt the old mixed bag of emotions. Old emotions that always lay dormant until she crossed the Texas border. A confusion of love and longing, disappointment and missed opportunity.

Some of her earliest memories were of her mother dressing her up for a pageant. The memories had blurred with age, the over-the-top pageant dresses and the piles of fake hair clipped to her head were just faded recollections. She remembered the feelings, though. She remembered the fun and excitement and the comforting touch of her mother's hand. She remembered the anxiety and fear. Wanting to do well. Wanting to please, but never quite pulling it off. She remembered the disappointment her mother tried and failed to hide each time her daughter won best "pet photo" or "best dress" but failed to win the big crown. And with each pageant, Sadie tried harder. She sang a little louder, shook her hips a little faster, or put an extra kick into her routine, and the more she tried, the more she went off key, off step, or off the stage. Her pageant teacher always told her to stick to the routine they'd practice. Go with the script, but of course she never did. She'd always had a hard time doing and saying what she'd been told.

She had a wispy memory of her mother's funeral. The organ music bouncing off the wooden church walls, the hard white pews. The gathering after the funeral at the JH, and the lavender-scented bosoms of her aunts. "Poor orphaned child," they'd cooed between bites of cheese biscuits. "What's going to happen to my sister's poor orphaned baby?" She hadn't been a baby or an orphan.

The memories of her father were more vivid and defined. His harsh profile against the endless blue of the summer sky. His big hands throwing her into a saddle and her hanging on as she raced to keep up with him. The weight of his palm on top of her head, his rough skin catching in her hair as she stood in front of her mother's white casket. His footsteps walking past her bedroom door as she cried herself to sleep.

Her relationship with her father had always been confusing and difficult. A push and pull. An emotional tug of war that she always lost. The more emotion she showed, the more she tried to cling to him, and the more he pushed her away until she gave up.

For years she'd tried to live up to anyone's expectations of her. Her mother's. Her father's. Those of a town filled with people who had always expected her to be a nice, well-behaved girl with charm. A beauty queen. Someone to make them proud like her mother or someone to look up to like her father, but by middle school she'd tired of that heavy task. She'd laid down that burden, and just started being Sadie. Looking back, she could admit that she was sometimes outrageous. Sometimes on purpose. Like the pink hair and black lipstick. It wasn't a fashion statement. She hadn't been trying to find herself. It was a desperate bid for attention from the one person on the planet who looked at her across the dinner table night after night but never seemed to notice her.

The shocking hair hadn't worked, nor the string of bad boyfriends. Mostly, her father had just ignored her.

It had been fifteen years since she'd packed her car and left her hometown of Lovett far behind. She'd been back as often as she could. Christmases here and there. A few Thanksgivings, and once for her aunt Ginger's funeral. That had been five years ago.

Her finger pushed the button and the window slid all the way down. Guilt pressed the back of her neck and wind whipped her hair as she recalled the last time she'd seen her father. It had been about three years ago, when she'd lived in Denver. He'd driven up for the National Western Stock Show.

She pushed the button again and the window slid up. It didn't seem like that long since she'd seen him, but it had to have been because she'd moved to Phoenix shortly after that visit.

It might seem to some as if she was a rolling stone. She'd lived in seven different cities in the past fifteen years. Her father liked to say she never stayed in one place long because she tried to put down roots in hard soil. What he didn't know was that she never tried to put down roots at all. She liked not having roots. She liked the freedom of packing up and moving whenever she felt like it. Her latest career allowed her to do that. After years of higher education, moving from one university to another and never earning a degree in anything, she'd stumbled into real estate on a whim. Now she had her license in three states and loved every minute of selling homes. Well, not every moment. Dealing with lending institutions sometimes drove her nutty.

A sign on the side of the road ticked down the miles to Lovett and she pushed the window button. There was just something about being home that made her feel restless and antsy and anxious to leave before she even arrived. It wasn't her father. She'd come to terms with their relationship a few years ago. He was never going to be the daddy she needed, and she was never going to be the son he always wanted.

It wasn't even necessarily the town itself that made her antsy, but the last time she'd been home, she'd been in Lovett for less than ten minutes before she'd felt like a loser. She'd stopped at the Gas and Go for some fuel and a Diet Coke. From behind the counter, the owner, Mrs. Luraleen Jinks, had taken one look at her ringless finger and practically gasped in what might have been horror if not for Luraleen's fifty-year, pack-a-day wheeze.

"Aren't you married, dear?"

She'd smiled. "Not yet, Mrs. Jinks."

Luraleen had owned the Gas and Go for as long as Sadie could recall. Cheap booze and nicotine had tanned her wrinkly hide like an old leather coat. "You'll find someone. There's still time."

Meaning she'd better hurry up. "I'm twenty-eight." Twenty-eight was young. She'd still been getting her life together.

Luraleen had reached out and patted Sadie's ringless hand. "Well, bless your heart."

She had things more figured out these days. She felt calmer, until a few months ago when she'd taken a call from her aunt Bess, on her mother's side, informing her that she was to be in the wedding of her young cousin Tally Lynn. It was such short notice she had to wonder if someone else had dropped out and she was a last-minute substitute. She didn't even know Tally Lynn, but Tally Lynn was family, and as much as Sadie tried to pretend she had no roots, and as much as she hated the idea of being in her young cousin's wedding, she hadn't been able to say no. Not even when the hot-pink bridesmaid's dress had arrived at her house to be fitted. It was strapless and corseted, and the short taffeta pickup skirt was so gathered and bubbled that her hands disappeared into the fabric when she put them to her sides. It wouldn't be so bad if she was eighteen and going to her prom, but her high school years were a distant memory. She was thirty-three and looked a little ridiculous in her prom/bridesmaid's dress.

Always a bridesmaid. Never a bride. That's how everyone would see her. Everyone in her family and everyone in town. They'd pity her, and she hated that. Hated that she still gave a damn. Hated that she didn't currently have a boyfriend to take her. Hated it so much she'd actually given some thought to renting a date. The biggest, best-looking stud she could find. Just to shut everyone up. Just so she wouldn't have to hear the whispers and see the sideway glances, or have to explain her current manless life, but the logistics of renting a man in one state and transporting him to another hadn't been real feasible. The ethics didn't trouble Sadie. Men rented women all the time.

Ten miles outside Lovett, a weather vane and a part of an old fence broke up the brown-on-brown scenery. A barbed wire fence ran along the highway to the rough log-and-wrought-iron entry to the JH Ranch. Everything was as familiar as if she'd never left. Everything but the black truck on the side of the road. A man leaned one hip into the rear fender, his black clothing blending into the black paint, a ball cap shading his face beneath the bright Texas sunlight.

Sadie slowed and prepared to turn up the road to her father's ranch. She supposed she should stop and ask if he needed help. The raised hood on the truck was a big clue that he did, but she was a lone woman on a deserted highway and he looked really big.

He straightened and pushed away from the truck. A black T-shirt fit tight across his chest and around his big biceps. Someone else would come along.

Eventually.

She turned onto the dirt road and drove through the gate. Or he could walk to town. Lovett was ten miles down the highway. She glanced in her rearview mirror as he shoved his hands on his hips and looked after her taillights.

"Damn." She stepped on the brake. In the state only a couple of hours and already the Texas in her reared its hospitable head. It was after six. Most people would be home from work by now, and it could be minutes or hours before someone else drove by.

But . . . people had cell phones. Right? He'd probably already called someone. Through the mirror, he raised one hand from his hip and held it palm up. Maybe he was in a dead zone. She checked to make sure her doors were locked and put the car into reverse. The early evening sunlight poured through the back window as she reversed out onto the highway, then drove up alongside the road toward the big truck.

The warm light bathed the side of his face as the man moved toward her. He was the kind of guy who made Sadie a little uncomfortable. The kind who wore leather and drank beer and crushed empties on their foreheads. The kind who made her stand a little straighter. The kind she avoided like a hot fudge brownie because both were bad news for her thighs.

She stopped and hit the power button on her door handle. The window slowly lowered halfway, and she looked up. Way up past the hard muscle beneath his tight black T-shirt, his wide shoulders and thick neck. It was an hour past his five o'clock shadow, and dark whiskers shaded the bottom half of his face and his square jaw. "Trouble?"

"Yeah." His voice came from someplace deep. Like it was dragged up from his soul.

"How long have you been stuck out here?"

"About an hour."

"Run out of gas?"

"No," he answered, sounding annoyed that he might be confused for the kind of guy who'd run out of gas. Like that somehow insulted his masculinity. "It's either the alternator or timing belt."

"Could be your fuel pump."

One corner of his mouth twitched up. "It's getting fuel. No power."

"Where you headed?"

"Lovett."

She'd figured that since there wasn't much else down the road. Not that Lovett was much. "I'll call you a tow truck."

He raised his gaze and looked down the highway. "I'd appreciate it."

She punched the number to information and got connected with B.J. Henderson's garage. She'd gone to school with B.J.'s son, B.J. Junior, who everyone called Boner. Yeah, Boner. The last she'd heard, Boner worked for his dad. The answering machine picked up and she glanced at the clock in her dash. It was five minutes after six. She hung up and didn't bother to call another garage. It was an hour and five minutes past Lone Star time, and Boner and the other mechanics in town were either at home or holding down a barstool.

She looked up at the man, past that amazing chest, and figured she had two choices. She could take the stranger to her daddy's ranch and have one of her father's men take him into town, or take him herself. Driving to the ranch would take ten minutes up the dirt road. It would take twenty to twenty-five to take him into town.

She stared into the shadow cast over his profile. She'd rather a stranger didn't know where she lived. "I have a stun gun." It was a lie, but she'd always wanted one.

He looked back down at her. "Excuse me?"

"I have a stun gun and I've been trained to use it." He took a step back from the car and she smiled. "I'm deadly."

"A stun gun isn't a deadly weapon."

"What if I set it really high?"

"Can't set it high enough to kill unless there is a preexisting condition. I don't have a preexisting condition."

"How do you know all that?"

"I used to be in security."

Oh. "Well, it will hurt like hell if I have to zap your ass."

"I don't want my ass zapped, lady. I just need a tow into town."

"Garages are all closed." She tossed her phone in the cup holder. "I'll drive you into Lovett, but you have to show me some identification first."

Annoyance pulled one corner of his mouth as he reached into the back pocket of his Levi's, and for the first time, her gaze dropped to his five-button fly.

Good Lord.

Without a word, he pulled out a driver's license and passed it through the window.

Sadie might have cause to feel a little pervy about staring at his impressive package if it hadn't been sort of framed in her window. "Great." She punched up a few numbers on her cell and waited for Renee to pick up. "Hi, Renee. It's Sadie again. Gotta pen?" She looked at the hunk of man junk in front of her and waited. "I'm giving a stranded guy a ride into town. So, write this down." She gave her friend the Washington driver's license number and added, "Vincent James Haven. 4389 North Central Avenue, Kent, Washington. Hair: brown. Eyes: green. Six foot and a hundred and ninety pounds. Got it? Great. If you don't hear from me in an hour, call the Potter County sheriff's office in Texas and tell them I've been abducted and you fear for my life. Give them the information that I just gave you." She shut the phone and handed the ID through the window. "Get in. I'll drop you off in Lovett." She looked up into the shadow of his hat. "And don't make me use my stun gun on you."

"No ma'am." One corner of his mouth slid up as he took his driver's license and slid it back into his wallet. "I'll just get a duffel."

Her gaze dropped to the back pockets of his jeans as he turned and shoved his wallet inside. Nice chest. Great butt, handsome face. If there was one thing she knew about men, one thing she'd learned from being single all these years, it was that there were several different types of men. Gentlemen, regular guys, charming dogs, and dirty dogs. The only true gentlemen in the world were purebred nerds who were gentlemen in the hopes of someday getting laid. The man grabbing a duffel from the cab of his truck was too good-looking to be a purebred anything. He was likely one of those tricky hybrids.

She hit the door locks, then he tossed a green military duffel into the backseat. He got in the front, and set off the seat belt alarm, filling up the

Saab with his broad shoulders and the annoying *bong bong bong* of the belt alarm.

She put the car into drive, then pulled a U-turn out onto the highway. "Ever been to Lovett, Vincent?"

"No."

"You're in for a treat." She pulled on a pair of sunglasses and stepped on the gas. "Put on your seat belt, please."

"Are you going to zap me with your stun gun if I don't?"

"Possibly. Depends on how annoyed I get by the seat belt alarm between here and town." She adjusted the gold aviators on the bridge of her nose. "And I should warn you in advance, I've been driving all day, so I'm already annoyed."

He chuckled and belted himself in. "You headed to Lovett yourself?"

"Unfortunately." She glanced at him out of the corners of her eyes. "I was born and raised here but I escaped when I was eighteen."

He pushed up the bill of his hat and looked across his shoulder at her. His driver's license had stated that his eyes were green and they were. A light green that wasn't quite spooky. More unsettling, as he stared back at her from that very masculine face. "What brings you back?" he asked.

"Wedding." Unsettling in a way that made a girl want to twist her hair and put on some red lip gloss. "My cousin's getting married." Her younger cousin. "I'm a bridesmaid." No doubt the other bridesmaids were younger, too. They'd probably arrive with a date. She'd be the only single one. Old and single. A "Welcome to Lovett, Texas, Y'all" sign marked the city limits. It had been painted a bright blue since the last time she'd been home.

"You don't look happy about it."

She'd been out of Texas too long if her "uglies" were showing. According to her mother, "uglies" were any emotions that weren't pretty. A girl could have them. Just not show them. "The dress is meant for someone ten years younger than me and is the color of Bubble Yum." She glanced out the driver's side window. "What brings you to Lovett?"

"Pardon?"

She glanced at him as they passed a used car lot and a Mucho Taco. "What brings you to Lovett?"

"Family."

"Who're your people?"

"Person." He pointed to the Gas and Go across the street. "You can drop me off there."

She cut across two lanes and pulled into the parking lot. "Girlfriend? Wife?"

"Neither." He squinted and looked out the windshield at the convenience store. "Why don't you go ahead and call your friend Renee, and tell her you're still in one piece."

She pulled to a stop in an empty slot next to a white pickup and reached into the cup holder. "Don't want the sheriff knocking on your door?"

"Not on my first night." He unbuckled the belt and opened the passenger door. His feet hit the pavement and he stood.

She could practically smell the popcorn from the Gas and Go as she punched in Renee's number. Lady Gaga's "Born This Way" played in her ear until her assistant answered. "I'm not dead." Sadie pushed her sunglasses to the top of her head. "I'll see you in the office on Monday."

The rear door opened and he pulled out his duffel. He dumped it on the curb, then closed the door. He placed his hands on the roof of the car, then leaned down and looked through the car at her. "Thanks for the ride. I appreciate it. If there's any way I can repay you, let me know."

It was the kind of thing people said and never meant. Like asking, "How are you?" when no one really gave a crap. She looked across at him, into his light green eyes and dark masculine face. Everyone in town had always said she had more nerve than sense. "Well, there is one thing."

Chapter Two

Vince Haven lowered the bill of his ball cap and watched the Saab pull out of the parking lot. Normally he didn't mind doing a favor for a beautiful woman. Especially one who'd saved him from humping it ten miles into town. Although compared to a thirty-mile jog or a hike in the Afghani mountains with at least sixty pounds on his back and enough ammo in his chest rig to blow up a small village, a ten-mile walk across the Texas panhandle was just a pleasant stroll through the country. Back in the day he'd have packed an M4A1 across his chest, his Sig on his hip, and a .45ACP 1911 custom sidearm strapped to his thigh.

He reached for his old Navy-issue pack and tucked it under one arm. He'd turned Sadie down and blamed it on not having a suit. Which was true but wasn't why he'd told her no. Blond-haired Sadie wasn't his type. She was certainly pretty enough. Beautiful really, but he liked his blondes easy. Easygoing, easy tempered, easy to be around, and easy to get in the sack. Brunettes and redheads, too. An easy woman didn't ask anything from him, like wearing a suit and attending a wedding where he knew no one. Easy didn't chew his ears off with talk of *feelings*. Easy didn't demand a commitment beyond sex, or any sort of stability, nor did easy expect the one hundred and one other things he was unable to give. Luckily for him, there were plenty of easy women who liked him as much as he liked them.

He didn't know what that said about him. Probably a lot. Probably things he wouldn't particularly like to admit. Good thing for him, he didn't particularly give a shit.

The rubber heels of his boots didn't make a sound as he moved toward the front of the store, passing a white truck with a big dent in the rear fender. The woman who'd dropped him off was far from dumb. A dumb woman wouldn't phone in his ID like he was a serial killer before she let him in her car. He'd actually been impressed by that, and the nonexistent stun gun had been a nice touch, too. He didn't know if she was easy. Sometimes smart women were just as easy as dumb, but he'd guess not. Her clothes—jeans and a big gray hoodie—hadn't given any clues, and he hadn't been able to tell if the body matched the face. Not that it mattered. Women like Sadie always wanted a relationship. Even when they said they didn't, and he wasn't in any position to commit to more than a one- or two-night stand. Possibly more if all the woman wanted was great sex.

He pulled open the front door, and the smell of popcorn, hot dogs, and Pine-Sol hit him. A cowboy stood at the counter loaded down with jerky and a twelve-pack of Lone Star, chatting it up with a woman with a pile of fine gray hair and deep wrinkles. A white "Don't Mess with Texas" T-shirt was tucked into the belted skirt beneath her breasts. She looked a bit like a skinny Shar Pei with long, dangly earrings.

"Hello, Aunt Luraleen."

"Vince!" His mother's sister glanced up from bagging the cowboy's jerky. "Well, aren't you just a handsome sight." Her blue eyes were bright as she came around the counter. She hurled herself into his chest and he dropped the pack at his feet. She wrapped her arms around as much of him as she could and squeezed him with the kind of free affection he'd never understood. His mother's Texas relatives were natural-born huggers, like it was part of them. Like it was in their DNA, but somehow neither he nor his sister had inherited the hugging gene. He raised a hand to pat her back. How many pats was enough? One? Two. He kept it at two.

She lifted her chin from his chest and looked up at him. It had been several years since he'd seen her, but she hadn't changed. "You're as big as hell and half of Texas," she said in that deep, tobacco raspy twang that had scared the hell out of him as a kid. How she'd lived so long was a testament to stubbornness rather than clean living. He guessed he'd inherited that particular strand of DNA because he hadn't exactly lived a clean life himself. "Good-lookin' as original sin, too," she added.

"Thanks." He smiled. "I get my looks from my Southern relatives." Which wasn't true. His Texas relatives were fair-skinned and redheaded. Like his sister. The only thing he'd inherited from his mother was green eyes and a penchant to roam from place to place. He got his black hair and roving eye from his father.

Luraleen gave him one last squeeze with her skinny arms. "Bend down here so I can kiss you."

As a kid, he'd always cringed. As a thirty-six-year-old man, and a former Navy SEAL, he'd endured worse than his aunt's Marlboro breath. He lowered his cheek.

She gave him a big smack, then rocked back on the heels of her comfortable shoes as the cowboy exited the Gas and Go. "Luraleen," he said as he passed.

"See ya tomorrow night, Alvin."

The cowboy colored a deep pink as he walked out the door. "Does he have a thing for you?"

"Of course." The soles of Luraleen's shoes squeaked on the linoleum as she turned and headed back behind the counter. "I'm a single woman with needs and prospects."

She was also in her late sixties with a bad smoker's wheeze and had about twenty extra years on the cowboy. Twenty hard, unattractive years. He laughed. "Aunt Luraleen, you're a cougar." Jesus, who would have thought? It just went to show that some men had no standards. Some women—mainly his sister—might consider Vince a dog but he did have his standards. Old ladies with smoker's hacks was one of them.

Luraleen's raspy laugh joined his and ended in a coughing fit. "You hungry?" She pounded on her bony chest. "I got Wound Hounds in the warmer. My jalapeño dogs are real favorites with the customers."

He was hungry. Hadn't eaten since Tulsa.

"And I got some regular all-beef franks. Folks like to load 'em up with Cheez Whiz, salsa, and chili."

Not that hungry. "Maybe I'll just have a Wound Hound."

"Suit yourself. Get a beer." She smiled and motioned toward the big coolers. "Get two and I'll join you in the back room."

While Vince's mother had been deeply religious, Aunt Luraleen had worshipped at her favorite bar with a bottle of cheap booze and a pack of smokes. He moved to the cooler and opened the glass door. Cool air brushed his face as he grabbed a couple of Shiner Blondes. He hadn't had a Shiner since he'd been in San Antonio visiting Wilson's mother. Pete Bridger Wilson had graduated BUD/S with Vince and was one of the smartest guys Vince had ever met. He'd had a big round head stuffed with everything from the trivial to the profound. He'd been a tall, proud

Texan, a teammate, and a SEAL brother. He'd also been the best and bravest man Vince had ever known, and the accident that had changed Vince's life had taken Wilson's.

On the way to the back room, Vince stuck one bottle beneath his arm and snagged two Wound Hounds out of the warming drawer. Those jalapeño and all-beef dogs rolled up and back on one of the nastiest-looking wiener grills he'd ever seen.

"I expected you hours ago," Luraleen said as he walked into the room. She sat at an old battered desk with a Marlboro clamped between her fingers. Obviously smoking in the workplace was acceptable at the Gas and Go. It probably didn't hurt that she owned the place.

He handed her the beer, and she held the neck as he twisted off the top. "I had a little trouble with my truck about ten miles outside of town." He twisted off his own top and took a chair across the desk. "It's still parked out there on the side of the road."

"And you didn't call?"

He frowned. Still unable to believe what he had to confess. "My phone's dead." He was Mr. Prepared. Always made sure his gear was in tip-top working order. There had been a time in his life when preparation had been a matter of living or dying. "I think something is wrong with the charger."

She took a long drag and blew it out. "How'd you get here? You didn't have to walk, did ya?"

"Someone stopped and gave me a lift." He pulled back the foil on his hot dog and took a bite. It wasn't the best meal, but he'd certainly eaten worse. Silkworm pupas from a street vendor in Seoul came to mind.

"Someone from around here?"

It had either been the pupas or dog meat stew. The pupas had been smaller. He swallowed and took a drink from the bottle. It had helped that he'd been blind drunk.

"Who?"

"Her name was Sadie."

"Sadie? The only Sadie from around here is Sadie Jo Hollowell, but she doesn't live in Lovett these days." Luraleen poured her beer into a Tweety Bird coffee mug. "She took off right out of high school. Abandoned her poor daddy."

"She mentioned that she doesn't live here anymore."

"Huh. Sadie's back, then." She took a drink.

"Probably on account of Tally Lynn's weddin' this weekend over at the Sweetheart Palace Weddin' Chapel at six o'clock. It's a big doin's." She set the mug on the desk. "I wasn't invited, of course. No reason I would be. Except maybe I went to school with her cousin on her daddy's side and Tally Lynn and her friends used to try and buy beer from me with fake IDs. Like I haven't known them all their lives."

Luraleen sounded bitter so he didn't mention that he'd been invited. "If you aren't invited, how do you know so much about it?" He took another bite.

"People tell me everything. I'm like a hair-dresser and bartender all rolled into one."

More likely she pried a lot. He swallowed and took a long drink of his beer. The door chimed, indicating a customer, and Luraleen snubbed out her smoke. She placed her hand on the desk and rose.

"I'm gettin' old." She moved toward the door and said over her shoulder, "Sit tight and enjoy your dinner. When I get back, we'll talk about that business proposition I have for you."

Which was why he'd driven to Texas. She'd called him a few weeks ago when he'd been in

New Orleans, helping a buddy re-side his house. She hadn't told him anything else, just that she had a proposition for him and that he wouldn't be sorry. He figured he knew what the proposition was, though. For the past five years, he'd worked a regular job in security, and on the side, he'd bought a run-down Laundromat. He'd fixed it up and turned it into a real cash-rich business. No matter the dip in the economy, people washed their clothes. With the money he'd made, he'd invested in a recession-proof pharmaceutical company. While others saw their stocks wiped out, his were up twenty-seven percent from when he'd bought in. And six months ago, he'd sold the Laundromat for a nice profit. Now he was taking his time, looking at other recession-proof stocks and cash-rich businesses in which to invest.

Before joining the Navy, he'd taken a few business classes in college, which came in handy. A few classes weren't a business degree, but he didn't need a degree to look at a situation, run a cost-benefit analysis in his head, and see how to make money.

Since Luraleen didn't seem to need highly trained security, he figured she had some sort of fixing-up job for him.

Vince took a bite and washed it down. He glanced about the office, at the old microwave and refrigerator and the boxes of cleaning products and Solo cups. The old olive-colored counters and ancient cabinets. The place was run-down, that was for sure. It could use a coat of paint and new ceramic floor tiles. The counters here and in the store needed a sledgehammer.

He polished off a Wound Hound and balled the foil hot dog wrapper in his hand. At the moment, he had the time to help out his aunt. Since leaving his security job in Seattle a few months ago, he had some time on his hands. Since leaving the teams a little over five years ago, his future was pretty much wide open. A little too wide open.

A few months after he'd been medically retired from the SEALs, his sister gave birth to his nephew. She'd been alone and scared, and she'd needed him. He'd owed her for taking care of their terminally ill mother while he'd been gone, down range in Iraq. So he'd been living and working in Washington State, looking after his little sister and helping her raise her son, Conner. There were only a few things in Vince's life that caused him guilt; his baby sister taking care of their mother, who could be difficult at the best of times, was one of them.

That first year out had been a tough one, for him and Conner. Conner screaming from bellyaches, and Vince wanting to scream from the damn ringing in his head. He could have stayed in the teams. He'd always planned to do his full twenty. Could have waited it out until things got better, but his hearing would never be what it had been before the accident. A SEAL with hearing loss was a liability. No matter his expertise in armed and unarmed combat, his mastery of everything from his Sig to a machine gun. No matter his underwater demolitions skills nor that he was the best insertions guy in the teams, he was a liability to himself and the rest of the guys.

He'd missed that adrenaline-fueled, testosterone-driven life. Still did. But when he'd left, he took on a new mission. He'd been away for ten years. His sister, Autumn, had dealt with their mother all alone, and it had been his turn to take care of her and his nephew. But neither of them needed him now, and after a particularly bad bar brawl at the beginning of the year that had left Vince bruised and bloody and in lockup, he had needed a change of scenery. He hadn't felt that kind of rage in a long time. The pent-up kind just beneath the surface of his flesh, like a pressure cooker. The kind that blew him apart if he let it, which he never did. Or at least hadn't for a very long time.

He tossed the foil into the garbage can and started on the second hot dog. For the past three months, he'd been traveling a lot, but even after months of reflection, he still wasn't real clear on why he'd taken on a bar filled with bikers. He wasn't real clear on who had started it, but he was clear about waking up in jail with a sore face and ribs, and a couple of battery charges. The charges had all been dropped, thanks to a good lawyer and his sparkling military record, but he'd been guilty. As sin. He knew he hadn't picked the fight, never did. He never went looking for a fight, either, but he always knew where to find one.

He reached for the beer and raised it to his mouth. His sister liked to tell him that he had anger problems, but she was wrong. He swallowed and set the beer on the desk. He had no problem with his anger. Even when it crawled across his skin and threatened to blow, he could control it. Even in the midst of a firefight or a barroom brawl.

No, his problem wasn't anger. It was boredom. He tended to get into trouble if he didn't have a goal or mission. Something to do with his head and hands, and even though he'd had his day job and the Laundromat to fill up his time, he'd felt at loose ends since his sister had decided to remarry the son of a bitch ex of hers. Now that the SOB was back in the picture, Vince was out of one of his jobs.

He took a bite and chewed. Deep down, he knew that it was best for the SOB to step up to the plate and be a good father, and he'd never seen his sister happier than the last time he'd been at her house. He'd never heard her happier than the last time he'd talked to her on the phone, but her happiness had created a big vacuum in Vince's life. A vacuum he hadn't felt since he'd left the teams. A vacuum that he'd filled at the time with family and work. A vacuum he'd been trying to fill this time with driving across the country visiting buddies who understood.

The squeak of Luraleen's shoes and her smoker's hack announced her entry into the office. "That was Bessie Cooper, Tally Lynn's mama. The weddin's got her nervous as a cat with a long tail." She moved around the side of the desk and lowered herself into the rolling chair. "I told her Sadie made it to town." She lit the snubbed-out smoke and grabbed her Tweety mug. As a kid, Luraleen had always brought him candy cigarettes when she'd visited. His mother had thrown a fit, which Vince suspected was why his aunt had done it, but he'd always loved his pack of wintergreen Kings. "She'd wanted to know if Sadie had packed on the pounds, like the women on her daddy's side tend to do."

"She hadn't looked fat to me. Of course I didn't get a real good look at her." The most memorable thing about Sadie had been the way her blue eyes had gotten all wide and dreamy when she'd talked about zapping his ass with her imaginary stun gun.

Luraleen took a drag and blew it toward the ceiling. "Bessie says Sadie still isn't married."

Vince shrugged and took a bite. "Why did you call me a month ago?" he asked, changing the subject. Talk of marriage usually led to talk of when *he* was getting married, and that just wasn't in his foreseeable future. Not that he hadn't thought about it, but being in the military, where the divorce rate was high, not to mention his own parents' divorce, he'd just never met a woman who made him want to risk it. Of course, that could have something to do with his preference for women with low expectations. "What's on your mind?"

"Your daddy told me he called you." Luraleen set the cigarette in the ashtray and a curl of smoke trailed upward.

"Yeah. He did. About four months ago." After twenty-six years the old man had called and evidently wanted to be a dad. "I'm surprised he called you, though."

"I was surprised, too. Shoot, I haven't talked to Big Vin since he left your mama." She took a drag off her cig and blew it out in a thick stream. "He called 'cause he thought I could talk sense into you. He said you wouldn't hear him out."

Vince had heard him out. He'd sat in the old man's living room and listened for an hour before he'd heard enough and left. "He shouldn't have bothered you." Vince took a long drink from the bottle and sat back in the chair. "Did you tell him to fuck himself?"

"Pert near." She grabbed her mug. "Is that about what you told him?"

"Not about. That's exactly what I told him."

"You don't want to reconsider?"

"No." Forgiveness wasn't easy for him. It was something he had to work at, but Vincent Haven Senior was one person who wasn't worth the hard work he'd have to put into it. "Is that why you called me to come here? I thought you had a proposition for me."

"I do." She took a drink and swallowed. "I'm getting old, and I want to retire." She set the mug on the desk and closed one eye against the smoke curling from the end of her cigarette. "I want to travel."

"Sounds reasonable." He'd traveled the world. Some places were pure hell. Others so beautiful they stole his breath. He'd been thinking about going back to some of those places as a civilian. Maybe that was exactly what he needed. He had no strings now. He could go wherever he wanted. Whenever he wanted. For however long he wanted to stay. "What can I do to help?"

"You can buy the Gas and Go, is all."

Chapter Three

He'd turned her down. She'd asked a stranger to take her to her young cousin's wedding and he'd turned her down flat.

"Don't own a suit," was all he'd said before he'd walked away. Even if she hadn't seen his driver's license or heard the lack of twang in his voice, she would have known he wasn't a native Texan because he hadn't even bothered with a good lie. Something like his dog died and he was grieving or that he was scheduled to donate a kidney tomorrow.

The setting sun bathed the JH in bright orange and gold and filtered through the fine plumes of dust disturbed by the Saab's tires. He'd made the offer to repay her, but of course he hadn't meant it. Asking him had been a dumb, impulsive idea.

And dumb, impulsive ideas always got her into trouble. So, if she looked at it that way, Vince the stranded guy had done her a favor. After all, what was she supposed to do with a huge, enormously hot stranger all night long once he'd served her purpose? She clearly hadn't thought it through before she'd asked.

The dirt road to the JH took ten to twenty minutes depending on how recently the road had been graded and the type of vehicle. Any moment, Sadie expected to hear mad barking and see the sudden appearance of half a dozen or so cow dogs. The ranch house and outbuildings sat five miles back from the highway on the ten-thousand-acre ranch. The JH wasn't the largest spread in Texas, but it was one of the oldest, running several thousand head of cattle a year. The ranch had been settled and the land purchased on the Canadian River in the early twentieth century by Sadie's great-great-grandfather, Major John Hollowell. Through good times and lean, the Hollowells had alternately both barely survived and thrived, raising purebred Herefords and American paint horses. Yet when it came to securing the future of the family with a male heir, the Hollowells came up short. Except for a few distant cousins whom Sadie had rarely met, she was the last in the Hollowell line. Which was a source of grave disappointment for her father.

It wasn't quite grazing season and the cattle were closer to the house and outbuildings. As Sadie drove along the fence line, the familiar silhouettes grazed in the fields. Soon it would be branding and castration season, and since moving, Sadie did not miss the sounds and smells of that horrific, yet necessary, event.

She pulled to a stop in front of the four-thousand-square-foot house her grandfather had built in the 1940s. The original homestead was five miles west on Little Tail Creek and was currently occupied by foreman Snooks Perry and his family. The Perrys had worked for the JH for longer than Sadie had been alive.

She grabbed her Gucci bag from the backseat, then shut the car door behind her. Whippoor-wills called on a cool breeze that touched her cheeks and stole down the collar of her gray Pink hooded sweatshirt.

The setting sun turned the white stone and clapboard house golden, and she moved to the big double, rough oak doors with the JH brand in the center of each. Coming home was always unsettling. A tangle of emotion tugged at her stomach and heart. Warm feelings stirred with the familiar guilt and apprehension that always pulled at her when she came to Texas.

She opened the unlocked door and stepped into the empty entrance. The smells of home greeted her. She breathed in the scent of lemon, wood and leather polish, years of smoke from the huge stone fireplace in the great room, and decades of home-cooked meals.

No one greeted her and she moved across the knotty pine floors and Navaho rugs toward the kitchen at the back of the house. It took a full-time staff to keep the JH operating on a smooth schedule. Their housekeeper, Clara Anne Parton, kept things neat and tidy in the main house as well as the bunkhouse, while her twin sister, Carolynn, cooked three meals every day but Sunday. Neither had ever married and they lived together in town.

Sadie followed the steady *thump-thump* of something heavy being tossed about in a dryer. She moved through the empty kitchen, past the pantry, to the laundry room beyond. She stopped in the doorway and smiled. Clara Anne's considerable bottom greeted her as the housekeeper bent to pick up towels from the floor. Both twins had considerable curves and tiny waists that they liked to show off by cinching in their pants and wearing buckles the size of dessert plates.

"You're working late."

Clara Anne jumped and spun around, clutching her heart. Her high stack of black hair teetered a bit. "Sadie Jo! You scared me to death, girl."

Sadie smiled and her heart got all warm as she moved into the room. "Sorry." The twins had helped raise her and she held out her arms. "It's good to see you."

The housekeeper hugged her tight against her huge bosom and kissed her cheek. The warmth around her heart spread across her chest. "It's been a coon's age."

Sadie laughed. The twins were holdouts when it came to high hair and clichéd old sayings. And if Sadie were to mention to Clara Anne that some people might consider that old expression a little racist these days, the housekeeper would be shocked because there wasn't a racist cell in Clara Anne's body. Once, as a kid, she'd smart-mouthed Clara Anne and asked exactly how long a coon's age was. The housekeeper had looked her straight in the eye and answered seriously, "Six to eight years. That's how long a raccoon lives in the wild." Who knew there'd actually been an answer?

"It hasn't quite been a raccoon's age."

"Close." She leaned back and looked into Sadie's face. "Lordy, you look just like your mama."

Without the poise and charm and everything that made people just naturally love her. "I have Daddy's eyes."

"Yep. Blue as Texas bluebells." She ran her rough hands up Sadie's arms. "We've missed you around here."

"I missed you, too." Which was true. She missed Clara Anne and Carolynn. She missed their warm hugs and the touch of their lips on her cheek. Obviously she didn't miss it enough to move back. She dropped her hands to her sides. "Where's Daddy?"

"In the cookhouse eating with the boys. Are you hungry?"

"Starving." Of course he was eating with the ranch hands. That's where he'd usually eaten because it made sense. "Did he remember that I was coming?"

"Sure he remembered." The housekeeper reached for a stack of towels. "He wouldn't forget a thing like you coming home."

Sadie wasn't so sure. He'd forgotten her high school graduation. Or rather, he had been too busy vaccinating cattle. The care of animals had always taken precedence over the care of people. Business came first, and Sadie had accepted that long ago. "How's his mood?"

Clara Anne looked at her over the stack of towels in her arms. They both knew why she asked. "Good, now go find your daddy, and we'll catch up tomorrow. I want to hear all about what you've been doin' with yourself."

"Over lunch. Maybe Carolynn will make us her chicken salad on croissants." It wasn't something the cook made for the ranch hands. They tended to like more hearty sandwiches for lunch, like thick slices of meat on heavy bread. But Carolynn used to make chicken salad especially for Sadie's mother and later for Sadie.

"I'll tell her you mentioned it. Although I think she's already planned on it."

"Yum." Sadie took one last look at Clara Anne, then walked back into the kitchen and outside. She moved down the same concrete path she'd walked along thousands of times. Most meals were eaten in the cookhouse and the closer she got to the long cinder-block and stucco building, the more she smelled barbecue and baked bread. Her stomach growled as she stepped onto the long wooden porch. The hinges on the screen door announced her arrival, and a few of the ranch hands looked up from their plates. Roughly eight cowboy hats hung on hooks by the front door. The room looked exactly as it had the last time she'd stepped inside. Pine floor, whitewashed walls, red and white gingham curtains, and the same duo of Frigidaire refrigerators. The only thing different was the shiny new stove and oven.

She recognized a few of the men's faces as they rose to their feet. She motioned for them to remain seated and then her gaze found her father, his head bent over his plate, wearing the same classic Western work shirts he always wore. Today it was beige with white pearl snaps. Her stomach got tight and she held her breath a little. She didn't know quite what to expect. She was thirty-three and still so unsure around her father. Would he be warm or unavailable?

"Hi, Daddy."

He looked up and gave her a tired smile that

didn't quite work its way to the wrinkles at the corners of his blue eyes. "There you are, Sadie Jo." He placed his hands on the table and rose, and it seemed to take him longer than normal. Her heart fell to her tight stomach as she moved toward him. Her father had always been a thin man. Tall. Long-limbed and high-waisted, but he'd never been gaunt. His cheeks were sunken and he looked like he'd aged about ten years since she'd seen him in Denver three years ago. "I expected you about an hour ago."

"I gave someone a ride into town," she said as she wrapped her arms around his waist. He smelled the same. Like Lifebuoy and dust and the clean Texas air. He lifted one gnarled hand and patted her back. Twice. It was always twice, except on special occasions when she'd done something to garner three pats.

"You hungry, Sadie girl?"

"Starving."

"Grab a plate and sit down."

She dropped her arms and looked up into his face as a selfish fear settled on her shoulders like a thousand-pound weight. Her daddy was getting older. Looking every bit of his seventy-eight years. What was she going to do when he was gone? What about the JH? "You've lost weight."

He returned to his seat and picked up his fork. "Maybe a pound or two."

More like twenty.

She moved to the stove across the room and dished herself rice and grabbed a piece of freshly baked bread. Other than raising a few sheep and Herefords for 4–H years ago, Sadie didn't know a lot about the day-to-day running of a cattle ranch. And in the pit of her traitorous soul, down deep where she kept dark secrets, was the fact that she had no interest in knowing, either. That particular Hollowell love of the land had totally skipped her. She'd rather live in town. Any town. Even Lovett: population ten thousand.

The screened back door slammed against the frame as Carolynn Parton stepped into the cookhouse. She squealed and threw her hands in the air, and except for the prairie skirt and ruffled blouse, she looked just like her sister. "Sadie Jo!" Sadie set her plate on the chipped counter a second before she was smashed against Carolynn's big, soft bosom.

"Lord, girl, it's been a coon's age."

Sadie smiled as Carolynn kissed her cheek. "Not quite."

After a few moments of chitchat, Carolynn took Sadie's plate and loaded it with ribs. She poured a glass of sweet tea and followed Sadie across the room to the table. A few of the cowboys left, and she took a chair next to her father.

"I'll catch up with you tomorrow," Carolynn told Sadie as she set the tea on the table. Then she turned her attention to Clive. "Eat," she ordered, then walked back across the room.

Clive took a bite of cornbread. "What are your plans while you're here?"

"I have the rehearsal dinner tomorrow night and the wedding is at six on Saturday." She took a bite of Carolynn's Spanish rice and sighed. The warm comfort of the familiar settled in her stomach along with the rice. "I'm free all day tomorrow. We should do something fun while I'm here." She thought about what she and her father had done together in the past. She took another bite and had to think hard. "Maybe shoot traps or ride over to Little Tail and shoot the breeze with Snooks." She used to love to shoot traps with her daddy and ride the trail to Snooks. Not that she had that often. Usually if she nagged him, he'd make one of the hands take her.

"Snooks is in Denver looking over some stock

for me." He took a long drink from his sweet tea. "I'm leaving tomorrow for Laredo."

She wasn't even surprised. "What's in Laredo?"

"I'm taking Maribell down there to breed with a Tobiano stud named Diamond Dan."

Work came first. Come rain or shine, holiday or homecoming. She understood that. She'd been raised to understand, but . . . the JH employed a lot of people. A lot of people who were perfectly capable of dropping off a mare to be bred in Laredo. Or why not just have some of Diamond Dan's semen shipped overnight? But Sadie knew the answer to the question. Her daddy was old and stubborn and wanted to oversee everything himself, that's why. He had to see the live coverage with his own eyes to make sure he was getting the stud he paid for.

"Will you make it back for the wedding?" She didn't have to ask if he'd been invited. He was family, even if he wasn't a blood relation, and even if her mama's people really didn't care for him.

He shook his head. "I'll be back too late." He didn't bother to look heartbroken. "Snooks should be home Sunday. We can ride over then."

"I have to leave Sunday morning." She picked

up a rib. "I have a closing Monday." Renee could probably handle the closing just fine, but Sadie liked to be there just in case something unexpected came up. She paused with the rib in front of her face and looked into her daddy's tired blue eyes. He was just a few years shy of eighty. He might not be around in another five years. "I can move appointments around and leave Tuesday."

He picked up his tea, and she realized she was holding her breath. Waiting like always. Waiting for him to show her a sign, a word or touch . . . anything, anything at all that he cared what she did. "No need to do that," he said, and took a drink. Then in typical Hollowell fashion, he changed the subject away from anything that might touch on important. "How was your drive?"

"Great." She took a bite and chewed. Small talk. They were good at small talk. She swallowed past the lump in her throat. She suddenly wasn't very hungry and set her rib on the plate. "There's a black truck on the side of the road," she said, and wiped her fingers on a napkin.

"Could be one of Snooks's."

"He wasn't from around here and I dumped him off at the Gas and Go."

Her dad's shaggy white brows lowered.

"Lovett isn't the same small town as when you were growing up. You have to be careful."

Lovett was almost exactly the same. "I was careful." She told her father about taking the guy's information. "And I threatened him with a stun gun."

"Do you have a stun gun?"

"No."

"I'll get your twenty-two out of the safe." Which she supposed was her daddy's way of saying he cared if a serial killer hacked her up.

"Thanks." She thought of Vince and his light green eyes, looking at her from the shadow of his ball cap. She didn't know what had gotten into her when she'd asked him to take her to her cousin's wedding. Her mother's people were very conservative, and she didn't know anything about him. For all she knew, he really could be a serial killer. Some sort of homicidal maniac, or worse.

A Democrat.

Thank God he'd turned her down, and thank God she'd never have to see Vincent Haven again.

Chapter Four

Sadie pulled the Saab into the Gas and Go and stopped beneath the bright lights of the gas pumps. A dull thump pounded her temples. The rehearsal dinner hadn't been the complete hell she'd feared. Just a warm-up version for the following night.

She got out of the car and pumped premium into her tank. She'd been right about one thing. All the other wedding attendants were about ten years younger than Sadie, and they all had boyfriends or were married. Some had children.

The groomsman she walked down the aisle with was Boner Henderson's cousin Rusty. She wasn't sure if Rusty was his real name or a nickname. The only thing that was for sure was that the name fit him. He had red hair and freckles and was pale as a baby's butt. He was about four inches shorter than Sadie and mentioned that maybe she should wear "flat shoes" to the wedding.

As if.

She leaned against the car and crossed her arms over her beige trench coat. A cool night breeze played with her high ponytail and she hugged herself against the chill. Her aunt Bess and uncle Jim had seemed genuinely happy to see her. During dessert, Uncle Jim stood and gave a really long speech about Tally Lynn. He began with the day his daughter was born and finished with how happy they all were that she was marrying her high school sweetheart, an all-around "great guy," Hardy Steagall.

For the most part, Sadie had evaded questions about her love life. It wasn't until the dessert plates were cleared that her uncle Frasier's wife, Pansy Jean, warmed to the topic. Thank God it had been several hours after cocktail time and Uncle Frasier had been tanked and talkative and he'd interrupted Pansy Jean with his stupid jokes. It was no secret that Frasier controlled his drinking by waiting until after five to tank up. It had been past eight when he'd unwittingly saved Sadie from Aunt Pansy Jean's interrogation.

The gas shut off and Sadie returned the nozzle to the pump. She couldn't imagine getting married so young and to someone from high school. She hadn't had a high school sweetheart. She'd been asked out, gone on some dates, but she'd never been serious about anyone.

She screwed on the gas cap, then opened her car door and grabbed her purse from the seat. She'd had her first real relationship her freshman year at UT at Austin. His name had been Frank Bassinger, but everyone called him Frosty.

Yeah, Frosty.

He'd been beautiful, with sun-kissed hair and clear blue eyes. A true Texan, he'd played football and had been clean-cut, like a someday senator. He'd taken her virginity, and he'd made it so good, she'd gone back for more that very same night.

They'd dated for almost a year and, in hindsight, he was probably the only real good guy she'd ever dated, but she'd been young and started to feel trapped and restless and wanted to move on from Frosty and Austin and Texas altogether.

She'd broken his heart, and she'd felt bad about that, but she'd been young with a wide-open future. A future even more wide-open than the flat Texas plains she'd always known.

The heels of her four-inch pumps tapped across the parking lot as she made her way to the front of the store. She wondered what had become of Frosty. Probably married to one of those perfect, perky Junior Leaguers, had two children, and worked in his father's law firm. He probably had the perfectly perfect life.

She moved between a white pickup and a Jeep Wrangler. After Frosty, she'd had a series of boyfriends at different universities. Only one of them had been what she'd consider a serious relationship. Only one of them had twisted and broken her heart like a pretzel. His name had been Brent. Just Brent. One name. Not two. No nickname, and she'd met him at UC Berkeley. He hadn't been like any guy she'd ever known. Looking back now, she could see that he'd been a rebel without a clue, a radical without a cause, but in her early twenties, she hadn't seen that. Hadn't seen that there'd been nothing behind his dark, broody moods. The son of privilege with nothing but pretentious anger against "the system." God, she'd been crazy for him. When he'd dumped her for a black-haired girl with soulful eyes, Sadie had thought she was going to die. Of course she hadn't, but it had taken her a long time to get over Brent. These days, she was much too smart to love so blindly. She'd been there and done that and had no interest in emotionally unavailable men. Men like her dad who shut down when anyone got too close.

She opened the door to the Gas and Go, and a little chime rang somewhere in the store. Her nostrils were assaulted by the smell of popcorn, hot dogs, and pine cleaner. She moved down a row of chips to the glass refrigerator cases. Her last relationship had been short-lived. He'd been successful and handsome, but she'd had to kick him to the curb because his sexual technique hadn't improved after three months. Three frustrating months of him falling asleep before he finished the job. She didn't need a man for his money. She needed him for things she couldn't do for herself like lift heavy objects and knock boots.

Simple, but it was always shocking how many guys weren't that great at knocking boots. Which was just baffling. Wasn't sex their number one job? Even above actually *having* a job?

She grabbed a six-pack of Diet Coke and slid past a middle-aged cowboy reaching for a case of

Lone Star in the next cooler. Beneath his hat, his big mustache looked somewhat familiar, but she didn't stop for a close look. She was tired, and after the rehearsal dinner, preceded by lunch with the Parton twins, she was talked and tuckered out.

Tuckered out? Lord, she hadn't used, or even thought of, that expression in a raccoon's age. Maybe a raccoon and a half even.

She grabbed a bag of Chee-tos and set it by the six-pack on the counter in front of Luraleen Jinks. If it was possible, Mrs. Jinks had even more wrinkles. She wore a neon pink blouse and pink skull earrings with jeweled eyes.

"Well Sadie Jo," she greeted, her voice as rough as sixty-grit sandpaper.

"Hello, Mrs. Jinks."

"You're just as pretty as your mama."

She guessed she should return the compliment, but that would require lying skills she didn't possess. Even for a native. "Thank you, Mrs. Jinks. I really like your skull earrings." Which was still a lie but not as big as telling Luraleen she was pretty.

"Thank you. One of my gentlemen gave them to me."

She had gentle*men*? As in more than one?

"How's your daddy?" She scanned the Diet Coke and placed it in a plastic bag. "I haven't seen him in a while."

"He's good." She set her Gucci bag on the counter and pulled out her wallet.

"I hear you're in town for Tally Lynn's weddin'."

"Yes. I just came from the rehearsal dinner. Tally looked very happy." Which was true. Happy and glowing with young love.

She rang up the Chee-tos. "Vince told me you helped out and gave him a ride into town last night."

She looked up. "Vince? The guy stranded out on the highway?" The one who'd turned down the chance to escort her to her cousin's wedding? The last guy on the planet she'd hope to see again?

"Yeah. He's my nephew."

Nephew? When she'd left the JH earlier, she'd noticed that his truck was no longer on the side of the road.

Luraleen hit total. "He's in the back puttin' boxes away for me. I'll get him."

"No really I—"

"*Vince!*" she called out, then broke out in a coughing fit.

Sadie didn't know whether to run or to jump across the counter and pound on the woman's back. Running really wasn't an option, and she wondered if she pounded on Luraleen's back, would smoke signals pour out of her ears with each thump?

From the back of the store she heard the slight squeak of a door and the heavier thud of boot heels a second before the deep rumble of masculine voice. "You okay, Aunt Luraleen?"

Sadie glanced to the left, at the tall dark presence moving toward her. A shadow of black scruff covered the bottom half of his face, making his eyes a more vivid light green. If it was even possible, he looked bigger and badder than he had the night before. Without his ball cap, he was even hotter. His dark hair was cut short, about an inch shy of a crew cut.

He stopped when he saw her. "Hello, Sadie."

He'd remembered her name. "Hi, Vincent." And even though he obviously found her resistible, she once again fought the ridiculous urge to twist her hair and check her lip gloss. Which just proved to her that she needed to start thinking about a new relationship. This time with a man who was good in the sack. "I didn't see your truck on the side of the highway. So I take it you got a tow."

"Everyone calls me Vince." He continued behind the counter and stood next to his aunt. "I got a tow this morning. The alternator went out, but it should be fixed by Monday."

No doubt the guy in front of her would know what to do and get the job done. Guys like him always knew the ins-and-outs of bed. Or against the wall, on the beach in Oahu, or in the car overlooking L.A. Not that *she* knew. Of course not. "So you're here until Monday?" And why was she thinking of Vince and the sack anyway? Maybe because he looked so sackable in his brown T-shirt stretched across his hard chest.

He slid a gaze to his aunt. "I'm not sure when I'm shipping out."

Sadie pushed a twenty across the counter. She looked up into Vince's light green eyes within his dark, swarthy face. He just didn't seem like a small-town kind of guy. Especially a small-town *Texas* kind of guy. "Lovett isn't quite the Seattle area." She guessed him to be in his midthirties. The women of Lovett would *love* him, but she wasn't sure how many of those women were single. "There isn't a lot to do."

"Well, I . . . I beg to differ with you," Luraleen sputtered as she made change. "We don't have big museums and fancy art galleries and such, but there's lots of goin's and doin's."

Sadie had obviously hit a nerve. So she didn't argue that there was little in Lovett to go and do. She took her change and put it in her wallet. "I only meant that it's a family-oriented town."

Luraleen slid the cash drawer shut. "Nothing wrong with family. Family's important to most folks." She pushed the bag of Diet Coke and Chee-tos toward Sadie. "Most folks come visit their poor old daddies more than once every five years or so."

And most daddies stayed home when their daughters came to visit after five years. "My daddy knows where I live. He's always known." She felt her face turn hot. From anger and embarrassment, and she didn't know which was worse. Like most of the people in Lovett, Luraleen didn't know what she was talking about, but that didn't keep her from talking like she did know. She wasn't surprised that Luraleen knew how long it had been since her last visit. Small-town gossip was just one of the reasons she'd left Lovett and never looked back. Sadie dropped her wallet into her purse and glanced up at Vince. "I'm glad to hear you got towed into town."

Vince watched Sadie grab her bag of Diet Coke and Chee-tos. Watched her cheeks turn a darker shade of pink. There was something going on behind those blue eyes. Something more than anger. If he was a nice guy he might make an effort to think of something nice to say to soothe the obvious sting of Luraleen's comment. The woman had done him a favor, but Vince didn't know what to say, and had never been accused of being a nice guy. Except by his sister, Autumn. She'd always given him a lot more credit than he deserved, and he'd always figured if his sister was the only female on the planet who thought he was a nice guy, then he was pretty much an asshole. Which was surprisingly okay with him. "Thanks again for the ride," he said.

She said something but he didn't catch it because she turned her face away. Her blond ponytail swung as she turned on her heels and marched out the door. His gaze slid down the back of her coat, down her bare calves and ankles to a pair of red fuck-me heels.

"She always did think she was too good for her raisin's."

Vince glanced at his aunt, then his gaze returned to Sadie's back as she moved across the parking lot. He wasn't sure what raisins had to do with anything, but he was sure that he was a huge fan of fuck-me heels. "You were rude to her."

"Me?" Luraleen put an innocent hand on her skinny chest. "She said there was nothin' to do in town."

"And?"

"There's lots!" Not a gray hair on her head moved as she vigorously shook her head. "We got the Founder's Day picnic, and the Fourth of July is a big whoop-de-do. Not to mention Easter is coming up in a month." She motioned for Alvin, who stood back with his case of Lone Star. "We got some real nice restaurants and fine dining." She rang up the beer. "Isn't that right, Alvin?"

"Ruby's serves a real good beefsteak," the cowboy agreed as he handed over two folded bills. His big hat seemed to be held up by his jug-handle ears. "Seafood's not too great though."

Luraleen waved away the criticism. "This is cattle country. Who cares about seafood?"

"What are you doin' after you close up for the night, Luraleen?"

She cast a sideways glance at Vince and he tried not to notice. "I got my nephew in town."

"If you want to go out with friends, that's fine with me." After last night and most of today, he could use a break from his aunt. He still had to think over her offer. His first instinct had been to turn her down, but the more he thought about it, the more he was tempted to take her up on it. He didn't plan to stay in Lovett, Texas, for the rest of his life, but maybe he could turn the Gas and Go into another nice investment. A few minor improvements here and there, and he could sell it and make a pile of cash.

"Are you sure?"

"Yeah." He was sure. His aunt's idea of a good time was Tammy Wynette plugged into the "cassette player" and a fifth of Ten High. He wasn't much of a bourbon drinker, especially *cheap* bourbon, and he didn't know if his liver could take much more.

She slapped the change into Alvin's outstretched palm. "Fine, but make sure everything is operatin' this time or don't bother."

Operating?

Alvin turned red but managed a wink. "You got it, darlin'."

What the . . . ? Vince had been exposed to some real disturbing shit in his life, most he stored away in the black locker of his soul, but his wrinkled aunt, heels to Jesus, with Alvin was right near the top of the disturbing shit list.

Luraleen shoved the cash drawer closed and announced, "We're closin' up early. Shut down the hot dog roller, Vince!"

Less than an hour later, Vince was dropped off at his aunt's house. She'd slapped some pink, Pepto-colored lipstick on her wrinkly, horsy lips and jumped in Alvin's truck, off to do things Vince didn't even want to contemplate.

Vince was left alone to sit in an old iron chair on the screened porch. He raised a bottle of water to his mouth, then set it on the warped wood by his left foot. He'd never been good at relaxing. He'd always needed something to do. A clarity of purpose.

He tied the laces on his left running shoe and then switched to his right. When he'd been a member of the teams, there was always something that needed doing. He'd always been downrange or training and preparing for the next mission. When he'd come home, he'd kept himself busy with work and family. His nephew had been only a few months old and his sister had needed a lot of help. His purpose had been clear. There hadn't been a mental vacuum. Not a lot of time to think. About anything.

He liked it that way.

The screen door slammed behind him as he set off into the cool March air. A sliver of a moon hung in the black night crammed with stars. Seattle, New York, and Tokyo had stunning skylines, but none of them could compare with the natural beauty of billions of stars.

The soles of his running shoes thumped a silent, steady pace against the paved street. Whether in Afghanistan, Iraq, or the deck of an oilrig in the calm waters of the Persian Gulf, Vince had always found a certain peace within the dark blanket of night. Ironic, he supposed, given that, like most Special Forces, he'd often operated in the dead of night, the familiar *rat-tat* of an AK–47 in the distance, and the reassuring answer of an M4A1. This dichotomy of equal parts comfort and fear of the night was something that men like him understood: taking it to the enemy was much better than waiting around for the enemy to bring it to them.

In the calm Texas night, the only sound to reach his ears was the sound of his own breathing and a dog barking in the distance. Rottweiler maybe.

On nights like this, he could fill his head with either the future or the past. With the faces of his buddies. Those who'd made it out and those who hadn't. He could let his mind recall the guys in Team One, Alpha Platoon. Their fresh faces changed over the years by the things they'd seen and done. He'd grown up in the Navy. Grown into a man, and the things he'd seen and done had changed him, too.

But tonight he had other things on his mind. Things that had nothing to do with the past. He had to admit the more he thought about buying the Gas and Go from Luraleen, the more the idea appealed to him. He could buy it, fix it up, and sell it in a year. Or hell, he could become the next John Jackson, the owner and founder of about a hundred and fifty convenience stores throughout the Northwest.

True, he didn't know shit about convenience

stores, but John hadn't known that much, either. The guy had been a Chevron marketer from a small town in Idaho and was worth millions now. Not that Vince wanted to be a mogul. He just wasn't a suit-and-tie kind of guy. He didn't have the temperament for the boardroom. He knew himself well enough to know that he wasn't very diplomatic, if at all. He liked to cut through the bullshit and get things done. He'd much rather kick a door down than talk his way through, but he was thirty-six and his body was pretty beat up from too many years of kicking down doors, jumping from airplanes, and fighting waves like a bronc rider and dragging his Zodiac up the beach.

He passed beneath a weak streetlamp and turned north. He'd made it through BUD/S hell week, and served for ten years with SEAL Team One out of Coronado. He'd been deployed around the world, then moved to Seattle to help raise his nephew. A job that had sometimes made him long for the days of relentless sandstorms, putrid swamps, and teeth-rattling cold. He could manage one small convenience store, and truth be told, he wasn't doing anything else right now anyway.

Rescue Me

A car headed toward him and he moved closer to the curb. He hadn't felt so aimless in a long time. Not since his father had walked out on him and his mother and sister. He'd been ten when his old man walked out and never looked back. Ten when he'd first felt confused about his place in the world. He'd been too young to help his mother, been too old to cry like his sister. He'd felt helpless. A feeling he hated to this day.

At the time, they'd been living in a little house on Coeur d'Alene Lake in northern Idaho. To escape the pain of his father's abandonment and his mother's inability to cope, he'd spent most of that first summer exploring the underwater world of those freezing waters. Every morning he made his sister breakfast and watched her until his mother got out of bed. Then he put on his trunks, grabbed his fins and goggles, and pushed himself. He'd swim farther than he had the day before, dive deeper, and hold his breath longer. It was the only thing that gave him purpose. The only thing that made him feel not so helpless. The only thing he could control.

Over the next eight years, he and his mother and sister moved four more times. Sometimes they'd stay in the same state, but never in the same county or school district. Every place they moved, he got a job delivering newspapers before school. Because of his size and natural athletic ability, he'd played some football, but preferred lacrosse. During the summers he worked, and in his free time, he hung out at the closest body of water. Swimming, diving, or making Autumn pretend she was a drowning victim so he could tow her to shore. On the occasions his sister wasn't with him, he checked out the girls.

The summer of his sixteenth year, they'd been living in Forest Grove, Oregon, and he'd spent most days at Hagg Lake. He'd lost his virginity on the beach, beneath the stars and full moon. Her name had been Heather, and she'd been eighteen. There might be some people who'd consider the age difference a problem. Vince hadn't been one of them. He'd had no problem having sex all night with Heather.

He'd always known he wanted to join the military, but he'd promised his mom he'd try college first. He got a lacrosse scholarship to the University of Denver, and he'd played for two years. But he'd never really felt as if it was where he needed to be. The day he walked into a Navy recruiter's office, he felt like he was coming home. He'd taken one look at a mural of a SEAL team, deep blue ocean in the background, fast roping from a CH–53 onto the deck of a ship, and he'd felt like his whole life was on that wall.

These days, there was no clarity. No purpose. He was restless, which was never good. Restless led to bar fights and worse. And there were worse things than getting your ass kicked by a bar full of bikers. Worse things than an explosion that ended everything you worked so hard to accomplish. Worse things than the loss of hearing in his left ear.

He was a SEAL. A shadow warrior, and getting his ass kicked by nightmares, waking up freezing with a pool of sweat on his chest, was worse than anything he'd ever faced.

But was a little convenience store in bum-fuck Texas what he needed to give him clarity? Did he really want to hang out in a small Texas town? For at least a year? Selling beer and gas and Wound Hounds while fixing the place up?

He'd run the idea past his sister, Autumn. She owned a successful events planning business in Seattle, and he'd be interested to hear her take on Aunt Luraleen's offer. The last time he'd talked to Autumn, she'd been all slap-happy about planning her own wedding. To the son of a bitch ex of hers.

The same son of a bitch who'd bailed him out of jail after the biker bar butt whupping, and had given him the name of a kick-ass attorney. Which meant he owed the guy, and Vince hated owing anyone.

There were a few rules that Vince lived by, and they were set in stone. Keep your head clear and your equipment in clean working order. Never leave a buddy behind, and never leave owing anyone anything.

Chapter Five

Sadie stood to one side of the heart-shaped arbor, the second in a line of bridal attendants covered in hot-pink taffeta. The wood and wire arbor was covered in roses and tulle. Sadie fought the urge to yank up the top of her strapless dress. When she had the dress fitted, she hadn't had it on for more than a few minutes, and she'd never realized the dress was so low across her breasts. The other girls in the wedding party didn't seem to think anything of it, but Sadie had never been a fan of short and tight. It just wasn't comfortable or, in her line of work, appropriate. She wasn't used to anything that pushed her up and out, but she supposed if she were still in her early twenties, she'd think the pink taffeta dress was cute. The other wedding attendants looked cute, but she was thirty-three and felt ridiculous.

"If there is anyone who can show just cause why these two should not be joined in holy matrimony, let them speak now or forever hold their peace," the minister said as he neared the middle of the ceremony.

Directly behind Sadie, bridesmaid number three, Becca Ramsey, whispered something, then sniffed softly. The night before, Becca's boyfriend, Slade, had been caught cheating with "that slut Lexa Jane Johnson," and Becca wasn't taking it well. She'd arrived at the Sweetheart Palace Wedding Chapel with puffy red eyes and runny nose. As they'd all sat in salon chairs getting their hair and makeup done, Becca had cried and carried on until Tally Lynn had had enough. She'd stood, big hot rollers in her blond hair, one false eyelash freshly glued into place, and white "I'm the Bride" robe around her skinny shoulders.

"You will *NOT* ruin my day, Becca Ramsey!" she'd said in a voice so scary even Sadie had pushed back in her chair. Tally Lynn's eyes narrowed and a vein popped out on her smooth forehead as she pointed one perfectly manicured finger at her bridesmaid. "This is *MY* day, not yours. Everyone knows Slade'll hump any hound that'll hunt. He's been skirtin' around on you for two years. You've been puttin' up with that no-good dog, so shut the hell up about Slade. And if any of the rest of y'all are thinkin' of ruinin' my day, you can follow Becca out the dang door." Then she'd sat back down and motioned for the makeup artist to continue as if she hadn't just turned into a female Satan. "More eyeliner, please."

Sadie had smiled, proud of the fierce little cousin she didn't know very well. Proud despite the fact that Tally was making her wear a mini prom dress and big Texas hair. The kind she'd never even worn when she'd considered herself a Texan.

"You may kiss your bride," the minister announced, signaling the groom to grab Tally Lynn, bend her over his arm, and lay one on her. A little twinge of something fluttered across Sadie's heart. It wasn't envy. It was more like a reminder that someday she'd like to find someone who wanted to stand in front of a minister, promise to love her forever, and bend her over his arm.

"Ladies and gentlemen, Mr. and Mrs. Hardy Steagall."

Sadie turned and prepared to follow the bride and groom back down the aisle and into the foyer. Maybe mixed with the little twinge was that tiniest dab of melancholy.

She moved from the arbor and wove her free hand through Rusty's arm. She wasn't quite sure why she felt even the tiniest dab of melancholy. She wasn't sad about her life. She *liked* her life.

"Ready to party?" Rusty asked out of the side of his mouth as they moved down the aisle.

"Yeah." She could use a glass of wine. Maybe it was seeing her cousin and Aunt Bess and Uncle Jim so happy. Maybe it was her bubble gum dress and the small bouquet of pink and white flowers in her hand. Maybe it was being back in Lovett where the purpose in life was to marry and have children. She wasn't quite sure of the origin of her sudden mood, but felt very *single* and alone. Even Rusty was on loan to her. His girlfriend was in the crowd somewhere. As far as she knew, she and newly single Becca were the only solo girls at the Sweetheart Palace. Even her cougar aunt Charlotte had managed to find herself a date.

Sadie took her place in line for pictures. She smiled for the photographer and pretended that her mood hadn't flatlined. She was happy for her cousin. Truly. But she couldn't wait to get back to her real life where she didn't feel like quite the manless loser.

After the pictures were taken, they all moved to the dining room swathed in pink and gold and white. Tally Lynn grabbed Sadie in a tight hug against her white meringue of a dress. "I'm so glad you could come." Her face all lit up with love and plans of a happy future ahead of her, she added, "Gosh, Sadie, I just know you're next."

Her cousin meant it as a kindness, a reassurance, and Sadie pushed up the corners of her lips and managed a cheery "Maybe."

"I had you seated at a table with a couple of the aunts." She pointed to one of the round tables tricked out with roses and pink tea light centerpieces. "They're just so happy you're here and it will give y'all a chance to catch up."

"Fabulous." The aunts. Sadie walked between the tables covered in white linen and crystal, Caesar salad on each china plate. She moved slow and steady toward the inquisitioners with white cotton candy hair and red rouge on their octogenarian cheeks. "Hi, Aunt Nelma and Ivella." She placed a hand over her cleavage and bent forward to kiss each of them on their thin skin. "It's wonderful to see you two again."

"Lord, you look like your mama. Nelma, doesn't she look just like Johanna Mae when she won Miss Texas?"

"What?"

"I said," Ivella shouted, "doesn't Sadie look just like Johanna Mae!"

"Just like," Nelma agreed.

"It's the hair." She sat across from her aunts and next to a bigger girl who looked a little familiar.

"Such a sad thing," Ivella said with a shake of her head.

What was a sad thing? Her hair?

"Poor Johanna Mae."

Oh that sad thing. Sadie placed her linen napkin on her lap.

"Her heart was just too big," Nelma yelled. She might have problems with her hearing, but there was nothing wrong with her voice.

The older Sadie got, the more her memories of her mother faded. And that was a very "sad thing."

"Too big," Ivella agreed.

Sadie turned her attention to the woman on

her right and offered her left hand. "Hi, I'm Sadie Hallowell."

"Sarah Louise Baynard-Conseco."

"Oh, Big Buddy's daughter?"

"Yes."

"I went to school with Little Buddy. What's he up to these days?" She picked up her fork and took a bite of lettuce.

"He's working in San Antonio for Mercury Oil." Like all the people around Sadie, Sarah Louise's voice was thick, and words like "oil" came out sounding like "ole." Sadie used to sound like that, too, but not so much these days. "He's married and has three kids."

Three? He was a year younger than Sadie. She signaled a server, who poured her a glass of merlot. She took a long drink before she set the glass back on the table.

"How's your daddy?" Nelma loudly asked.

"Good!" She took a few more bites of her salad, then added, "He went to Laredo this morning to breed a horse."

Ivella put her fork down, a frown pulling her thin white eyebrows together. "Why on earth would he leave while you're in town?"

She shrugged, remembered her neckline, and

pulled up the top of the dress. He'd left before sunup and she hadn't even told him good-bye. She knew him well enough to know that he intended to tell her good-bye before she left Texas, but he'd put her on the back burner until he got back.

While they ate, everyone chitchatted about the wedding. The dress and vows each had written and that kiss at the end.

"Very romantic," Sarah Louise said as the salad plates were taken away and the entrée was placed on the table.

"When I married Charles Ray, we had our first kiss in front of the preacher," Nelma confessed loud enough to be heard in Dalhart. "Daddy didn't let us girls go around with the boys."

"That's true," Ivella agreed.

Sadie took a close look at the dinner plate. Steak, whipped potatoes, and asparagus tips.

"There was none of this sleeping around before the marriage!"

If not for sleeping around before the marriage, she'd still be a virgin. She took a bite of her steak. Although lately, she'd seen so little action, she might as well be a virgin. She'd reached the point in her life when quality mattered most. Not that it hadn't always mattered, but these days she'd just gotten less tolerant of lousy lays.

"Are you married?" Sarah Louise asked.

She shook her head and swallowed. "Are you?"

"Yes, but my husband lives out of town. When he gets out, we're going to start our family."

Out? "Is he in the military?"

"San Quentin."

Sadie took another bite instead of asking the obvious question. Sarah Louise provided the answer anyway.

"He's in for murder."

Sadie's shock must have shown on her face.

"He's totally innocent, of course."

Of course. "Did you know him before he . . . he . . . left?"

"No. I met him through a prison pen pal site. He's been in for ten years and has ten more to go before he's up for parole."

Good God. Sadie was always amazed that, one: any woman would marry a man in prison, and, two: she'd talk about it like it was no big deal. "That's a long time to wait for a man."

"I'll only be thirty-five, but even if it's longer, I'll wait for Ramon forever."

"What'd she say!" Nelma asked, and pointed a fork at Sarah Louise.

"She's tellin' Sadie about that murderin' man she hooked up with!"

"Well bless her heart."

Sadie kind of felt sorry for Sarah Louise. It had to be rough living in a small town and being known for marrying "that murderin' man."

Aunt Nelma leaned forward and yelled, "Do you have a boyfriend, Sadie Jo?"

"No." She raised a glass of red wine to her lips and took a sip. It was past seven and she'd actually managed to avoid that question until now. "I don't really have time for a man right now."

"Are you just being notional? Are you one of those women who thinks you don't need a man?"

Growing up, whenever her thoughts and ideas had seemed different from the herd, she'd been accused of being notional. "Well, I don't *need* a man." There was a difference between wanting and needing.

"What did she say?" Nelda wanted to know.

"Sadie doesn't need a man!"

Great. Now the whole room knew, but the aunts weren't through yet. They were such matchmakers that they looked at each other and nodded. "Gene Tanner is available," Ivella said. "Bless her heart."

Gene Tanner? The girl who wore a crew cut and flannel all through high school? "She still lives in Lovett?" Sadie would have bet good money that Gene would have moved and never come back. The girl had fit in even less than Sadie had.

"She lives in Amarillo but still visits her mama just about every weekend."

Sadie stilled and waited for the jab about her infrequent visits with her father.

"She works for the park service and probably has a good health plan."

Sadie relaxed. This was her mother's side of the family, and they'd never cared a great deal for Clive Hollowell. They'd made no secret that they'd found him too cold and unfeeling for their Johanna Mae. "Dental, do you think?" she asked to be a total smart aleck.

"I would imagine." Before Nelma could ask, Ivella cupped her hands around her mouth and yelled, "Sadie Jo wants to know if Gene Tanner has a dental plan!"

"A girl could do worse than a lesbian with a

dental plan," she mumbled, and took a bite of potato. "Too bad I'm leaving in the morning."

Sarah Louise looked a bit horrified that she might possibly be sitting next to a lesbian, but who was she to judge? She was married to "that murderin' man" who wasn't even up for parole for ten years.

After dinner, everyone followed the bride and groom into the ballroom and Sadie escaped the aunts. Beneath the room-glittering chandeliers, the newlyweds took their first turn on the dance floor to "I Won't Let Go" by Rascal Flatts. It was really a beautiful moment of young love on the brink of a wide-open future, and again, it made Sadie feel old.

She was only thirty-three. She took a glass of wine from a passing tray and stood beside a ficus tree draped in pink and white ribbon. She was old and alone at thirty-three.

Next, Tally Lynn danced with Uncle Jim to "All-American Girl." They smiled and laughed and Uncle Jim looked at his daughter with undeniable love and approval. Sadie didn't ever recall her own daddy looking at her that way. She liked to think that he had and she just didn't remember.

She turned down a dance with Rusty, mostly

because she didn't want to fall out of her dress, but also because he looked to be really into his girlfriend.

"Hey, Sadie Jo."

Sadie turned and looked into a pair of deep brown eyes. Over the sound of the band she said, "Flick?"

Her tenth grade boyfriend spread his arms wide and showed his slight paunch beneath his American flag dress shirt. "How are you, girl?"

"Good." She offered her hand but of course he grabbed her in a hug that sloshed her wine. She felt his hand on her butt and remembered why she'd dated Flick Stewart for only a short time. He was a groper. Thank God she'd never slept with him. "What have you been up to?"

"Got married and had a couple of kids," he answered next to her ear. "Got divorced last year."

Married *and* divorced? She extracted herself from his arms.

"Wanna dance?" he asked above the music.

With Flick the groper? Suddenly, hanging with her aunts sounded like a great time. "Maybe later. It was good to see you again." She moved out into the foyer and found Nelma and Ivella chatting at a table with Aunt Bess. Bess was her mother's youngest sister by ten years, which put her in her midsixties.

She sat down to take a load off her four-inch pumps, and within seconds, the three aunts started quizzing her again about her life and lack of a relationship. She took a drink of her wine and wondered how much longer she had to stay before she could go home and get out of her tight dress and shoes. Pack her bags, wait for her father to get home, and go to bed. She wanted to hit the road at daybreak.

"I'm so glad you're here, Sadie Jo," Aunt Bess said as a sad smile pulled at her lips. "It's like having a piece of Johanna Mae back."

At least it was a change of topic, but Sadie never knew what to say to that. She'd always felt like she should know, but she didn't. Like she should just naturally know how to comfort her mother's family for their loss, but she was clueless.

"I remember the night she won Miss Texas. It was in Dallas and she sang 'Tennessee Waltz' for her talent."

Ivella nodded. "She sang like an angel. Miss Patti Page couldn't have done a better job."

"Well, that's where the similarities between my mother and me end. I can't sing."

"Huh! What'd she say?"

"She said she can't carry a tune in a bucket! Bless her heart."

Aunt Bess rolled her eyes and cupped her hands around her mouth. "Where are your hearing aids, Nelma?"

"On my nightstand! I took my ears out so I wouldn't have to listen to Velma Patterson's yappy dog, Hector, all damn day, and I forgot to put 'em back in! I hate that dog! Velma makes it bark on purpose 'cause she's mean as a box of rattlers at a revival!"

A dull pain thumped Sadie's temples as the aunts bickered about hearing aids and evil dogs, but at least they'd moved off her lack of love life. For the moment, anyway.

Five more minutes, she told herself, and drained the last of her wine. She felt a warm hand on her bare shoulder and looked up past the end of her glass. Past a pair of pressed khaki pants, and blue dress shirt covering big shoulders. The collar was open around his wide neck, and she had to force herself to swallow the wine in her mouth. Her gaze continued over his square jaw and lips, to his nose, and into a pair of light green eyes.

"Sorry I'm late." His deep, mellow voice put an end to all conversation.

Sadie put her glass on the table and stood. She didn't know which she felt most. Shock or relief. Shock that he was actually at the wedding or relief that his unexpected appearance had put an end to her familial torture. All three aunts stared, wide-eyed, at the big hunk of hot male in front of them.

"I didn't think you were coming."

"Neither did I, but I guess I can't let you leave town knowing I still owed you. We wouldn't be square." He let his own gaze travel down the length of her. Over her bare throat and her breasts pushed together and encased in tight taffeta. Past her hips and down her legs to her feet. "And I had to get a good look at your Bubble Yum dress."

"What do you think?"

"About?" His gaze traveled back up her body to her eyes.

"The dress."

He laughed, a deep, rich sound that tingled her spine, for no reason other than she liked the sound. "Like you're going to a prom and need a date."

"Funny, that's how I feel."

"Who's your gentleman, Sadie Jo?"

She glanced over her shoulder and into the interested eyes of her three aunts. "This is Vince Haven. He's in town visiting his aunt Luraleen Jinks." She motioned to the three women staring back. "Vince, these are my aunts, Ivella, Nelma, and Bess."

"You're Luraleen's nephew?" Ivella struggled to her feet. "She said you were comin' to see her. It's a pleasure to meet you, Vince."

He moved around the table. "Please don't get up, ma'am." He bent over slightly and shook each aunt's hand like his mama had raised him right. Gone was his five o'clock shadow, and his cheeks were smooth and tan.

"Who is Sadie Jo's young man?" Nelma hollered.

"He's not mine. He's—"

"Luraleen's nephew, Vince!" Bess answered close to Nelma's deaf ear.

"I thought she said she liked women! Bless her heart!"

Sadie closed her eyes. *Just kill me now.* There was nothing wrong with being lesbian, but she just happened to be straight, and Nelma yelling that she liked women was as embarrassing as if she'd hollered that she liked men. It made her appear desperate. She opened her eyes and looked up into the dark, handsome face of the stranger in front of her, amusement adding a slight tilt to the corners of his mouth and creases to the corners of his eyes.

"Rescue me," she said just above a whisper.

Chapter Six

He stuck out his arm like he was used to rescuing women, and she threaded her hand between his elbow and ribs. Heat seeped through her palm and warmed her pulse. "It was nice to meet you, ladies."

"A pleasure, Vince."

"Thanks for coming."

"He's as big as Texas!"

Together the two of them moved down the hall to the ballroom, and Sadie said, "My aunts are a little crazy."

"I know a little something about crazy aunts."

Yes. He did. "Well, thank you for coming to-night. I appreciate it."

"Don't thank me yet. I haven't danced in so long, I'm not sure I remember how it's done."

"We certainly don't have to dance." She looked

down at her cleavage, then back up into his profile. With his chiseled jaw and swarthy skin and dark hair, what struck her most about Vince was that he was all *man*. A ridiculously good-looking man. "In fact, I'm afraid to raise my arms."

"Why?"

"I don't want to fall out of my dress."

He smiled and glanced down at her out of the corners of his eyes. "I promise to catch anything that falls out."

She laughed as his arm bumped hers, the brush of cotton and heat against her skin. "You'd rescue me twice in the same night?"

"It'd be tough, but I'd manage somehow." They moved into the ballroom and walked into the middle of the crowded dance floor. Beneath the glittering prisms of the crystal chandeliers, he took one of her hands in his and placed his big palm in the curve of her waist. The band played a slow song by Brad Paisley about little memories, and she slowly slid her other hand up his chest, over the hard planes and ridges, to his shoulder. Everything in her dress stayed inside, and he pulled her close, close enough that she felt the heat of his big chest, but not so close that they touched.

"But if you have to rescue me twice in one night, we won't be square," she said just above the music, and his gaze slid to her lips. "I'd owe you before I leave town."

"I'm sure you can think of something."

How? She didn't know anything about him. Other than his aunt was crazy Luraleen Jinks, he was from Washington, and he drove a big Ford. "I'm not going to wash your truck."

He chuckled. "We could probably figure out something more fun for you to wash than my truck."

She'd set herself up for that one, but hadn't her mind been running down the same track since the first or second time she'd seen him? On the side of the highway? Her window framing his package? She purposely changed the subject. "How do you like Lovett so far?"

"I haven't seen that much in the daylight." He smelled like cool night air and crisp cotton, and his breath brushed the left side of her temple when he spoke. "So it's hard to say. It seems nice at night."

"Have you been going out?" There was little to do in Lovett at night but hit the town bars.

"I run at night."

"On purpose?" She pulled back and looked into his face. "No one is chasing you?"

"Not these days." His soft laughter touched her forehead. Prisms of sharp, colored light slid across his cheeks and into his mouth when he spoke. "Jogging at night relaxes me."

She preferred a glass of wine and the entire *Housewives* franchise to relax her, so who was she to judge? "Before you got stranded on the side of the road Friday, what were you doing with yourself?"

"Traveling." He looked over the top of her head. "Visiting some buddies."

There were those in town who assumed she had a trust fund. She did not. Her daddy had wealth. She didn't. How much wealth, she didn't know, but she had a fairly good idea. "Are you a trust fund baby?" He didn't look like a man who lived off a trust fund, but traveling in a big gas-guzzling truck wasn't free, and looks got a person only so far in life. Even him.

"Pardon?" He returned his gaze to her face and watched her mouth as she spoke, which, she had to admit, she found kind of sexy. When she repeated her question, he laughed. "No. Before I left Seattle a few months ago, I worked as a security consultant at the port of Seattle. Part of my job was to identify holes and weakness in the system and report them to Homeland Security." His thumb brushed her waist through the smooth silk. "Which meant that I dressed like regular security guards or maintenance workers or truck drivers and looked for security breaches in the container terminals."

Knowing that someone was looking out for America's ports made her feel safer, and she told him so.

One corner of his mouth lifted. "Just because I filled out some paperwork doesn't mean anyone paid attention or anything changed."

Great.

"Working for the government is a lesson in frustration." He brushed her waist again, back and forth as if he was testing the smooth fabric against the print of his thumb. "Doesn't matter the branch. Same shit. Different wrapper." He folded her hand against his chest and slid his free palm to the small of her back. While the band dug into another slow song by Trace Adkins about every light in the house turned on, the unexpected pleasure of Vince's touch spread a tingling warmth up and down Sadie's spine.

He brought her a little closer and asked, "When you're not dressed in a Bubble Yum dress like a prom queen, what do you do for a living?" His warm breath touched the shell of her right ear, and the crease of his khakis brushed her bare thigh.

Maybe it was the wine, or maybe the exhaustion of the day, but she settled into his chest. "Real estate." She'd had only a few glasses of merlot, so it probably wasn't the wine. "I'm an agent." And she wasn't all that tired. Certainly not tired enough to have to rest against a hard, muscular chest. She should probably take a step back. Yeah, probably, but it felt good to be held in a pair of big arms against a big chest. His hand slid up her zipper, then back down, spreading all the tingling heat across her skin.

He turned his face into her hair. "You smell good, Sadie Jo."

So did he, and she breathed him in like a tingly drug. "The only people who call me Sadie Jo have Texas accents." She liked the way he smelled and felt against her and the way he made her heart pound in her chest, making her feel young and alive. With just a touch on her back, he did things to her body that she hadn't felt in a long time. Things she shouldn't be feeling for a stranger. "Everyone else on the planet just calls me Sadie." She slid a hand to the back of his neck and brushed his collar with her fingers.

"Is Sadie Jo short for something?"

"Mercedes Johanna." The tips of her fingers slipped across the top of his collar and touched his neck. His skin was hot, warming up the tips of his fingers. "No one has called me that since my mama died."

"How long ago did she die?"

"Twenty-eight years."

He was silent for a moment. "Long time. How'd she die?"

So long she hardly remembered her. "Heart attack. I don't remember a lot about it. Just my daddy calling her name and the sound of the ambulance and a white sheet."

"My mother died almost seven years ago."

"I'm sorry." Her knee bumped his. "Your memories are fresher than mine."

He was quiet for several more heartbeats, then added, "I was in Fallujah at the time. My sister was with her when she died."

Her fingers on his collar stilled. It had been a while, but she remembered the nightly news reports and pictures of the fighting in Fallujah. "You were a soldier?"

"Sailor," he corrected. "Navy SEAL."

She guessed she'd been schooled. "How long did you serve?"

"Ten years."

"I dated a Ranger once." For about three weeks. "He was a little crazy. I think he had PTSD."

"Happens to a lot of good guys." She was nosy enough to *want* to ask if it had happened to him, but she was tactful enough not to.

Her fingers slid into the short dark hair at the base of his skull. There was just something about a strong, capable man. Something appealing about knowing that if a girl fell and broke her leg, he could throw her over his shoulder and run twenty miles to a hospital. Or hell, make a splint out of a little mud and sticks. "The Ranger guy said that SEALs are even more arrogant than Marine Recon."

"You say that like it's a bad thing," he said next to her ear, scattering those warm tingles down her neck and across her chest. "People confuse arrogance and the truth. When President Obama ordered a counterterrorism unit to take down bin Laden, he sent three SEAL teams because we're the best." He shrugged his big shoulders. "That's not arrogance. It's the truth." The music stopped and he pulled back far enough to look down into her face.

"We should maybe get a drink."

A drink would lead to other things and they both knew it. Knew it by the way his green eyes looked into hers and how her body responded. She didn't know him. She wanted to know him, though. Wanted to know all the bad things that would feel so good. If just for a little while, but she had more sense and a lot to do in the morning. "I've got to go."

Purple and blue chandelier light sliced across his nose and cheeks. "Where?"

"Home." Where she was safe from good-looking strangers with too much charm and testosterone. "I'm leaving early in the morning and I need to spend a few hours with my daddy before I go."

She half expected him to angrily point out that he'd barely arrived at the wedding as a favor to her, and now she was leaving. "I'll walk you out."

"Thank you again for coming to my cousin's wedding," Sadie said as she and Vince moved down the hall toward the bride's room inside the Sweetheart Palace. "I feel bad that you got dressed up for so short a time."

"I'm not all that dressed up, and I owed you," he said, his deep voice filling the narrow passage toward the back of the facility.

Together they entered the bride's room, and light from the hall spilled through the door and on the rows of salon chairs and empty garment bags. Within the rectangle of hall light, her coat and overnight bag sat in one of the chairs and she moved to it. "You didn't owe me, Vince." She picked up her coat and looked at him through the salon mirror. The light cut across her throat and his chest, leaving the rest of the room in variegated shadow.

He took her coat from her hands. "We square now?"

It seemed so important to him that she nodded, realized he probably couldn't see, and said, "Yes. We're square."

He held her coat open behind her, and she threaded one arm and the other into the sleeves. The backs of his fingers brushed her bare arms and shoulders as he helped her with the coat.

Sadie pulled her hair from the collar and looked

back across her shoulder at him. Her mouth just below his, she whispered, "Thank you."

"You're welcome." His breath brushed her lips. "Are you sure you want to go home?"

No. She wasn't sure at all. She felt him bend down the second before his mouth covered hers, warm and completely male. So completely male it was like a straight shot burning its way down her chest to the pit of her stomach. The tingles he'd ignited on the dance floor flared, and she opened her mouth. His tongue swept inside, hot and wet and good. Her toes curled in her shoes and she melted back into the solid wall of him. His arms circled her waist and he held her against him. Held her tight even as he pushed her into the lush descent of pleasure. She didn't know if she would have resisted. Didn't really get the chance to think about it before he turned up the heat, giving her deep, wet kisses. She tried to catch his tongue, tried to draw him deep into her mouth as her body turned hot and liquid, wanting more. More than just his tongue deep inside.

Desire curled around her, squeezing her with so much pleasure that she didn't resist when she felt his hands slide up her waist to cup her breasts. Through the thin taffeta his hot hands turned her nipples hard and she moaned deep in her throat. A shiver worked its way up her spine, and she turned to face him.

This was all happening so fast. Too fast, and her whole world narrowed and focused on his hot mouth and warm hands, touching her breasts and softly caressing the tips of her hard nipples. His mouth continued to devour hers in hot passion and greedy hunger, and she ran her hands all over his body. His shoulders and chest. The side of his neck and through his short hair.

She was in trouble, big trouble, but she didn't care. His warm hands on her aching skin felt good. His mouth luscious, the big erection pressed into her pelvis, hard and powerful.

He moved one warm palm to the inside of her cool, bare thigh and slipped his fingers beneath the hem of her short dress. His mouth slid to the side of her neck. "You're beautiful, Sadie." His mouth opened on the side of her throat and his hand moved between her thighs.

She gasped as he cupped her crotch through the lace and silk of her panties. This wasn't happening. This shouldn't be happening. She shouldn't let this happen. Not here. Not now.

"You're wet," he said against her throat.

Liquid heat, fiery and intense, poured through her veins, and her whole world was reduced to Vince's hot mouth on her throat and his fingers pushing aside the tiny scrap of lace and silk.

She moaned and her head fell back.

"Do you like this?"

"Yes." She had to stop him. Now, before there was no stopping. He parted her flesh and stroked where she was slick and wet inside and . . . "Oh God."

"More?"

"Yes."

"Wrap your legs around my waist."

"What?" She was mindless. Mindless to anything but his pleasure-giving hand.

"Wrap your legs around my waist and I'll fuck you against the door."

"What?" She opened her mouth to tell him they couldn't do anything against the door. He had to stop. Stop before—"Oh God," she moaned as a rush of liquid fire grabbed ahold of her and burned her up from the inside out. "Don't stop, Vince." It started between her thighs and spread across her flesh. Her head spun and her ears rang as hot wave after hotter wave of intense orgasm slammed into her. "Please don't stop."

She squeezed her thighs around his pleasure-giving hand. Her body pulsed with pure lust, over and over; it rushed across her skin until the last ounce of the hot pleasure flowed from the tips of her fingers and toes. Only then did she slowly become aware of where she was and what she'd just allowed to happen. "Stop!" She stepped away. "Stop!" She pushed at his hands and chest. What was she doing? What had she done? "What are you doing?"

"Exactly what you wanted me to do."

She tugged her top up and the hem of her dress down. This was her cousin's wedding. Anyone could have walked in. "No. I didn't want that." Thank God she couldn't see his face and he couldn't see hers.

"You just begged me not to stop."

Had she? "Oh God."

"You said that a couple of times, too."

The burning in her cheeks spread to her ringing ears. She closed her coat over her dress and grabbed her overnight case. "Did anyone see us?"

"I don't know. You didn't seem too concerned about that a minute ago."

"Oh God," she said again, and raced from the room.

* * *

Sexual frustration pounded Vince's head and groin. Was she really leaving? When he wasn't finished? "Wait a minute!" he called out as the tails of her coat disappeared from sight. He stood in the bride's room in some wedding place in Texas with a huge hard-on. What the hell had just happened? He'd hardly touched her, was just getting into touching her, and she'd gone off.

"Shit." He let out a breath and looked down at himself, at the tent in the front of his pants. He'd known she'd be trouble. He just hadn't figured her for a dick tease. Not after she'd shoved her body against his chest on the dance floor. Not after she'd looked up at him like she was thinking about sex. He'd been around enough women to know when they were thinking about getting naked, and she'd been thinking about it plenty.

He sat in a salon chair, adjusted himself to the right, and then leaned his head back into the darkness. He couldn't leave. Not quite yet. Not until he wasn't leading with a hard-on. He couldn't remember the last time he'd had his hand up a girl's dress and she'd left him throbbing and alone. High school maybe.

Earlier, when he'd pulled her close so he could

hear her over the band, she'd just melted into him, reminding him that he hadn't had sex since he'd left Seattle. By the time they'd entered the room alone, he'd been half hard and he'd acted on it. He wouldn't have kissed Sadie if he hadn't looked into the mirror, into that slice of light cutting across her pretty mouth and incredible cleavage that had been riding his chest. So maybe it hadn't been one of his finest ideas, but she hadn't exactly objected, and he'd gone from half to fully stiff in less than a second.

He leaned forward and rested his forearms on his knees. Through the darkness, he looked down at the toes of his loafers. She hadn't owed him sex, but if she hadn't wanted to go heels to Jesus, she should have stopped him before he slid his hands to her full breasts. She was old enough to know where kissing and having a man's hand in her panties ended. She was old enough to know it ended in *both* people getting something out of it. And yeah, this probably wasn't the best place to get naked, but there were hotels in town. He'd seen them. He would have let her take her pick, but instead she'd run off like her tail caught on fire. Leaving him with nothing but a hard-on. Nothing but frustration. Nothing. Not even a thank-you.

The light flipped on and Vince looked up as a girl in a Bubble Yum dress walked in. She had long tubes of blond hair pinned about her head. She stopped in her tracks and her eyes widened. One hand went to the top of her strapless dress and she gasped. "What are you doing in here?"

Good question. "Meeting someone." Vince was used to thinking quick and coming up with plausible lies. He'd been trained to give up just enough information to pacify interrogators. "But I guess she must have left." He also knew how to change the subject and pointed to her dress. "I see you're in the wedding."

"Yeah. My name's Becca, what's yours?"

"Vince." He still didn't want to risk standing and scaring young Becca.

"Who were you meetin'?"

"Sadie." The dick tease.

"I just saw her leaving." She sat in the chair next to his. "She stood you up."

In ways he didn't want Becca to know about, which was why he stayed seated.

"Love sucks," she said, then, to Vince's horror, burst into tears. She shook her head and her curls bobbed as she told him all about her boyfriend, that dirty no-good dog, Slade. She rambled about

Rachel Gibson

how long they'd dated and the plans she'd had for
their future. "He ruined everything. He cheated
on me with that slut Lexa Jane Johnson!" Becca
reached for a Kleenex on the counter behind her.
"Lexa Jane," she sobbed. "She's as dumb as a wad
of hair and been rode more than a rented mule.
Why do men go for women like that?"

Instantly Vince's erection went soft and he
was almost grateful for Becca and her hysteria.
Almost, but he'd never been the kind of guy who
could tolerate emotional females.

"Why?" she asked again.

He figured that had been a rhetorical question.
Or at the very least obvious, but she was staring
at him through watery eyes like she expected an
answer. "Why do men go for easy women?" he
asked, just to make sure they were on the same
page.

"Yes. Why do guys mess around with sluts?"

He'd never liked the word "slut." It was thrown
around too much and implied that a woman was
dirty because she liked sex. Which wasn't always
true.

"Why do guys want that?"

He might be a good liar, but no one had ever
accused him of being tactful. "Because some

women are a sure thing and don't play games. You know what she wants, and it isn't dinner and a movie."

A frown puckered Becca's forehead. "Isn't that emotionally shallow for both people?"

"Yes." He placed his hands on the arms of his chair and prepared to stand. "That's exactly the point. Emotionally shallow sex. You get in, you get out, and no one gets hurt." He rose halfway out of the chair, and Becca burst into hysterics again. Shit. "Well, a . . . It was nice to meet you, Becca." This was Sadie's fault, and it was a good thing she was leaving town in the morning and he'd never see her again. He'd sincerely love to wring her neck.

"That's so immature and dis-disgusting, Vince."

It was convenient and mutually beneficial, he could have argued, but he didn't feel like a discussion on sex and morality with Becca, and he wondered how much longer he had to sit there. Thirty seconds? One minute? "Can I get you something before I go?"

"Don't go." She swallowed and shook her head. "I need someone to talk to."

What? Did he look like a girl? Or even one of

those guys who liked to chat about shit? "Why not find one of your girlfriends? I'll go find one of them if you'd like." Not that he would actually put much effort into it once he escaped out the door.

"They'll just tell me to get over it because everyone knows Slade's a dog." She shook her head again and wiped her nose. Her red watery eyes narrowed. "I want both of them to catch the crabs and die in a fiery crash."

Whoa. That was harsh and exactly why he steered a wide path around women who wanted relationships.

"I want them maimed and mangled and I have a hankering to run them over with my uncle Henry Joe's Peterbilt!"

A pain settled in the back of Vince's head and he suddenly had a hankering of his own. A hankering for the taste of gunmetal in his mouth.

Chapter Seven

The *tap-tap* of Sadie's heels echoed in the old ranch house as she followed the light toward the kitchen. She didn't even want to think about what she'd just done in the bride's room at Tally Lynn's wedding. She hadn't meant for anything to happen. She hadn't meant to embarrass herself more than she'd ever been embarrassed in her life, but it all had happened so fast. He'd kissed her and touched her and wham *bam*. It was over almost before it began.

The only bright spot, the only thing that gave her a modicum of relief, was that no one besides her and Vince knew what she'd done. After she'd run from the room, she'd said a quick good-bye to Aunt Bess and Uncle Jim, and she was sure that if anyone had seen her and Vince, it would have spread faster than a Texas wildfire. Faster than her feet could run from it.

She hadn't stuck around to say good-bye to her other relatives. She hadn't wanted to risk running into Vince. She'd send Tally Lynn and the others a nice note once she got home, excusing her rude exodus on a headache or broken ankle or heart failure. The last wasn't far from the truth. Just the thought of Vince's big, hot hands all over her made the blood rush from her head and made her feel faint out of sheer humiliation. Although if she was a man, she probably wouldn't be beating herself up about it. She'd probably consider herself "lucky" and forget it.

The quicker she got out of Texas, the better. Obviously, Texas made her lose her mind, and it just went without saying that never seeing Vincent Haven again was a big, fat bonus.

She moved past the formal dining room and into the brightly lit kitchen, with its stone floor and yellow daisy wallpaper her mother had hung in the sixties. She expected to see her father sitting at the breakfast nook, nursing a glass of sweet tea. It wasn't real late and he had probably just returned from Laredo, but instead of her father, the Parton twins sat at the nook, chipped mugs sitting on the table in front of them.

"You two are staying late tonight." Sadie slipped off her shoes, and the tails of her coat brushed the floor as she bent to pick them up. With the straps of her heels hooked in her fingers, she moved to the refrigerator. She'd said her good-byes to both of them earlier. They really shouldn't have waited for her. Nice, but unnecessary.

"Oh Sadie, I'm so glad you're finally home."

With her free hand on the refrigerator handle, she looked at the two women over her shoulder. "Why?" She glanced from one worried face to the other, and the events of the past hour melted away.

Clara Anne, the more emotional twin, burst into noisy tears.

"What?" Sadie turned toward them. "Is Daddy home yet?"

Carolynn shook her head. "No, honey. He's in the hospital in Laredo."

"Is he okay?"

Again she shook her head. "That stallion kicked him and broke some of his ribs and punctured his left lung." Her lips drew together. "He's too old to be messing with those stallions."

Sadie's shoes fell to the floor with a *thump-thump*. There had to be a mistake. Her father was always very careful around high-strung stallions because they were so unpredictable. He was as tough as an old saddle, but he was almost eighty. She shook off her coat and moved to the nook. "He's been around those horses all his life." Breeding American paint horses had always been more than just a hobby to Clive. He loved it more than raising cattle, but cattle ranching paid better. She hung the coat on the back of a chair and sat next to Carolynn. "He's always so careful." He'd been kicked and stepped on and thrown many times but never seriously hurt. Never anything that required more than a few hours in the hospital getting stitched back up. "How could something like this happen?"

"I don't know. Tyrus called a couple of hours ago with a few of the details. He said something happened with the lead rope. Your daddy was fixing it and somehow got in between Maribell and Diamond Dan."

Tyrus Pratt was a foreman in charge of the JH remuda. Which not only included the paints, but a fair number of cattle horses, too. "Why didn't anyone call me?"

"Don't have your number." Clara Anne blew her nose, then added, "We've just been sittin' here, waitin' for you to come home."

And while they'd been waiting, she'd been getting felt up by a guy she hardly knew. "What's Tyrus's number?"

Clara Anne pushed a piece of paper toward Sadie and pointed to the top. "Here's the number of the hospital in Laredo, too. Tyrus's number is below. He's staying the night at a hotel."

Sadie stood and picked up the landline hooked to the wall. She dialed the hospital, identified herself, and was connected with the emergency room doctor who initially treated her father. The doctor used a lot of big words like "traumatic pneumothorax" and "thoracic cavity," which translated meant Clive had a collapsed lung due to blunt force trauma and had a chest tube. He had four fractured ribs, two displaced, two nondisplaced, and he also had damage to his spleen. The doctors were guardedly hopeful that he wouldn't require surgery for either injury. He was currently in ICU on a ventilator, and they were keeping him deeply sedated until he could breathe on his own. The doctor's biggest concern was Clive's age and the risk of pneumonia.

Sadie was given the name and number of the pulmonologist treating her father, as well as the geriatric physician overseeing his care.

Geriatric physician. Sadie waited on hold while being transferred to the nursing station in ICU. A doctor specializing in the care of the elderly. She'd always thought of her dad as old. He'd always been older than the daddies of other girls her age. He'd always been old-fashioned. Always old and set in his ways. Always old and grouchy, but she'd never considered him *elderly*. For some reason the word "elderly" had never seemed to apply to Clive Hollowell. She didn't like to think of her father as elderly.

Her father's nurse answered questions and asked if Clive was on any medication other than the blood pressure medicine they'd found in his overnight bag.

Sadie hadn't even known he had high blood pressure. "Is Daddy on any medication other than for his blood pressure?" she asked the twins.

They shrugged and shook their heads. Sadie wasn't surprised that the women who'd known Clive Holloway for over thirty years didn't know of possible health issues. That just wasn't something her father would have talked about.

The nurse assured Sadie that he was stable and resting comfortably. She'd call if there was any change. Sadie left messages with his doctor's answering service, and made airline reservations on the first flight to Laredo, via Houston. Then she sent the Parton sisters home with the promise that she would call before her nine A.M. flight.

With adrenaline pumping in her veins and exhaustion pulling at her limbs, she moved up the back stairs to her bedroom at the end of the hall. She moved past generations of stern Hollowell portraits. As a child, she'd taken the somber faces for scowling disapproval. She felt like they all knew when she ran in the house, didn't eat her dinner, or shoved her clothes under her bed instead of putting them away. As a teen, she'd felt their disapproval when she and some of her friends played the music too loud, or when she'd crawled home after a party, or when she'd made out with some boy.

Now as an adult, even though she knew that the somber faces were more a reflection of the times, missing teeth, and bad oral hygiene, she felt the same disapproval for crawling home from her cousin's wedding. For leaving Texas and staying gone. For not knowing that her elderly father had high blood pressure and what medications he took. She had a lot of guilt about leaving and staying gone, but she felt the most guilt for not loving the ten-thousand-acre ranch that she would someday own. At least not like she should. Not like all the Hollowells staring down at her from the gallery hall.

She moved into her room and flipped on the light. The room was just as she'd left it the day she'd moved away fifteen years ago. The same antique iron bed that had belonged to her grandmother. The same yellow and white bedding and the same antique oak furniture.

She unzipped her dress and tossed it on a wingback chair. Wearing just her bra and panties, she moved down the hall to the bathroom. She flipped on the light and turned on the faucet to the claw-foot bathtub.

She caught a glimpse of her face as she opened the medicine cabinet and looked inside. The only items there were an old bottle of aspirin and a box of Band-Aids. No prescription bottles.

Her panties and bra hit the white tile floor and

she stepped into the tub. She shut the curtain around her and turned on the shower.

The warm water hit her face, and she closed her eyes. This whole night had gone from bad to worse to horrendous. Her daddy was in a hospital in Laredo, her hair was as stiff as a helmet, and she'd let a man stick his hand up her dress and down her panties. Out of the three, her hair was the only thing she could deal with tonight. She didn't want to think about Vince, which wasn't a problem because she was consumed with worry for her father.

He had to be okay, she told herself as she shampooed her hair. She told herself he would be okay when she wrapped a towel around her body and went through the medicine cabinet in his bathroom. All she found was a half tube of toothpaste and a pack of Rolaids. She told herself he'd be fine when she went to bed. She woke a few hours later and grabbed the small bag she'd packed before leaving Arizona. She told herself he was strong for his age. She called Renee on the drive to the airport and filled her in. She estimated that she'd be gone a week and instructed her assistant on what to do while she was away.

* * *

As she boarded the flight from Amarillo to Houston, she thought about all the times her father had been thrown from horses, or knocked around by twelve-hundred-pound steers. He might have walked a bit stiff afterward, but he'd always survived.

She told herself that her daddy was a survivor as she waited three hours in the Houston airport for the hour flight to Laredo. She kept telling herself that as she rented a car, plugged the coordinates into the GPS and drove to Doctor's Hospital. As she took the elevator to the ICU, she'd half convinced herself that the doctors had overestimated her father's condition. She'd half convinced herself that she'd be taking her father home that day, but when she walked into the room and saw her daddy, gray and drawn, with tubes coming out of his mouth, she couldn't lie to herself anymore.

"Daddy?" She moved toward him, to the side of his bed. He had a bruise on his cheek and dried blood at the corner of his mouth. Machines dripped and beeped, and the ventilator made unnatural sucking sounds. Her heart squeezed and she pulled a ragged breath into her lungs. Tears pinched the backs of her eyes, but her eyes remained dry. If there was one thing her father had taught her, it was that big girls didn't cry.

"Suck it up," he'd say as she lay on the ground, her bottom sore from getting bucked off one of his paint horses. And she had. She couldn't remember the last time she'd cried.

She stuffed everything way down and moved to the side of his bed. She took her father's cool, dry hand in hers. He had a pulse oximeter clipped to his index finger, turning the tip a glowing red. Had his hand looked so old just yesterday? The bones so prominent, the knuckles big? His cheeks and eyes looked more sunken, his nostrils pinched. She leaned closer. "Daddy?"

The machines beeped, the ventilator moved his chest up and down. He didn't open his eyes.

"Hi there," a nurse said as she breezed into the room. "I'm Yolanda." Happy rainbows and smiley suns decorated her scrubs; the cheery fabric was in direct opposition to the dire cast of the room. "You must be Sadie. The nurse you talked to last night told us you'd be here this afternoon." She looked at all the mechanical readouts, then checked the IV tube.

Sadie placed her father's hand on the sheet and slid out of the way. "How's he doing?"

Yolanda glanced up and read a tag on the IV bag. "Have you talked to his doctors?"

Sadie shook her head and moved to the foot of the bed. "They returned my calls while I was on the plane."

"He's doing as well as can be expected for a gentleman his age." She moved to the other side of the bed and checked his catheter bag. "We interrupted his sedation this morning. He was fairly combative."

Of course he was.

"But that's normal."

"If it's normal, why interrupt the sedation?" she asked. It just seemed unnecessary to her.

"Sedation vacations help orient him to his sur-roundings and situation, and it helps with his weaning process."

"When will he be weaned?"

"Hard to say. It'll depend on when he can sup-port his own breathing, and when he's getting enough oxygenation." Yolanda raised the head of his bed and checked a few more lines and dials. "I'll let his doctors know you're here. If there is anything you need, let me know."

Sadie took a chair next to his bed and waited. She waited until after five when the pulmonologist showed up to tell her exactly what she pretty much already knew. Clive had broken ribs and a punctured lung and a damaged spleen, and they had to wait and see how he responded to treatment. The geriatrician was more informative, although he said things that were hard to hear. Elderly patients presented a whole different spectrum of concerns, and the doctor talked to Sadie about the increased risk of acute atelectasis and pneumonia and thrombosis. People over the age of sixty were twice as likely to die from their injuries as younger patients.

Sadie scrubbed her face with her hands. She wasn't going to think about acute atelectasis and pneumonia and thrombosis. "Presuming he doesn't present those risks, how long will he have to stay in the hospital?"

The doctor looked at her and she knew she wasn't going to like the answer. "Barring a miracle, your father has a long recovery ahead of him."

Her father was old but he was very strong, and if anyone could have a miraculous recovery, it was Clive Hollowell.

That night after she left the hospital, she found a local mall. She bought underwear at Victoria's

Secret and some comfy sundresses and yoga gear at Macy's and the Gap. She'd booked a room at a Residence Inn close to the hospital and sent her new clothes to the hotel's laundry service. She checked her e-mail and read carefully through a buyer's offer on a multimillion-dollar property in Fountain Hills. She called her client with the offer, made a counter, and tightened up some of the language. She eFaxed the revised changes to the buyer's agent. She might be stuck in Laredo, but she was on top of things. She waited to hear back from the agent, then called her clients back and they accepted the deal. Renee could handle the rest of the closing, and Sadie went to bed and slept solid until eight the next morning.

Her new clothes were clean and waiting for her outside her hotel room door. She showered, did a bit of work on her computer, and was at the hospital when the doctors made their first rounds of the day. She was there when they suctioned out his breathing tube and when they restrained his hands and feet and brought him out of sedation for a brief time. They told him where he was and what had happened to him. They told him that Sadie was there.

"I'm here, Daddy," she said as he pulled at the

restraints holding his wrists. His blue eyes, wild and confused, rolled toward the sound of her voice. A distressed moan rumbled his throat as the ventilator forced air into his lungs. *Suck it up, Sadie.* "It's okay. Everything is going to be okay," she lied. As they put him back under, she leaned close to his ear and said, "I'll be here tomorrow, too." Then she wrapped her arms around herself and walked from the room. She held herself tight, just like when she'd been a kid and there'd been no one there to hold on to. When there'd been no one there to hold her whenever her life felt like it was coming apart. She moved toward a set of windows at the end of the corridor, and she looked out at a parking lot and some palm trees without seeing a thing. Her body shook and she squeezed herself tighter. *Suck it up, Sadie.* Big girls didn't cry, not even when it would have been so easy. So easy just to let it out rather than push it down deep.

She took a deep breath and let it out, and when she entered her father's room again, he was resting quietly.

The next day was much like the day before. She spoke with the doctors about his progress and care, and like the day before, she forced herself to stand by his bed as they brought him out of sedation. She was her father's daughter. She was tough, even when she was falling apart inside.

A week after the accident, Sadie had to adjust her work schedule. She talked to the broker and had all her clients moved to other agents. She had to face the fact that there would be no miracle recovery for her father. He was in for a long recovery, and she was in for a long absence from her real life.

Each day, he spent a bit more time off sedation, and they started the process of weaning him off the ventilator. When she entered the room a week and a half after the accident, the ventilator was gone, replaced by a nasal cannula. Her father lay in bed, asleep. A little touch of relief lifted her heart as she moved to the side of his bed.

"Daddy?" She leaned over him. He was still hooked to monitors and bags of saline and medication. His skin was still pale and drawn. "Daddy, I'm here."

Clive's eyelids fluttered open. "Sadie?" His voice was a painful rasp.

She smiled. "Yes."

"Why . . ." He coughed, then grabbed his side with shaky hands. "Son of a bitch!" his croaky voice swore. "Jesus, Joseph, and Mary! My god-damn side is on fire."

Yolanda, of the smiley rainbow scrubs, was back on duty. "Mr. Hollowell, do you need some water?"

"I don't need"—he broke into another cough-ing fit, and Sadie cringed—"any goddamn water. Goddamn it!"

Yolanda turned to Sadie as she poured the water anyway. "Some patients wake up cranky," she warned. "It's just stress and confusion."

No. It was just Clive Hollowell's natural dis-position.

The Monday after the ridiculous fuckery at the wedding palace from hell, Vince called a bank in Amarillo and made an appointment to talk to a business loan officer in two weeks' time. Years ago, he'd borrowed money to buy a Laundro-mat, and he knew the drill. This time, though, he wouldn't be using the VA loan program. This time he'd need more cash than the half-million-dollar cap.

In anticipation of the meeting, he got the names of a commercial inspector and appraiser and set up appointments with both. He wrote out a business plan and got his financial documents in order. Everything from his banking history, retirement savings, and stock accounts. He got the financial records for the Gas and Go for the past five years, and he had his sister go to his storage shed in Seattle and send him his tax records for the past two years. For some reason, she'd also sent a few boxes of personal stuff. Loose photos and medals and patches and commendations. The Trident Wilson's mother had given him on the day he'd buried his friend.

By the time he walked into the bank with the appraisal and inspection in hand, he was prepared. Just as he liked to live his life. Prepared. Not like a Boy Scout. Like a SEAL. If anything was going to hold back the sale, it was Aunt Luraleen's loosey-goosey way of keeping records. Her assets and liabilities sheets were a mess, but the Gas and Go had passed inspection with flying colors. Luraleen's financials might be lax, but she was in complete compliance when it came to environmental infractions. The building itself might need some attention, but the fuel tanks were solid. And the fact that Luraleen was offering the business several hundred thousand dollars below appraisal made Vince fairly confident that the loan would be approved. Of course, there were always unknowables that could stall the process.

Vince hated unknowables even more than he hated owing anyone anything.

While he waited to hear from the bank, he learned as much as he could about running a convenience store. He met the store's suppliers and Luraleen's two employees, Patty Schulz and George "Bug" Larson. Both seemed capable enough, but nether struck him as particularly having a fire in their bellies for anything. Except maybe jalapeño cheese dogs. If and when he took over the Gas and Go, Patty and Bug were going to do more for their ten bucks an hour than sit on stools and ring up cigarettes and beer. He was going to make other changes, too. First, he would take a sledgehammer to the place. As a member of the SEAL teams he'd been an insertion specialist, but he did love to demo. Second, when he reopened, the Gas and Go would close at twenty-four hundred hours. Not twenty-two-hundred or whenever the *mood* struck Luraleen.

His second week in Lovett, he took over his aunt's night shifts and the responsibility of closing the place. And over the next few nights he discovered that the people of Lovett gossiped like it was a natural reflex. Like breathing and saying y'all.

One night over a Snickers and a cup of decaf, Deeann Gunderson told him that Jerome Leon was "skirtin' around" behind his wife's back with Tamara Perdue. Deeann owned Deeann's Duds and was a pretty thirtysomething divorced mother of two. She let him know she was interested in more than a candy bar and gossip and that she was free every other weekend. As long as she wasn't looking for a daddy for her kids, he might take her up on it. He didn't have anything against kids. Just mamas who wanted a new husband.

He heard that someone ran over Velma Patterson's little dog, and that Daisy and Jack Parrish were expecting a baby girl. He learned that Sadie Hollowell was in Laredo with her sick father. Everyone seemed to have an opinion about the Hollowells in general and Sadie in particular. Some, like Aunt Luraleen, thought she was an ungrateful daughter. Others that her father was neglectful, more concerned with his cattle and horses than his own child. Whatever the opinion, they all loved to talk.

Like Vince gave a shit.

Besides the average customers who just stopped when they needed a fill-up, the Gas and Go had regulars. People who stopped in every day or so at the same time for a fountain Coke or gas or beer.

One of those regular customers who stopped by for a nightly fountain Coke turned out to be Becca Ramsey. Which he did mind.

"Vince!" she'd shrieked as if they were old friends the first time she'd seen him in the Gas and Go. "Are you stayin' in Lovett?"

He wondered if he could get away with lying to her. "For a while yet." After that, she came in for a pack of gum, a candy bar, and a Rockstar on her way home from the Milan Institute in Amarillo. Apparently young Becca was going to beauty school, and for some reason thought Vince gave a flying fuck.

"If I have to give one more old lady a perm," she said, her words drawn out, "I swear I'm goin' to flip the freak out!"

"Uh-huh." He rang up her energy drink.

"I saw Slade drivin' around in that slut Lexa Jane's truck. He's so broke down he can't even afford his own vehicle."

He felt a sudden stabbing pain in his left eye. Like a nail driven into his iris. The next day, she stopped in to tell him she'd cut her first wedge. Apparently it was a type of woman's hairstyle, and for the first time in six years, he could imagine an upside to his hearing loss. Maybe if he turned his bad ear toward her, he could block out her voice. Or maybe she'd run out of words and shut the hell up.

"And she didn't look like she had dog ears when I was done." She laughed. "You just can't believe the number of girls who can't cut a wedge."

No such luck. Vince had been trained by the finest military in the world on how to escape and evade. He could get out of tight spots, but there was no way to E and E Becca without putting her in a sleeper hold.

"Next week I'm having a birthday party."

"How old are you going to be?" he asked as he rang up her Big Hunk. Vince would guess, barely legal. Some men might find a young, attractive girl fair game. Vince wasn't one of those guys. He liked mature women who didn't weep all over him.

"Twenty-one."

When he'd been twenty-one, he'd just finished SQT and was headed to the teams. He'd been full of himself and riding high on testosterone and invincibility. He'd been arrogant and tenacious with a full bag of skills to back it all up.

"You should come and take shots with me." She dug in her wallet and handed him a five.

"I don't think so."

"Why not? We're friends now."

He made change, then looked at the silly girl in front of him. She actually thought they were friends. "Since when?"

"Since we talked at Tally Lynn's wedding. You were there for me, Vince."

Jesus, she thought he'd sat in that bride's room because of her. He'd been there because he'd had a hard-on for Sadie Hollowell and he'd had to wait it out.

"You helped me see that Slade is shallow and that I'm better off without him."

"I did?" He didn't remember saying that.

She smiled. "I want more. I *deserve* more, and I've moved on."

Suddenly he had a very uncomfortable feeling. Like someone had a bead between his eyes and he was caught completely unarmed.

The chime above the door rang and he looked from the big brown eyes in front of him to the woman strolling into the Gas and Go. Into the face of the woman who'd made his life uncomfortable in more ways than one. Her blond hair was pulled back into a loose, messy ponytail. She wore a rumpled dress and zip-up hoodie. She looked like shit, but for some reason, his body responded like he was in junior high and the prettiest girl in school just walked into sex ed class.

Chapter Eight

Sadie pushed open the door to the Gas and Go and hitched her bag onto her shoulder. She was beyond exhausted. She'd spent the past two weeks inside a hospital in Laredo, and she'd just deplaned about an hour ago in Amarillo. She'd had a four-hour layover in Dallas, and she was not only exhausted, she was cranky as hell. Her ponytail was falling to one side and her eyes were scratchy. She looked like crap and she just didn't care.

She glanced up through her scratchy eyes at Becca and beyond to the man scowling like a black storm cloud was sitting above his dark head and big shoulders. Great. Vince was still in town. She didn't have the energy to care or be embarrassed about what had happened at Tally Lynn's wedding or how she looked. She'd be embarrassed tomorrow after her brain rested and she could recall every humiliating memory of his warm mouth and hot touch.

"Hi, Sadie," Becca moved toward her and gave her a big hug like they were old friends. "I heard about your daddy. How's he doing?"

She was a little surprised by how good Becca's hug felt. "Cranky." She pulled back and looked into the younger woman's brown eyes. "Thanks for asking." The doctors said it would be a few more weeks until he could be moved to a care facility in Amarillo, followed by months of rehabilitation. "He's going to be moved to a rehab facility in Amarillo soon." Which was why she was back home. To talk to the administrator and determine what care was best for him. Best for a cranky old rancher with anger issues.

"I know you were planning on going home. Are you in town for a while now?" Becca asked.

"Yeah, probably a few more months." She was stuck in Lovett for *months*. Taking care of her father who didn't want anyone taking care of him, it seemed, least of all her. Sadie dropped her arms to her sides and moved past Becca toward the coolers. Her mind might be too tired to retrieve every memory of that night in the bride's room, but the testosterone rolling off Vince like a tsunami reminded her body in a crashing wave that created a bit of turbulence in her chest.

"The night of Tally Lynn's wedding, everyone wondered why you ran off before the bouquet toss. Now we know why you were in such a hurry."

Her tired feet stopped and she looked over her shoulder at Vince. "We do?" Had Vince told Becca, or had someone seen them in that room?

He didn't say a word. Just raised a dark brow up his forehead.

"Yeah. If my daddy had been hurt, I would have run out without saying good-bye to anyone, too."

Relief dropped her shoulders and Vince laughed. A deep, amused rumble. She was too tired to care.

"Well, I gotta go," Becca announced. "See you around, Sadie."

"Bye, Becca." She snagged a big bag of Cheetos and headed to the coolers. When she returned to the front of the store, she was alone with Vince. A tight white T-shirt hugged his big shoulders and chest and was tucked into a pair of beige cargo pants. A rack of various brands of cigarettes hung behind him. Had he looked that hot the night of the wedding? No wonder she'd let him stick his hand up her skirt.

She set her Coke and Chee-tos on the counter next to a box of Slim Jims. Hopefully, he wouldn't mention the other night. "So you work here now?"

"Yeah." He looked her up and down, his green gaze pausing for the briefest of moments on the front of her dress. "You look like shit."

"Wow." And here she'd been thinking he looked hot. "Thank you."

His long fingers punched numbers on the cash register. "Just saying maybe you should brush your hair before you go out in public."

She pulled her wallet out of her purse. "Didn't they teach you charm in SEAL school?"

"Yeah, at Camp Billy Machen. It was taught between recon and demolition."

"Well, you obviously flunked." So far so good. He hadn't brought up the other night. Talking about how bad she looked was much preferable.

"Can't flunk any part of SQT or you ring the bell." He pushed total.

"What's SQT?" She watched him shove her Chee-tos into a bag.

"SEAL qualification training."

"And exactly what do SEALs train for?" Not that she was all that interested, but it was a safe topic.

"Hunting down bad guys. Fixing the world."

"I guess they didn't teach you how to fix broken-down trucks on the side of the road. I thought SEALs were trained to go all MacGyver in any situation."

"Yeah, well, I was all out of paper clips and sticks of gum that day."

She almost smiled. "What do I owe you?"

He looked up at her and smiled, but it wasn't the nice, pleasant smile she'd seen the night of Tally Lynn's wedding. Gone was the nice guy. "At the very least, a thank-you."

She pointed at her purchases. "You want me to thank you for buying a Diet Coke and Chee-tos?"

"For the Coke and Chee-tos, five dollars and sixty cents."

She handed him six bucks.

"But you still owe me for the other night."

She guessed she'd hoped for too much. He wanted to talk about it. Fine. "Thank you."

"Too little, too late."

His gaze lowered to her mouth. The other

night she'd found him watching her lips sexy. Tonight, not so much. "How much is an orgasm worth these days?"

"That one?" She'd been raised to be nice. To be a lady, no matter how rudely she was being treated. To smile, say, "Bless your heart," and walk away, but she'd hit her quota of nice. She was all filled up with smiling at obnoxious, rude men. "Keep the change and we'll call it good."

One corner of his mouth slid up. "Honey, you think that orgasm was worth forty cents?"

"I've had better." Maybe, but none faster.

"Still worth more than forty cents. You said, 'Oh God' at least twice."

"If it'd been a really good orgasm, I would have said it more than twice."

"I barely touched you and you went off." He held out her change and dropped it in her palm. "That makes it worth more than forty cents."

She closed her hand around the coins and shoved them in the pocket of her hooded jacket. "So, I take it we're not square anymore."

His lids lowered over his light green eyes, a smile turned up his lips, and he shook his head. "Payback's hell."

She grabbed her bag as the door chime rang. She pointed to the ceiling and said, "Saved by the bell."

"For now."

"Sadie Jo?"

Sadie looked across her shoulder at the woman carrying a toddler on one hip while two other little kids trailed behind. Her blond hair had an inch of brown roots and was pulled on top of her head. "RayNetta Glenn?"

"It's RayNetta Colbert now. I married Jimmy Colbert. Remember Jimmy?"

Who could forget Jimmy Colbert? He'd had a taste for Elmer's Glue and smoked pencil shaving wrapped up in lined paper. "You have three kids?"

"And two on the way." She moved the little girl she held to one side. "Twins due in September."

"Oh God!" Sadie's mouth fell open. "Oh my God!"

"That's two 'oh gods,'" Vince said from behind the counter. "You owe that woman forty cents."

She ignored him.

"I heard about your daddy." RayNetta adjusted the toddler on her hip. "How's he doin'?"

"Better." Which was true, but still not good. "I'm moving him to a rehab hospital in Amarillo."

"Bless his heart." The two little boys behind RayNetta ran around her and headed to the candy rack. "Only one," she called after them. "Kids." She shook her head. "You married?"

There it was. "No." And before RayNetta asked. "Never been married and don't have any kids." She adjusted the plastic bag in her hand. "It was good to see you."

"Yeah. We should get together and catch up."

"I'll be in town for a while." She glanced over her shoulder. Vince had planted his hands on his hips, and her gaze climbed up the ladder of chest muscles, past his square jaw, to his green eyes. "Good-bye, Vince."

"See you around, Sadie." It wasn't a good-bye as much as a warning.

She bit her lip to keep from smiling. She supposed she should be scared or at least apprehensive. Vince was definitely big and overpowering, but she didn't feel the least threatened by him. If he'd wanted to use his strength to get a "payback," he would have at Tally Lynn's wedding.

She moved out into the deep shadows of night toward her Saab. She'd be in town for only a few days before she headed back to Laredo, so she doubted she'd run into Vince. Especially if she stayed away from the Gas and Go.

Other women might crave chocolate, but she craved Chee-tos, and on the fifteen-minute drive to the ranch, she ripped open the bag and chowed down, careful not to leave cheese fingers on her steering wheel. She cranked up her iPod and filled the car with My Chemical Romance. Sadie had been a fan since their first album, and she sang "Bulletproof Heart" at the top of her lungs. Sang like her life hadn't turned to utter crap. Sang like she was carefree.

Rocks crunched beneath her tires as she pulled to a stop in front of the dark ranch house. She hadn't let anyone know she was coming home. She didn't want anyone waiting for her. She just wanted to go to bed early.

Not a single light burned within the house, and Sadie walked carefully into the living room and flipped a switch. An enormous chandelier made of a tangle of antlers lit up the cowhide furniture and huge rock fireplace. Framed photographs of her with her mother and father were placed on the different tables. Those same photos hadn't moved since her mother's death twenty-eight years ago. Above the fireplace hung a painting of her father's biggest accomplishment and his greatest love: Admiral, a Blue Roan Tovero. He'd been Clive's pride and joy, but he'd died of colic after just five years. The day the horse died was the only time she'd ever seen her father visibly upset. He hadn't shed a tear in public, but she imagined he'd cried like a baby in private.

She made her way to the kitchen, snagged a glass of ice, and continued upstairs. She moved past the ancestral portraits and into her bedroom. A lamp sat on the stand beside her bed and she turned it on. Light spilled across the bed, and she tossed the bag from the Gas and Go on the yellow and white spread.

Everything about her room was cozy in a familiar sort of way. The same clock sat on the nightstand next to the same lamp with the same floral shade. The same painting of her and her mother when she was born still sat on the dresser next to a tin holding miscellaneous perfume samples she'd collected over the years. The same volleyball and 4–H ribbons were tacked to the corkboard next to the shelf holding all the runner-up sashes and crowns she'd won.

It was familiar, but it wasn't home. Currently,

home was a townhouse in Phoenix. She'd bought the Spanish-inspired house at the bottom of the market for an insanely reduced price. Her mortgage payment wasn't all that much, and she had enough money in her account to keep up on the payments for a while.

She was a top earner at her current brokerage and shared sixty-five-percent commissions. The agency had assured her that she always had a job with them, but she didn't want to be gone so long that her compensation package rolled back to a fifty/fifty split. She'd worked very hard for that fifteen percent increase.

The problem was, she didn't know when she would be able to return to Arizona. Four weeks? Six? She didn't know if it would be as much as two months before she was able to pick up the pieces of her life. The only real thing she did know was that she would make sure her life would be waiting for her.

Intact. As much as possible.

The next morning, she met with the administrator of the Evangelical Samaritan Rehabilitation Center in Amarillo. They assured Sadie that they were capable of providing the proper rehabilitation and care her father needed. They also assured her they were used to difficult patients. Even ones as difficult as Clive Hollowell.

A week after she spoke to them, Clive arrived in Amarillo, fifty miles southeast of Lovett, which was sixty miles closer to home. She thought he'd be happy about the move.

"What are you doing here?"

She looked up from her magazine as a male nurse wheeled her father into his room, a tank of oxygen hooked to the back of the chair. He'd been at Evangelical Samaritan for twenty-four hours and looked more drawn than before. And clearly not happier, but he was clean-shaven and his hair was wet from his bath. "Where else would I be, Daddy?" God, why did he have to hassle her every day? For once, couldn't he just be glad she was there? Couldn't he just look at her and say, "I'm glad you're here, Sadie girl." Why did he always have to act like he couldn't wait for her to leave?

"Wherever in the hell it is that you live these days."

He knew where she lived. "Phoenix," she reminded him anyway. "I brought you more socks." She held up a bag from the Target a few miles away. "The fuzzy kind with traction on the soles."

"You wasted your money. I don't like fuzzy socks." The nurse moved the footrests and he set his long, bony feet covered in the red plaid socks with the nonskid soles she'd bought him in Laredo. The nurse helped him rise from the chair. "Son of a bitch!" He sucked in a breath and sat on the edge of the bed. "Goddamn!"

When she'd been younger, the tone of his voice would have sent her from the room. Instead, she moved to the side of his bed. "What can I do for you, Daddy? Anything you need from the house? Mail? Invoices? Reports?"

"Dickie Briscoe is on his way," he answered, referring to the ranch manager. "Snooks is coming with him.

She was dismissed. "Isn't there something *I* can do for you?"

His blue eyes cut into hers. "Get me out of here. I wanna go home."

He needed too much care to go home just yet. Too much for her to return to Arizona, too. "I can't."

"Then there is nothing you can do for me." He looked behind her and smiled. "Snooks, it's about goddamn time."

Sadie turned and looked at her father's foreman. She'd known him all her life, and like her father, he was a real cowboy. Work shirt with pearl snaps, Wranglers, and boots covered in cow shit and dust. He was hard and grizzled from the Texas wind and sun and a pack-a-day habit.

"Hey, Snooks." Sadie opened her arms as she moved toward him.

"There's my girl." He was the father of six boys, in his mid to late sixties, and like Clive, was showing his age. But unlike Clive, Snooks had a belly and a sense of humor.

"You look as handsome as ever," she lied. Even on a good day, Snooks had never been handsome, mostly because he was allergic to ragweed and dust. As a result, his eyes glowed an eerie red. "How're your boys?"

"Good. I got eight grandkids."

"Good Lord!" She really was the last person in Lovett over the age of twenty-five who was childless. Her and Sarah Louise Baynard-Conseco, but that was only because Mr. Conseco was a guest of San Quentin.

"And I don't have a single one," grumbled Clive from behind Sadie.

Was that why her father was crabby all the

time? Because she hadn't spanked out six grand-children? What had been his excuse when she'd been twelve? "You've never mentioned grand-kids before."

"Didn't think I had to."

"Well, I'll let you two catch up," she said, and made her escape.

She spent the afternoon tending to exciting de-tails like having her car serviced. She was lucky enough to find a hair salon that looked halfway decent, and she made an appointment to come back and have her roots touched up. She re-turned to the hospital to check in on Clive, then drove home. She ate dinner with the ranch hands and filled them in on her father's progress.

She watched television in bed. Mindless real-ity shows with people whose lives sucked worse than hers. So she didn't have to think of the real-ity of her own sucky life.

The whir of a ceiling fan stirred the cool night air across Vince's bare chest. Slow, even breaths filled his lungs. Within the guest room of Lura-leen's seventies ranch-style house, he slept in the frilly twin bed, but behind his closed eyes, Vince was back in Iraq. Back in the huge cavity of the

C–130 Hercules, stowing the last of the team's essential gear. Dressed in light combat gear, desert khakis, and Oakley assault boots, he stowed his tired body in a thick mesh hammock. Several hours before he'd been ordered to join Team Five at the U.S. air base in Bahrain, he'd been knocking in doors and rounding up terrorist leaders in Baghdad. The more they rounded up, the more seemed to pop up in their place. Al Qaeda, Taliban, Sunni, Shiite, or a half dozen other insurgent groups filled with hate and fanaticism and hell-bent on killing American soldiers, no matter how many innocent civilians got in the way.

"Haven, you ugly son of a bitch. What are you doing up there? Jerkin' off?"

Vince recognized that voice and cracked open his eyes. He turned his head toward the bald SEAL cramming his body into a mesh seat across from him. "Sorry to disappoint you, you dirty hooker, but I already took care of my business."

Wilson shook his head. "Yeah, I heard about that ammo dump business this morning."

Vince winced. He'd been sent out with three other SEALs to secure an insurgent ammo dump and blow it the fuck up. There hadn't been time to wait for an explosive ordnance disposal tech, and the dump was small, or so they'd thought. They'd planted their own explosives and lit that building up and up and up. Concrete and dust and debris had rained down for several minutes. "We may have underestimated the English we put on it." Actually they hadn't known about a hidden room under the mud and concrete building, filled with grenades and bombs, until they'd lit it up and the explosion grew bigger and bigger and they'd dived for cover. No one wanted to talk about the oversight though. It was just a damn good thing they'd moved way back and no one got hurt.

Wilson laughed. " 'There's enough bang in there to blow us to Jesus.' " He was a lieutenant, smart as hell, and the king of movie quotes. Vince hadn't seen Pete for a while, and it was good to see his buddy.

"*Hooyah!*" The two had gone through BUD/S together, almost drowned in the surf, and had their asses chewed by Instructor Dougherty. He'd stood next to Wilson as they'd both had their Tridents pinned on their dress uniforms, and he'd stood up with Pete when Pete married his high school sweetheart. The marriage hadn't lasted past the five-year anniversary, and Vince had been there to help his buddy drown his sorrows. Divorce was a reality of military life, and operational SEALs were no exception to that reality.

The loading ramp rose, and the pilot fired up the huge turbo-prop freighter, filling the cavity with the rattle of steel and horsepower and ending any further conversation.

He fell asleep somewhere over the Gulf of Oman. The last untroubled slumber he would have for several years. Once the Hercules touched down in Bagram, his life would change forever in varied and unforeseeable ways.

His life was different now, but the dream was always the same. It started in the mountains in the Hindu Kush with him and the guys on a routine mission. Then the dream changed, with him scrambling for cover, loaded down with enough firepower to fight his way out of any Taliban fight. It ended with him kneeling over Wilson, his head spinning and ringing, nausea turning his stomach and the dark corners of his vision closing in on him as he thumped his best friend's chest and forced his own breath into Pete's lungs. The unmistakable beat of howling U.S. airpower, rotors screaming, thundering and whipping the dust into sandstorms. The ground shuddered as the military blew the hell out of slopes and crevasses of the Hindu Kush Mountains. Blood stained his hands as Vince thumped and breathed and watched the light fade from Pete's eyes.

Vince woke, his heartbeat pounding in his head as it had that day in the hell of the Hindu Kush. He stood somewhere, disoriented, his eyes wide, lungs pulling air like bellows. Where was he?

In a room. A soft streetlamp burned in the distance and lacy curtains were wrapped about his fist.

"You okay, Vince? I heard thumpin'."

He opened his mouth but a gaspy wheeze came out. He swallowed. "Yeah." He purposefully opened his shaking hands and the curtain fell to the floor, the thin rod a tinny clang.

"What was that?"

"Nothing. Everything is okay."

"Is someone climbing in your window? If so, have her use the front door."

Which would explain why she wasn't busting down his door.

"No one's in here but me. Good night, Aunt Luraleen."

"Well, night then."

Vince scrubbed his face with his hands and sat on the too small, too frilly bed. He hadn't had that dream in a while. Not for a few years now. A Navy shrink had once told him that certain things could trigger posttraumatic stress. Change and uncertainty were two of the big ones.

Vince was a SEAL. He did not have PTSD. He wasn't jumpy or nervous or depressed. He had a recurring nightmare.

One. That was it.

That shrink had also told him that he'd shut down his feelings. And that as soon as he started to feel, he would heal. "Feel to heal" had been that shrink's favorite catchphrase.

Well fuck that. He didn't need to heal from anything. He was fine.

Chapter Nine

Every year on the second Saturday in April, the Lovett Founder's Day kicked off at nine A.M. with the Founder's Day parade. Ever year, the reigning Diamondback Queen rode a huge rattlesnake made of tissue and toilet paper. Its big head and bejeweled eyes looked out at the crowd while its forked tongue flicked the morning air. The queen sat atop the coiled body, waving for all she was worth, like she was the Rose Queen making her way down Colorado Boulevard in Pasadena.

This year, the float was hauled down Main by a classic 1960 Chevy F–10 furnished by Parrish American Classics car restorers. A second restored car followed behind the float. Twenty-three-year-old Nathan Parrish drove the completely restored 1973 Camaro; its big V–8, 383 engine pounded the morning air and vibrated the Diamondback so bad the tongue fell out around Twelfth Street. Marching closely behind and sucking up fumes, the Lovett High School band played the "Yellow Rose of Texas" while the dance team shimmied in their sequins and fringe.

After the parade, Main Street was closed off to cars. Vendors' booths ran up and down both sides of the street selling everything from jewelry and hair bows to pepper jelly and knitted cozies. The beer court and food vendors were set up a block off Main on Wilson and were crammed with people from as far away as Odessa.

The Lovett Historical Society members dressed in period costumes. By noon it had warmed up to sixty-three degrees; by five, it was a balmy seventy-two and the society was looking a bit damp. In the Albertson's parking lot, artists and cloggers performed throughout the day. That night, a local favorite, Tom and the Armadillos, was set to play at one end of the big lot while a pool tournament took place at the other end.

At seven P.M., Sadie pulled her Saab into a parking slot in front of Deeann's Duds and hit the vendors down the street. What else was she going to do? Go home and stare at the walls?

Watch more television? Check out YouTube until her eyes bled? God, how many talking dog and teenage prank videos could she watch?

She needed a life beyond the rehab center. Her father had always refused to give her responsibilities at the JH. Granted, at the moment she couldn't analyze grazing reports and animal tracking data, but she'd taken plenty of college courses and was sure she could read graphs if someone took the time to show her.

There had to be something for her to do besides making her bed and washing her own dishes. Something easy. Something to keep her occupied that didn't carry with it a big weight of responsibility. The responsibility of maintaining ten thousand acres, over a thousand head of cattle, and a herd of breed horses. Not to mention two dozen or so employees. Because she was a girl, her father had never taught her the business. Beyond just the basics she learned from living at the JH for eighteen years, she didn't know a lot. She didn't know what she would do once her daddy died. She'd been thinking about it a lot lately, and just the thought of the responsibility made her fidgety and filled her with an overwhelming urge to jump in her car and get the hell out of town.

After she'd visited her dad earlier, she'd gone home and changed into jeans, blue T-shirt, and a Lucky zip-up sweatshirt with a Buddha on the back. She dug out the white cowboy boots and white Stetson she'd worn in high school. The boots were a bit tight, like maybe her feet had grown half a size, but the hat fit like she'd worn it just the day before. She found her old custom-made belt with the JH brand worked into the leather and "SADIE JO" etched in the back. It was a bit stiff, but thank God it still fit.

She might live in Arizona, but she was a Texan and Founder's Day was no joke. It was an occasion to "dress." As she walked to the food vendors, she was glad she'd duded up. Given the size of the hats and belt buckles, teased hair and tight Wranglers, no one was messing around.

At the food booths, she bought a hot dog with mustard and a bottle of Lone Star.

"How's your daddy?" Tony Franko asked as he handed her the beer.

She knew Tony from somewhere. She wasn't quite sure where. Just like most everyone else around her, she'd grown up knowing them and they her. "Better. Thanks, Tony." It had been a week since she'd moved him from Laredo.

As she moved down Main, she was stopped several times by well-meaning people who asked about her dad. She paused at the bead booth long enough to buy two coral bead bracelets for the Parton twins.

"How's your daddy?" the woman asked as she took Sadie's money.

"Better. I'll tell him you asked." She slipped the bracelets into her pocket and moved past the pottery and beeswax candle booths. As she looked at little armadillos and corncobs carved from stone, she polished off her hot dog and felt a hand on her shoulder.

"Dooley and me was real sorry to hear about your daddy, Sadie Jo. How's he doin'?"

She looked across her shoulder at a woman she recognized from her childhood. Dooley? Dooley? Dooley Hanes, the veterinarian. "He's doing better, Mrs. Hanes. How's Dooley?"

"Oh dear, Dooley died five years ago. He had the cancer in his testicles. It was advanced by the time they found it." She shook her head and her big gray dome wavered. "He suffered something fierce. Bless his heart."

"I'm sorry to hear that." She took a drink of her beer and listened as Mrs. Hanes listed all the poor misfortunes that had befallen *her* since the demise of Dooley. Suddenly, sitting at home watching dog videos didn't sound so bad. Dog videos and a hammer upside the head sounded like heaven.

"Sadie Jo Hollowell? I heard you were in town." Sadie turned and looked into a face set with dark brown eyes and a huge smile.

"Winnie Bellamy?" She'd sat behind Winnie in the first grade and had graduated with her. They hadn't been best friends, but they'd hung out with the same group. Winnie had always had long dark hair, but she'd obviously given in to the Texas in her and had dyed it blond and poufed it up.

"Winnie Stokes now." She pulled Sadie against her chest. "I married Lloyd Stokes. He was a few years ahead of us in school. His little brother Cain was our age." She dropped her hands. "Are you married?"

"No."

"Cain's single and he's a catch."

"If he's such a catch, why didn't you marry him instead of his brother?"

"He's a catch *now*." Winnie waved the question away. "He and Lloyd are playin' in the pool tournament. That's where I'm headed. You should come and say hey."

The offer sounded better than Mrs. Hanes, dog videos, or a hammer. "Excuse me, Mrs. Hanes," she said, and she and Winnie caught up on old times as they made their way to the Albertson's parking lot a few blocks away.

Orange and purple streaked the endless Texas sky as the giant sun sank lower west of town. At one end of the grocery store's parking lot, two rows of five pool tables were set up beneath strings of Christmas lights. Cowboy hats crowded the spaces around each table, broken up by the occasional trucker's hat. Only one man braved the event out of costume.

Beneath the white Christmas lights, Vince Haven leaned a big shoulder into one of the square posts. He wore non-issue, beige cargo pants, plain black T-shirt without any sort of flag ironed or embroidered on it, and his head was bare. Obviously the man didn't know the seriousness of the day, and he stuck out like a sinner among the converted. He held a pool cue in one hand and his head was cocked to the side as he listened intently to the three women gathered about him. Two wore straw cowboy hats; the other had teased her red long hair into a massive pouf like the Little Mermaid. She held a cue in one hand, and as she bent over the table, her hair flowed down her back to her butt in a pair of tight jeans.

"Sadie Jo Hollowell!" someone yelled.

Vince lifted his gaze from the women in front of him and his eyes locked with hers. He watched her for several long seconds before she turned just in time to be caught up in a big hug that lifted her off her heels.

"Cord?" Cordell Parton was three years younger than Sadie and had taken odd jobs at the JH off and on with his aunts.

"It's good to see you, girl." He lifted her up higher and his hat fell to the ground.

He'd gotten huge since she'd seen him fifteen years ago. Not fat. Just solid, and he squeezed her tight. "Lord love a duck, Cord. I can't breathe." Had she just said, "Lord love a duck"? If she wasn't careful, she'd be saying "crying all night and pass the tea towels." Maybe it was the hat. She was starting to sound like a Texan.

"Sorry." He set her back on her feet and bent to retrieve his Stetson. "How's your daddy?"

"Getting better."

"My aunts said you've been spending a lot of time in Laredo with him."

"He was moved to Amarillo last week." She looked over Cord's shoulder and her gaze landed on Vince's butt as he leaned across the next table over and took a shot. Lord love a duck, he was hot. Judging by the three women watching his butt, too, she wasn't the only one who thought so. He made those non-issue cargo pants look good.

"Come say hey to Lloyd and Cain," Winnie said, and took Sadie's elbow.

"It was great to see you, Cord. Come out to the ranch and have a beer with me one of these days soon. We'll catch up."

"Sounds good." He slid his hat back on his head. As she walked away, he called after her, "You're still as pretty as a Sunday sermon. I always had a crush on you, you know."

Yeah. She'd known. She smiled and glanced at Vince out of the corners of her eyes. He lined up another shot, then laughed at something one of the women said to him. She wondered which one was his girlfriend, because, after all, he'd been in town for over a month. In Lovett, that was plenty long enough to meet someone, get married, and start a family.

"Hey. It's Sadie Jo Hollowell," Cain Stokes said as she and Winnie approached the table. He leaned over and lined up the white ball, and Sadie got a chance to look at him. She didn't know if he was a catch, but he'd certainly improved since high school. He was taller. Leaner. And somewhere he'd developed a killer smile that filled his blue eyes with mischief. He also knew how to dress for Founder's Day in a pair of tight Wranglers that outlined his package. Not that she cared to know.

"Hey, Cain." She turned to his brother. "How's it going, Lloyd?"

"Can't complain." Lloyd wasn't as handsome as his brother, but he was better husband material. Sadie could tell just by the way he looked at his wife.

"I heard you were back in town." He gave her a quick hug. "How's your daddy doin'?"

"Good and getting better."

She pointed to the pool table. "Who's winning?"

"Cain." Lloyd raised a beer to his lips. "He's a hustler."

In more ways than one. Cain came around the table and gave her a hug that lingered a bit longer than his brother's. "Lookin' good, Sadie Jo."

"Thanks."

Winnie followed Lloyd as he moved around the table and eyed his next possible shot. She told him exactly where he should hit the ball and how hard. "I was doing fine before you walked up," Lloyd complained.

"Where ya' been hangin' your hat these days?" Cain asked.

"Phoenix."

He wrapped his arm around her shoulders. "Wanna play me next after I finish kicking Lloyd's behind?"

"You gonna let me win?"

"No, but if you kick my butt I'm gonna tell everyone that I let you win."

She laughed and shook her head. She was in Texas. Flirting was just another form of conversation. She glanced at Vince as he rose up from the table. Another time, another day, she might have flirted back a little with Cain. Tonight she just didn't feel like it. Not that it had anything to do with the SEAL with the light green eyes. She just wasn't in the mood and didn't want to give Cain ideas. "Maybe next time," she said, and moved from beneath his arm. Within the crowd surrounding the tables, she stood ten feet from Vince. Close enough to recognize the deep timbre of his voice and the answering laughter of the three women she was now close enough to identify.

The two women in the matching straw hats were the Young sisters. Not twins, but they looked enough alike that they could pass. Sadie recognized the redhead playing pool, too. Deeann Gunderson. All three women were close to Sadie's age, but had been raised in Amarillo. She'd gone to charm school with them. They'd passed due to skill. She'd passed due to her last name, and the Young girls had never failed to point that out.

"I'm runnin' to the girls' room inside the Albertson's. I hate those Porta Potties," Winnie announced, and pointed to a row of blue portable outhouses across the parking lot. "You gonna be here for a while yet?"

"I think so."

She watched Winnie move between the tables and past a skinny teen in full dress code compliance. He wore a big black Stetson and a Texas flag shirt with one enormous star on the back.

She took a step back out of Lloyd's way and bumped into someone. "Excuse me," she said, and looked over her shoulder into Jane Young's hazel eyes.

"Sadie Jo Hollowell," Jane said, drawing out her vowels. "It's been forev-ah."

It had been a long time, and Sadie didn't believe in holding anyone's nasty teenage past against them. Lord knew, she hadn't always been so sweet herself. "Hello, Jane and Pammy." She gave the sisters a hug, then turned to the third woman standing with them. "How are you, Deeann?"

"I have nothing to complain about." She laughed, and her smile was genuine. "But that never stops me. How's your daddy?"

"Good and getting better. Thanks for asking." She turned her attention to Vince, who twisted a small cube of blue chalk on the tip of his cue. "I see you're making friends." It had been almost two weeks since she'd seen Vince at the Gas and Go. Two weeks since he'd told her she looked like shit and that she owed him. Two weeks since she'd told him that her orgasm was worth only forty cents.

"Sadie."

"Y'all know each other?"

She glanced at Jane, then returned her gaze to

Vince. "Yes. He had trouble with his truck and I gave him a ride into town." Since she didn't want to discuss the other ways she knew Vince, she turned the subject. "Jane, Pammy, and Deeann and I went to Ms. Naomi's Charm School together," she told Vince. "They were much better at the Texas dip than I was."

Vince looked at all four women. "What's in it?"

Jane and Pammy laughed. "That's funny."

"The Texas dip is a debutante curtsy," Deeann explained as she handed her cue to Pammy. She moved to a clear spot several feet away, then she extended her arms out to her sides and slowly bowed like a swan until her forehead almost touched the ground.

Sadie looked up from Deeann's flowing red hair to Vince, who watched with one brow cocked. He set the chalk on the edge of the table, then moved to the other side. He leaned his big body over the table and lined up a shot. The long cue slid between his knuckles as the Christmas lights shone in his dark hair and black shirt. She couldn't tell if he was impressed with Deeann or not.

Deeann rejoined them and took her cue. "I can still dip."

"Wow, I wasn't even that limber at seventeen. Very impressive."

"Remember when you tripped on your train at the Cotton Cotillion and your rose headdress fell off?" Pammy reminded Sadie, like she'd ever forget. After that, she hadn't really bothered to pile and pin and spray her hair into a headdress of any kind. She'd just worn her hair straight, which had caused a bigger scandal than the headdress debacle.

"That was tragic." Both sisters laughed as they had years ago, and Sadie guessed they hadn't changed much over the past ten years. What the women didn't know was that Sadie didn't care. They no longer had the power to make her feel bad about herself.

"But you were always so pretty it didn't matter," Deeann said, genuinely trying to make Sadie feel better.

"Thank you, Deeann," she said, and thought to return the favor. "I parked my car in front of your shop. It looks like you have some real nice stuff. I'll have to stop by before I leave town."

"I hope you do. I make my own jewelry, and if you decide to stay in Lovett, and don't want to live out there at the ranch, let me know. I sell real estate, too."

Her interest piqued, she said, "I'm an agent in Phoenix. How's the market around here?"

"I'm not getting rich, but it's picking up slightly. Brokering a lot of short sales."

Short sales weren't what agents bragged about the most. "Me too." Sadie liked that about Deeann.

"Goodness, are you going to bore us with shop talk?" Pammy asked.

Sadie glanced at her watch and pretended she had somewhere to be. Just because she didn't care what the sisters said, didn't mean she wanted to hang out with them. "It sure was great to see y'all." Lord, had she just said "y'all"? It had taken years to extract that contraction from her vocabulary. She looked at Vince, who lined up another shot. "Good night, Vince."

He shot the six ball in the side pocket and rose. "See ya around, Sadie," he said, more interested in his game than in her.

She said good-bye to Lloyd and Cain and headed toward the beer vendor. Overhead, dark blue and orange streaked across the night sky. She ran into JH employees and former employees, and by the time she made it to the vendor, it was full dark and Tom and the Armadillos took the stage at one end of the parking lot. She was tired but didn't want to go home. She didn't always mind being alone. She'd been raised on a ranch filled with people, but she'd always been alone. But lately she'd either been in a hospital room alone or listening to her grumpy daddy.

She was Sadie Jo Hollowell. Most people knew her name. Knew she was Clive's daughter, but they didn't know her. Her whole life, people either loved or hated her depending on how they felt about her daddy.

She took a drink from her Lone Star bottle and turned, almost running into a massive chest. She instantly recognized those defined muscles and big biceps. He grabbed the top of her arm to keep her from toppling over.

"How many of those have you had?" he asked.

"Not enough." She looked up past Vince's square chin and mouth into his eyes staring straight back into hers. "This is my second." She glanced about. "Where are your friends?"

"What friends?"

"The Young sisters and Deeann."

"Don't know." He slid his hand down her arm

and took her beer from her hand. He swallowed a big drink, then gave it back. "Where are yours?"

"Friends?" She took a much smaller drink, then handed it back. "I haven't seen Winnie since she went to the bathroom a while ago."

"Not her. The cowboy with the tight Wranglers choking his nuts."

What? "Oh, Cain. I don't know. Are you worried about his nuts?"

"More like disturbed."

She grinned. "Why aren't you playing pool?" They moved a few feet from beneath the vendor tent.

"I got knocked out of the tournament by a skinny fifteen-year-old wearing a Texas flag shirt."

She tilted her head back and looked up at him. At the light illuminating half of his face and casting a shadow over the other half. "You're a big bad SEAL. Aren't you supposed to kick ass?"

He chuckled, low and masculine and completely secure with himself. "Guess it isn't my ass-kicking day if I got whooped by a kid with acne."

"Do you mean that geeky boy with the big hat?"

"That sounds like him."

"Seriously? You lost to him?"

"Don't let the pimples fool you. He was a shark."

"That's just embarrassing." She took a drink, then handed Vince the bottle. "He wasn't much bigger than the pool cue."

"Usually I'm better with my hands." His gaze slid to hers and he raised the bottle to his lips. "But you know that."

Yeah, she knew that. "Hey, Sadie Jo. How's your daddy?" someone called out to her.

"Good. Thank you," she hollered back. She put her hands in the pockets of her jacket and moved farther away from the vendor and Tom and the Armadillos' version of "Free Bird." The first time she'd met Vince, she'd been under the impression that he wasn't staying in town long. "Are you still working for your aunt?"

"No. I work for myself."

He handed her the bottle and she took a sip.

"Luraleen sold me the Gas and Go."

She choked on the mouthful of beer. Vince hit her back with the heel of his hand as she coughed and gasped and sputtered. "No shit?"

"No shit. Just signed the papers yesterday." He

grabbed the near-empty bottle, drained it, then tossed it in the garbage behind her.

She wiped her nose and mouth with the back of her arm. "Congratulations." She guessed.

"How are you doing?"

She blinked. "Better. I just had a little beer go down the wrong pipe."

He placed a hand beneath her chin and raised her face to the light. "I heard about your dad. How are you holding up?"

She looked into the eyes of this man she hardly knew and realized that he was the first person to ask after her. Really ask after her. "I'm doing good." Her gaze slid to his chin, and her stomach kind of felt weird. Maybe it was chugging that beer.

He tilted her face a bit more. "You look tired."

"Last time I saw you, you said I looked like shit."

He smiled with one corner of his mouth. "I might have been a little annoyed with you."

Her gaze returned to his. "And you're not now?"

"Not as much." His thumb brushed her cheek. "Take off the hat, Sadie."

Her hair appointment wasn't scheduled for

several more days and the hat nicely covered her darker roots. "I have bad roots."

"Me too. You met Luraleen."

Sadie laughed. "I'm talking about my hair."

"I know. Take it off."

"Why?"

"I want to see your eyes." He took the hat from her head and handed it to her. "That's been irritating me all night. I don't want to talk to your chin."

For the most part, he acted like he didn't even like her, and she wondered why he was talking to her at all. "I'm sure Deeann and the Young girls aren't so irritating."

"Those women are looking for a boyfriend."

"You're not interested?"

He looked out at the crowd near the stage. "I'm not really a relationship guy."

Surprising. Most guys didn't cop to that until after they got a girl into bed a few times. "What kind of guy are you?" And if they did admit it up front, they gave the BS answer about having a lot going on in their lives or some horrid bitch had hurt them in the past and so they couldn't commit.

He shrugged his big shoulders. "The kind who gets bored. The kind who doesn't want to pretend I'm in it for anything but sex."

"That's honest, I guess." She gave a startled laugh. "Do you have commitment issues?"

"No."

"How many relationships have you been in?"

"Enough to know I'm not good at them."

She supposed she should ask why, but it really wasn't her business. Just like her past relationships weren't his business. "You want just sex. No dinner? No movie? No conversation?"

"I like conversation . . . during sex."

She looked up into his face, the strong angles of his jaw and cheeks. His dark skin and darker hair and those light green eyes. If he wasn't so massively male, he might almost be confused for pretty. He looked like just what she needed to pass the time while she was in town. Much better than junk television and videos. She figured she had a month, perhaps two, to kill before her daddy was well enough for her to leave. Not nearly enough time for her to form any sort of feelings. She looked at her watch. It was a little after ten and the thought of going home alone was like a lead ball in her chest. "What are you doing for the next few hours?"

He looked at her. "What do you have in mind?"

She was an adult. She hadn't had good sex in

a really long time. She knew from experience he could get the job done. He was a sure thing. "Poor decisions we'll probably regret later. Interested?"

"Depends."

The lead ball fell to her stomach. "On?" Was he going to turn her down?

"Two things." He held up one finger. "If you can handle no strings." A second finger joined the first. "You don't leave me alone again with nothing but a hard-on like you did at your cousin's wedding."

Relief brought a smile to her lips. While they were making rules, she added a few of her own just to make it all square. Lord knew how he liked things squared up. "I can handle no strings. Just make sure you can." She thought of her last relationship. Just because a guy seemed like a sure thing didn't mean he could always go the distance. "If I get undressed, you better make it worth my time."

"Honey, I think it's pretty safe to say that I can make it worth your time even when you *are* dressed. Just make sure you make it worth *my* time."

Chapter Ten

Vince raised his hand to knock on the big oak doors just as one side swung open. The light from behind lit up Sadie's golden hair, and he could finally see her face. Either that stupid hat or the evening shadows had hidden her eyes from him all night. And he liked her eyes, along with other parts of her body.

"I thought you might have gotten lost." She was kind of breathy, like she'd been running. She'd lost her jacket and boots and wore a tight T-shirt that matched the blue of those eyes he liked.

"I don't get lost." He'd stopped at the Gas and Go long enough to grab a box of condoms and lock up behind himself. He stepped into the large entry and looked around. He got a quick impression of cowhides and antlers and old money.

"Anyone else here?" He knew her father was in the hospital, but that didn't mean the house was empty.

"It's just me."

"Big house for one girl."

"Yeah." She pushed him against the closed door and he let her. "I believe I owe you something." She slid her hands up his chest, and his scrotum drew up his testicles like a satin purse. "When we were in the bride's room at my cousin's wedding, I ran out and didn't say thank you." She pressed into him and kissed the side of his neck. "I was raised with better manners." She pulled at the bottom of his shirt. "You smell good. Thank you."

He didn't know if she was thanking him for not stinking or the orgasm. With her hands tugging at his shirt, it didn't matter. "My pleasure."

"In charm school I was taught to always make people feel welcome. It was pretty much a number one rule." Her fingers lightly raked his stomach and chest as she pushed the shirt up. "Do you feel welcome, Vince?"

He sucked in a breath. A lot of women had undressed him in his lifetime. He'd had no problem finding women who wanted to get naked and touch him, but her hands were more of a tease. He liked it. "Yeah. I might feel more welcome if you did that Texas bow. Naked. Over my crotch."

She laughed against the right side of his throat, and the heat of her soft breath spread down his chest. "Is that what you were thinking when Deeann was showing off her Texas dip?" She tugged his shirt over his head and tossed it behind her on the floor.

"Not about her. You."

She took a step back and sucked in a breath. Her gaze lingered on his chest and abdomen and lust pooled in the back of his throat. "Good God. You look airbrushed." She put her warm palm on his warm belly and it was his turn to suck in a breath. "Like someone photo-shopped all the good stuff and put you on a birthday card."

He placed his hands on the sides of her head and brought her face close to his. "You haven't seen the good stuff yet."

"I want your good stuff, Vince."

He opened his mouth over hers and kissed her. "I want your good stuff," he added, then kissed her more. Hot, open-mouth kisses that raised his blood pressure and heated his skin. Wet, thrusting kisses that made him hard and aching with need. Long, deep kisses that made him hungry for a lot more. She tasted good. Like long, deep, hot, wet sex. She ran her fingers across his pecs and her palms over his bare stomach. Then she grabbed his waistband and brushed her thumbs across his lower belly. Touching here. Brushing there. Light touches driving him crazy and turning him hard as stone.

She pulled back and looked up at him, her eyes bright blue and drugged at the same time. "You're beautiful, Vince. I want to eat you up." She kissed the hollow of his throat. "One juicy bite at a time."

And he wanted to return the favor. One bite at a time in all her juicy spots. If her hands weren't diving down his pants, he might have told her, but he was having a difficult time breathing. He reached for the bottom of her T-shirt, but she grabbed his wrists and pressed his palms against the door. "Grab wood, Vince. And I don't mean yours."

His laughter came out kind of choked. "What're you planning?" He wasn't much into bondage.

"Watch. You'll see."

And he did. He watched her undo his pants and slide them down his thighs. He'd worn a pair of gray boxer briefs and she pressed her hand against him. Against the soft cotton and the hard edge of his erection. She ran her hot mouth all over him. His shoulder and chest. Then she knelt before him and licked his belly. He groaned deep in his throat and fought the urge to tangle his fingers in her hair. To push her face deeper.

Her teasing fingers brushed his skin as she shoved down his underwear and he sprang free. The hot tip of his erect penis brushed her cheek. "Nice, Vince."

"You're not disappointed?" he asked, even though he knew the answer. He was no porn star but he had more than enough to get the job done.

"Not yet." She took him in her hand and looked up at him. "When I'm through, you're gonna owe me."

"Forty cents?" She stroked him in her soft hand and if he'd let himself, he could have come right then. But he had more control than that.

"At least a buck forty." She kissed the head of his dick, then licked him like a Popsicle. Just when he thought he couldn't stand the torture of her slick tongue, she opened her hot, wet mouth and took him inside. She sucked him deep and slid her hand up his shaft. He locked his knees and his head fell back against the door. *God, don't let her stop,* he thought as his fingers dug into the door to keep from grabbing her hair. *Don't let her stop even to talk.* He didn't mind dirty talk. Most of the time he liked it, but nothing ruined a BJ like conversation.

Years of training steadied his breathing. He sucked even breaths into his lungs as she sucked him closer to the edge. She worked him over with her hands and wet velvet mouth, and he tried to prolong the pleasure. Tried to make it last, but she pulled a fierce orgasm from center mass. From his core, that rushed from his body and into her mouth. He groaned long and deep and might have managed to say something as she stayed with him until the end. Then she re-dressed him and slid back up his body.

"Worth a buck forty?"

"A buck forty-five." He ran his hands up and down her back and bottom. "Thank you."

"You're welcome." She kissed the side of his throat as her hands moved over his shoulders and chest. She said something he didn't quite hear.

"Pardon?"

She pulled back and smiled. "Wanna beer?"

Jesus. A blow and a beer. Most guys would consider that a dream come true, but Vince wasn't most guys. There was something he liked better. He tugged her shirt over her head and lowered his mouth to hers. He liked oral sex. He liked a face full of cleavage, but it was just foreplay. Fun stuff leading up to the real deal.

Vince liked intercourse. Any position. He liked the give and take. The hard thrust and the smooth finesses. He was an insertion guy. "No. I have something better than beer in mind." He slid his hands to her bra clasp.

Sadie pulled back and looked up into Vince's green eyes, still drowsy with lust but fully alert. "Don't you need some recovery time?" All the men she'd ever known needed recovery time.

"No. I'm good to go." He slid her bra straps down her arms, then tossed it aside. She'd raced home and changed her underwear. She didn't have anything sexy, but she wanted to at least match. She'd thrown on a pair of white panties to match her white bra. He didn't seem to notice and settled her bare breasts against his warm chest. "Do you need recovery time?"

Her nipples tightened and he grabbed two handfuls of her behind. As if she weighed nothing, he lifted, and she wrapped her legs around his waist. Hot, liquid lust pooled between her thighs. Had pooled between her thighs even before she'd pulled his impressive erection from his pants. "I'm good to go."

He moved with her through the entry into the dark living room and set her on her feet. He kissed her throat and finished undressing her. His big, warm hands touched her all over as his mouth sucked a soft patch of her throat. Like that night in the bride's room, she felt herself going fast. This time, she pushed him away and toward her great-grandmother's settee. "Condom." She held out her hand.

"You have a choice." He put three in her palm. Red, green, or blue.

"It'll match your eyes," she said, and chose the green.

"You want my dick to match my eyes?"

She tossed the other one on the sofa and watched him strip. "Call me fashionable." He took off his boots and socks, and pushed his pants and underwear down his big, powerful thighs. There wasn't an ounce of fat or inch of loose skin anywhere on his tan body. When he was completely naked, she pushed at his chest until he sat. It wasn't the most romantic sex of her life, but she wasn't interested in romance.

"What's the hurry?"

She straddled his lap, and the plush head of his erection brushed her where she needed it most. A shiver worked every cell in her body, and she fought an urge not to go ahead and sit right down on his hot, naked penis. "You said you were good to go." He certainly looked good to go.

"I am."

"Then I want to go." She ripped open the condom and together they rolled it down the long, thick shaft.

He placed a hand on the side of her face and looked into her eyes as he shoved into her. It took a few thrusts and his voice was low and scratchy when he said, "Tight fit."

"Mmm." Her head fell back and she grabbed on to his shoulders. Heat spun through her, starting at the intimate place where they touched.

"You feel good up there." Vince slid his hand from her breasts down her sides to her hips. "Look good, too."

"Yeah, Vince." He lifted her, then pushed her back down. "That's good."

"Not a waste of getting naked?"

"No." God, was he going to talk all night? Nothing ruined sex faster than conversation. Especially if a guy said something dumb and broke her concentration. And sometimes it took a lot of concentration so the events of the day didn't pop into her head.

She rocked her hips and created some fiery friction. He groaned deep in his throat and slid in and out. He was big and powerful and plunged deep. Apparently he wasn't going to be one of those guys and she didn't have to try and concentrate on what he did to her. She was in the moment. Consumed by it. The house could have caught fire, and she wouldn't have noticed as she rode him like one of her daddy's prized stallions. Racing, long and hard, over and over forever, until the second she tumbled headfirst into a fierce, torrid orgasm that scrambled her brain. It went on out of control, controlling her, as he thrust into her again and again. Just as it began to let her go, he pushed down on her thighs and held her there with his big, strong hands.

"Hooyah," he groaned deep in his throat. She leaned forward and lightly bit his shoulder. Some people were silent when they orgasmed. Some praised God, while others yelled the F-word. She'd never heard "hooyah" before.

Sadie sliced a flaky croissant, then set it on the cutting board on the kitchen counter. "Do you want avocado on your sandwich?"

"Sounds good." Vince shook water from several pieces of lettuce, then set them on the counter beside the board.

She was dressed in her T-shirt and panties. He, in his cargo pants. After their workout, they'd worked up an appetite. "The man food is out in the cookhouse," she said as she spread mayonnaise on the croissants. "Carolynn would never feed the guys croissants."

"Who's Carolynn?" He tore off a paper towel and dried his hands.

"Carolynn is the ranch cook." She filled the croissants with turkey and lettuce and avocado. "She cooks two meals a day for all the hands. A big huge breakfast and a big dinner. Her sister Clara Anne does the housekeeping here and in the bunkhouse." She moved to the refrigerator and opened it. Cool air touched her bare thighs and she bent forward and grabbed dill pickles, a jar of pepperoncini, and sliced cheese. Since she'd been back, the sisters had kept the house refrigerator and pantry stocked with the sandwich stuff for her. "I think the sisters have been here about thirty years." She shut the door and turned.

He stood in the middle of the room, his head cocked to one side and eyes on her butt.

"What?"

"Nothing." He grinned like he'd been caught doing something but wasn't sorry. "How many men stay in your bunkhouse?"

She shrugged and tossed him the cheese. He caught it and followed her to the counter. "I don't really know." She set the jars on the counter and grabbed her mama's china plates from overhead. "When I was growing up there were probably fifteen. Now I think most of the people who work at the JH live in town." She stuffed the sandwiches with Swiss and pepperoncini. "Are you worried that one of my daddy's men might bust in here and kick your ass for messin' with the boss's daughter?"

He chuckled and she looked across her shoulder at him, all big and buff and bad. "No. I just wonder how safe it is for a woman out here all alone."

"Are you going to do something?"

"Other than what I've already done?"

She laughed. "I like what you've done. Should I worry you're going to do something I won't like?"

"I have a few positions I want to put you in, but I guarantee you'll like 'em."

"Do I need my stun gun just in case?"

He raised one brow up his forehead and set the cheese on the counter. "I didn't believe you the last time you threatened me with your make-believe stun gun."

She smiled but didn't admit anything as she pointed to the pantry. "Grab some chips, please." She set the croissants and a pickle on the blue Wedgwood. When he returned, she arranged the Lay's on the plate. "Water, beer, or sweet tea?"

"Water."

She poured a glass of tea and one of filtered water, and then together they carried the plates and glasses into the formal dining room. She set the table with her mother's best linen placemats and napkins. "We never really eat in here except for Christmas and Thanksgiving."

"Kind of fancy."

She looked around at the heavy mahogany furniture and damask draping. Company always ate in the dining room on the good china. It was a rule her mama had drilled into her head. Like chewing with your mouth closed and showing "uglies."

He picked up a chip. "Where do you eat?"

She placed her napkin on her lap. "Growing up, I always ate in the cookhouse or in the small breakfast nook in the kitchen." She took a bite of her sandwich, then swallowed. "I'm an only child, and after my mama died, it was always just me and Daddy." She took a drink of her tea. "It just made sense that we ate in the bunkhouse so Carolynn didn't have to run back and forth."

"How old were you when your mother died?" He took a big bite of his croissant.

"Five."

"Mmm." He took another bite and chewed. "This is really good, Sadie," he said after he swallowed. "I'm not usually a croissant kind of guy."

"Thanks. Sandwiches are easy. Seven-course meals are tough."

He reached for his water and paused with it before his mouth. "You can cook seven-course meals?"

"It's been a while, but yeah. Along with manners and charm, and all the many, many classes

I've taken in my life, I've taken a few cooking classes." She took a bite of her light, flaky sandwich. The turkey, avocado, and pepperoncini a perfect complement of tastes. "My mother was a fabulous cook and a stickler for manners. Not that I really remember. My daddy tried to raise me like he thought she would. Of course he often forgot."

He took a drink and set the glass on the table. "Are you like her?"

"She was Miss Texas and came really close to winning Miss America." Sadie popped a salty chip into her mouth and crunched. That's what she loved about Lay's: the salty crunch. Of course, Chee-tos were the best snack ever. "Mama was really beautiful and could sing."

"Can you sing?"

"Only if I want to piss people off."

He chuckled. "Then you must look like her." He took two more bites.

Was that a compliment? Was she really going to blush? "I don't know. People say I do, but I have my daddy's eyes." She took her own bite and chewed.

"Were you a beauty queen, too?"

She shook her head and reached for her tea. "I

have a few sashes and trophies, but no. I have a hard time walking and waving at the same time." She took a drink. "Queening is hard work."

He laughed.

"It is." She smiled. "You try singing, dancing, and sparkling and shining all at the same time. You think being a SEAL is tough? You think terrorists are hard-core? Piece of cake compared to the pageant circuit. Some of those pageant moms are brutal." Somewhere in her manners book there was a rule about talking about yourself too much. Besides, she wanted to know more about him. "Why did you join the Navy SEALs?"

"Blowing up stuff and shooting guns for Uncle Sam sounded fun."

"Was it?"

"Yeah." He shoved some chips into his mouth and reached for his water. He obviously wasn't much of a talker. At least not about himself. That was all right. One of the reasons she was such a successful real estate agent was that she got people to trust her enough to talk about anything. Sometimes about stuff she didn't care to know. Like bodily functions and strange behaviors. "Don't SEALs have to swim a lot?"

"Yeah." He took a drink, then offered, "We

train in the surf, but in the current conflict the teams spend most of the time on land."

"I'm not a great swimmer. I prefer to watch the tides from the beach."

"I love the water. When I was a kid, I spent most of my summers in a lake somewhere." He picked up the last bite of croissant. "I hate the sand, though."

"There's a lot of sand near lakes and oceans, Vince."

He smiled with one corner of his mouth. "In the Middle East, too. Sand and dust storms." He popped the last of the sandwich in his mouth.

"Did you have to learn Arabic?"

He shook his head and swallowed. "I picked up a few words here and there."

"Didn't that make it hard to communicate?"

"I wasn't there to talk."

He wasn't here to talk, either, and he didn't give a lot away about himself. That was okay. He was nice to look at with his big muscles and startling green eyes staring back at her from his handsome face. She'd been with fine-looking men. None as fine as Vince, but with all that fineness came a real reserve. A refusal to give anything to a woman but his body. Which was okay with

Sadie because that's what they'd agreed she'd get. And that's all she truly wanted.

"Why do you live in Phoenix when you could live here?" he asked.

Obviously they were done talking about him. "I know that ranching sounds romantic, in a sort of taming the Wild West sort of way, but it's *a lot* of hard work and isolation. I don't mind hard work, but growing up with your closest neighbor twenty miles away can be lonely. Especially if you're an only child. I couldn't exactly jump on my bike and head out to a friend's house." She took a bite and chewed. She'd never really had a best friend. Never ran around with other kids in a neighborhood. She'd hung out with adults or the calf or sheep she was raising for 4–H. "If you enjoy moving cattle and stepping in cow shit, then I guess the loneliness is worth it." Did she say lonely? She didn't consider herself lonely, but she supposed as a kid she'd been very alone.

He put his napkin on his empty plate. "Isn't this all going to be yours one day?"

Suddenly she wasn't hungry as the old feeling of dread landed like a ball in her stomach. "What makes you think that?"

"People talk, and working in a convenience

store is like being a bartender." He shrugged one shoulder. "Only not as many drunks and without the tips."

People loved to talk, especially in Lovett. "Yes, but I'm a girl."

He sat back in his chair and folded his big arms across his bare chest. His gaze moved from hers, down her chin and neck to the front of her shirt. He smiled and looked back up into her eyes. "That's obvious."

"My daddy wanted a boy." She took a drink of tea. "He doesn't want to leave the JH to me any more than I want a ten-thousand-acre ranch, but I'm the only child of an only child. There isn't anyone else."

"So you're going to inherit a ranch you don't want."

She shrugged. Her feelings about the JH were confusing. She loved and hated it all at the same time. It was a part of her like her blue eyes. "I don't know what my daddy has in mind. He hasn't told me and I haven't asked."

"And you don't think that's odd?"

"You don't know my daddy," she said just above a whisper.

He turned his head slightly to the left as she

noticed he did sometimes and watched her mouth. "How old is your father?"

"Seventy-eight." Why all the questions? He couldn't be that interested in her life. She was a one-night stand. Nothing more. She pushed her plate aside.

"Are you done eating?"

"I am."

He smiled. "Are you good to go again?"

Ah. He was just killing time with questions until she finished eating. She looked at the clock. It was a little after one A.M. The Parton sisters wouldn't arrive for five more hours. No, it wasn't the most romantic sex, but it was amazing. He wasn't much of a romantic guy, but she wasn't looking for romance. What he *was*, was a one-night stand and he'd given her something she hadn't had for a while.

A good time. "Hooyah."

Chapter Eleven

"Who buttered your muffin?"

Sadie turned and looked at her father, an oxygen cannula in his nose, glasses on the top of his head, and a new pair of nonskid purple socks on his feet. Had he found out about Vince? Had someone seen his truck leave at about three A.M. and ratted her out? "What?"

"You're humming."

She turned back to the sink filled with yellow daisies. "A person can't hum?"

"Not unless there's somethin' to hum about."

She bit the inside of her cheek to keep from smiling. She felt more relaxed than she had since the morning she'd headed her Saab toward Texas. For the first time since she'd arrived at the JH, she'd spent the night thinking of . . . well, thinking of nothing. Just feeling pleasure. Of doing something other than watching television, worrying about her daddy and her career and her future. And that was something to hum about.

She cut an inch off the stems and arranged them in a vase. "Is there anything I can do for you, Daddy?"

"Not a thing."

"I can take over some of the responsibilities at the ranch." For a while. Until he could go home. "You could show me your accounting software and I can do your payroll." Once she was shown what to do, it couldn't be that hard.

"Wanda does all that. If you take Wanda's job, she can't feed her kids."

Oh. She didn't know Wanda. "You'll be vaccinating and tagging the new calves soon. I could help out with that." One of her least favorite jobs, but it would give her something to do besides hang out in a rehab hospital with her grumpy daddy.

"You'd be in the way."

True, but he could have lied and spared her feelings. Wait. He was Clive Hollowell, no he couldn't. "I thought these flowers might cheer you up," she said and gave up trying. Daisies had been her mother's favorite flower.

"Going home will cheer me up." He coughed and grabbed his side. "Goddamn it!"

She glanced over her shoulder at him but knew there was nothing she could do. Her father's ribs were healing, but slowly. He was still in pain but refused to take pain medication.

"Why don't you take something," she said as she filled the vase with water.

His painful fit went on for several more moments. "I don't want to be a damn doper," he croaked between coughs.

He was seventy-eight, it wasn't like he was going to get addicted, and if on the off chance he did, so what? He'd live out the rest of his life pain-free and happy. It might be a nice change. "Daddy, you shouldn't have to live in pain," she reminded him, and turned off the water. She moved across the room and set the vase on his bedside table. "Mama's favorite flowers. I thought they'd add a little color to your room."

"Your mama loved white daisies."

She looked down at the yellow flowers. "Oh."

"White daisies and blue sky. I never saw her when she wasn't pretty as a silver dollar. Not even in the morning."

Sadie thought of her darker roots she was having retouched the next day. She'd pulled her hair into a ponytail and given her lashes a few swipes with mascara. That was it.

"Sweet as sugar and kind to everyone."

"I guess I'm not like her."

"No. You're not like her." Her father looked at Sadie. "You were never like her. She knew it when you were a baby and stubborn about everything."

No, her father would never lie to spare her feelings. "I tried, Daddy."

"I know, but it's not in you." He picked up the newspaper on the side of his bed and pushed his glasses from the top of his head to the bridge of his nose.

So maybe she didn't volunteer at hospitals or animal shelters. Maybe she didn't cook soup for sick old ladies, but she worked hard and supported herself. "You know, Daddy, the only time I feel like I'm never good enough is when I'm here. I know it might shock you, but there are people who think I'm a smart, capable woman."

"No one ever said you weren't smart and capable." He opened his paper. "Don't throw a wide hoop with a short rope. If you feel better about yourself someplace else, then go live your life, Sadie Jo."

She was tempted. Tempted to do just that. To just jump in her car and leave Lovett and Texas and her father and the memories and the disappointments.

Of course she didn't. She stayed for another hour before she left the hospital and headed home. To the empty house.

She'd had a good time the night before. There was freedom in a one-night stand. Freedom to be greedy and not worry about feelings or if he'd call again or any of the other things that went with building a relationship. Freedom to wake relaxed, with a smile on her face, and not wait around for a phone call.

Sadie drove through Lovett on her way home and was tempted to stop by the Gas and Go. She could always use a Diet Coke and a bag of Cheetos. She wasn't doing anything that night. Maybe he wasn't, either, but she'd rather watch prank videos on TV or on YouTube until her eyes bled than stop by the Gas and Go on the pretext of a munchies run.

When Vince had kissed her good-bye and

said thank you one last time, she knew he wasn't coming back for more. Oh, she knew he'd had a good time, but he hadn't asked to see her again, or even asked her for her number. She wasn't mad about it. She wasn't sad, okay maybe a little sad because she'd prefer to spend the night getting naked than bored out of her head, but she couldn't be upset. He'd told her it was just about sex. He was free to do other things, as was she, but she didn't have anything to do. Being back home made it woefully clear that she hadn't developed any deep friendships in the town where she'd been born and raised. There wasn't anyone she felt she could just call up for lunch, even if she knew their numbers. The person she'd talked to the most since she'd been back was Vince, and it wasn't his job to entertain her. Although that would be nice. She was just going to have to figure out something to do with her time before she went insane.

The next day, after her morning visit to the hospital in Amarillo, she drove three blocks south to the Lily Belle Salon and Spa. She sat in the chair of the owner of the salon and spa herself, Lily Darlington, and relaxed. It had been a while since she'd been in a salon, a black nylon cape covering her from throat to knees. The smell of shampoo and herbal-scented candles, punctuated with perming solution, made her forget her life for a while.

Sadie had chosen Lily because the woman had really good hair. Thick and healthy and with several different shades of natural-looking blond highlights. Like Sadie, Lily was blond-haired and blue-eyed, and once she started putting foils in Sadie's hair, they discovered they had something in common beyond butterscotch hair and sky-blue eyes. Lily had been raised in Lovett. She'd graduated from Lovett High five years before Sadie, and they knew some of the same people. And of course Lily knew of the JH and the Hollowells.

"My mama worked at the Wild Coyote Diner until she retired last year," Lily said as she painted thin strands of Sadie's hair. "And my brother-in-law owns Parrish American Classics."

Sadie had certainly heard of the Parrish brothers and knew of their business. "I used to eat at the Wild Coyote all the time. Open-face sandwiches and pecan pie." Through the salon mirror in front of her, she watched Lily wrap a foil. "What's your mama's name?"

"Louella Brooks."

"Of course I remember her." Louella was as big an institution as the Wild Coyote. "She always had tons of stories about everyone." Just like everyone else in Lovett, but what made Louella a standout was her ability to stop in the middle of a story, take an order at a different table, and then return without missing a syllable.

"Yep. That's Mama." The bell above the door rang and through the mirror, Lily looked up from Sadie's hair. "Oh no." A huge bouquet of red roses entered the business, hiding the person carrying them. "Not again." The delivery boy set the flowers on the counter and had one of the girls at the desk sign for them.

"Are those for you?"

"I'm afraid so."

Someone had dropped several hundred dollars on those roses. "That's sweet."

"No, it's not. He's too young for me," she said as a blush crept up her neck.

It was rude. She'd been raised better, but Sadie had to pry. "How old is he?"

She sectioned off a slice of hair. "He's thirty."

"That's only eight years. Right?"

"Yeah, but I don't want to be a cougar."

"You don't look like a cougar."

"Thanks." She shoved a foil beneath the hair she'd sectioned and added, "He looks about twenty-five."

"I think he has to be young enough to be your son before it's considered a cougar and cub relationship."

"Well, I don't want to date a man eight years younger." She swiped color out of one of the bowls. "But Lordy he's hot."

Sadie smiled. "Just use him for his body."

"I tried that. He wants more." Lily sighed. "I have a ten-year-old son, and I'm trying to run my own business. I just want a peaceful, calm life and Tucker is complicated."

"How?"

"He was in the Army and he saw a lot. He says he used to be closed off but isn't anymore." She painted strands of Sadie's hair. "But for a man who says he isn't closed off anymore, he doesn't share much about himself."

She thought of Vince. "And that scares you?"

Lily shrugged. "That and his age and the drama with my ex. I don't think I can take on more."

"Is your ex a real jerk?"

Lily glanced at Sadie through the mirror. "My ex is a rat bastard."

Which was considerably worse than a jerk.

After another hour of weaving color, Lily put a clear cap on Sadie's hair and sat her under the hair dryer. Sadie checked her cell phone for texts and e-mails, but there was nothing but junk. She used to get fifty or so business-related messages mixed with a few from friends throughout the day. It was like she'd fallen off the grid. Off the planet.

When she was done, her hair looked good. As good as in any of the salons she'd gone to in Denver or Phoenix or L.A. But Sadie was in Texas, and while Lily had managed just a slight trim to Sadie's straight, shoulder-length hair, she hadn't been able to control herself during the blow-out and Sadie had left with a slight pouf.

The thought of going home with her fabulous-looking hair was depressing so she stopped by Deeann's Duds to look at some sundresses she'd seen in the window. A bell above the door rang as she stepped inside, and she had the immediate impression of pink and gold and cowhides.

"Look at you!" Deeann came around the counter and gave Sadie a hug. "Just as cute as a bug's ear."

Sadie had never understood that expression. Since neither bugs nor ears were cute. "Thank you. I just had my roots touched up at Lily Belle Salon and Spa."

"Crazy Lily Darlington did it?"

She pulled back and looked into Deeann's brown eyes. "Lily's crazy?" She hadn't struck Sadie as off.

"Oh." Deeann waved a hand. "No. That's just what everyone used to call her. Especially when she was divorcing that skirt-chasing Ronnie Darlington. She's a few years older than me, but I always thought she was real sweet."

"And you were always the nicest girl at charm school. And pretty, too."

"Aren't you sweet."

Her daddy didn't think so. "Show me something cute. Most of my clothes are in my closet in Phoenix, and I'm getting tired of the same sundresses and jogging suits."

Deeann clapped her hands together. "Are you a size four?"

Who was she to argue? "Sure." The store was more narrow than wide, with racks and shelves stuffed with everything from skirts and shorts and T-shirts to sundresses and prom dresses.

There were a few cute things, but mostly Deeann's Duds weren't really Sadie's style. Too much
"embellishment." Which meant beads and silver
conchas and lace.

"I love your jewelry." Which she did.

"It helps pay the bills." Deeann looked at her
watch she'd made from a spoon. "I have a few of
the local girls coming in to look at prom dresses.
I hope they find something and don't go to Amarillo." She shook her head, and her long red hair
brushed her back. "My ex hasn't paid child sup-
port in a year, and I need the money."

Sadie set three T-shirts, two pairs of shorts,
and five pairs of earrings on the counter. "My
senior dress was a Jessica McClintock. Blue with
rhinestones on the bodice." She sighed. "I looked
fabulous. Too bad my date, Rowdy Dell, got hit in
the head with a flying tequila bottle and bled all
over me."

"Goodness. Did he have to have stitches?"
Deeann rang up the clothes.

"Yeah. A few." She chuckled. "I guess it was
horrible of me to be more worried about my dress
than his head."

Deeann bit her lip to keep from smiling.
"Not at all, honey. A dented head will heal. You

can't repair a bloody rhinestone-studded Jessica McClintock. Did Rowdy apologize for ruining your dress?"

"He obviously wasn't raised right." Sadie chuckled. "It was the prom night from hell."

"Bet it wasn't as bad as mine." Deeann handed her the bag of clothes. "I got knocked up on prom night and made matters worse by getting married three months later. Now I run this shop, sell jewelry and real estate on the side just to support my boys and me. All because I crawled into the back of Ricky Gunderson's truck."

Deeann was certainly a hard worker. Sadie liked that about her. "Can I help?" She wasn't licensed to sell real estate in Texas, but she could certainly show a home with Deeann. Give her some tips to close the deal. She was often the top-selling agent at her brokerage in Phoenix.

"You can sell prom dresses with me."

"What?" She'd been thinking real estate. Showing houses and talking up amenities.

"It's easy. Those girls are gonna want to try on every dress in the store. I sure could use another pair of hands."

It had been a long time since she'd bought a prom dress or been around teenagers. The twenty-year-olds at her cousin's wedding had been annoying enough. "I don't know . . ."

"It shouldn't take more than a couple of hours."

"Hours?"

Vince raised the sledgehammer over his head and brought it down on the counter. The sounds of splintering wood and whine of wrenching nails filled the air, and it felt good to go at something with all his force. His motto had always been, "Sometimes it is entirely appropriate to kill a fly with a sledgehammer." The man credited with the saying was a Marine, Major Holdridge. Vince loved the jarheads. Loved the wild grit and spit of the corps.

Of course, SEALs were trained a bit differently. Trained that it was easy to kill an enemy, but much more difficult to get intel from a corpse. Vince understood and walked the line between knowing that it was often vital to the mission to take enemy combatants alive, and loving a big explosion. And sometimes there was nothing quite like a sledgehammer to deliver a message and bring the point home.

A bead of sweat slid down his temple and he wiped it away with the shoulder of his T-shirt.

He hit an overhead cabinet and knocked it off the wall. He'd dreamed of Wilson again last night. This time the dream began before the firefight that took his buddy's life. He'd dreamed he was back in the rugged mountains and limestone caves. Of him and Wilson standing next to stockpiles of RPG launchers, AK–47 magazines, Russian-made grenades, Stinger missiles, and what someone claimed to be Osama bin Laden's very own personal copy of the Koran. Vince had always had a doubt or two about that, but it made for a good story.

The operation orders had called for the insertions of four SEALs and a seven-mile hump to the caves. Marine security covered their right and left flanks, watching for enemy snipers hiding in the cracks and crevasses. The assault took longer than expected because of the rough terrain and heat. They'd paused halfway to strip off the jackets they'd worn for the flight in, but that still left him packing water, MREs, H-gear, assorted weaponry, body armor, and ballistics helmet.

The first thing they'd noticed as they'd neared the objective was that the bombs the flyboys had dropped earlier to soften the area missed about eighty percent of their targets. The platoon patrolled up to the entrance and entered the caves like they would a house or ship. The lights on their weapons faded in the deep caverns.

"'Little surprises around every corner,'" Wilson said as they rounded the mouth of one cave. Before anyone asked, he added, "Willy Wonka. The original movie. Not the fucked-up Johnny Depp remake."

"Shit on rye. That's an ass-load of Gobstoppers." Vince shone the light from his weapon on boxes of Stingers. "Looks like someone planned on playing war with us."

Wilson laughed. That deep staccato *ha ha ha* that always brought a smile to Vince's face. The laugh he missed when he thought of his friend.

Vince set the sledgehammer on Luraleen's old desk, which he decided to keep for old times' sake, and grabbed pieces of busted-up wood and counter. Thinking about Wilson usually made him smile. Dreaming about him made him shake like a baby and run into walls.

He walked out of the office and through the back door he'd left wedged open with a brick earlier. He moved a few feet to a Dumpster and tossed the debris inside. He figured it would take a week or two to finish demolition and another three or four to renovate.

The fading evening sun lowered in the cloudless Texas sky as a red Volkswagen pulled to a stop in the back. A trickle of sweat slid down his temple and he lifted his arm and wiped at it with his shoulder. Becca cut the engine of the Bug and waved through the windshield at Vince.

"Sweet baby Jesus save me." For some inexplicable reason, she still stopped by on her way home a few times a week. He'd never done anything to encourage the "friendship."

"Hi, Vince," she called out as she walked toward him.

"Hey, Becca." He turned toward the building, then stopped and looked back. "You cut your hair."

"One of the girls did it at school."

He pointed to the left side. "It looks longer on one side."

"It's supposed to." She ran her fingers through it. "Do you like it?"

He supposed he could lie, but that just might encourage her to stick around. "No."

Instead of getting all upset and leaving, she smiled. "That's what I like about you, Vince. You don't sugarcoat things."

There was a reason. Sugarcoating encouraged relationships he didn't want. "You're not pissed about that hair?" The women he'd known would have freaked.

"No. I'll get it fixed tomorrow. Do you need your hair cut? I'm getting pretty good with the clippers."

Pretty good? "That's okay. I don't want my head lopsided."

Again she laughed. "I'd use a number two on you 'cause you look like you like it high and tight."

He thought of Sadie, and not for the first time since he'd left her house. He'd thought of her several times a day since then. If there'd been anything going on beyond mindless demo work, he might be worried about how much he thought about her.

"I need your advice on something."

"Me? Why?" He'd given his sister advice but she'd never listened to him. Becca wasn't even related, so why should he suffer?

She put her hand on his forearm. "Because I

care about you, and I think you care about me. I trust you."

Oh no. A bad feeling pinched the back of his neck. This was one of those times that called for finesse and a precision extraction. "Becca, I'm thirty-six." Much too old for her.

"Oh, I thought you were older."

Older? What? He didn't look old.

"And if my dad was still alive, I think he'd listen to me like you do. I think he'd give me good advice like you do."

"You think of me like your . . . *dad*?" What the hell?

She looked at him and her eyes rounded. "No. No, Vince. More like an older brother. Yeah, an older brother."

Sure. The only time he felt old was when the cold settled in his bones and cramped his hands. There'd been a time when the cold hadn't bothered him much, but he certainly wasn't *old*.

Behind Becca's Bug, Sadie's Saab rolled to a stop, and he forgot about being Becca's dad. Her running lights shut off and the door swung open. The orange sun shot golden sparks off her sunglasses and hair. She was all golden and shiny and beautiful.

"I stopped to get some super unleaded. What's up?" she asked.

"I'm closed for a while."

She shut the car door and moved toward him, the smooth walk she'd learned in charm school with a slight bounce to her step and breasts. A smile tilting the corners of her mouth. The mouth she'd used on him a few nights ago. A hot, wet mouth he wouldn't mind her using again. She wore a white dress he'd seen on her before. One he wouldn't mind taking off her.

"Hi, Becca."

"Hey, Sadie Jo."

The two gave each other hugs like the true Texans that they were. "Your hair looks good," Becca said as she pulled back.

"Thanks. I just got the roots touched up today." Sadie ran her gaze over Becca's hair. "Your hair is . . . darling." She glanced at Vince. "Short and long at the same time. Very clever."

"Thanks. I'm in beauty school and we practice on each other. When I get better, you should let me color your hair."

Since Sadie wouldn't be around when that happened she said, "Fabulous."

Becca dug her keys out of her pocket and

looked at Vince. "I'll stop by tomorrow and say hey."

"Fabulous."

Sadie turned and watched Becca scoot into her Volkswagen and drive away. "How often does she stop by to say 'hey'?"

"A couple times a week on her way home from school."

"Well, that haircut is just tragic." She looked up at Vince through her sunglasses. "I think Becca has a crush on you."

"No. She doesn't."

"Yes. She does."

"No, really. Just take it from me."

"As we say in Texas, 'She's sweet on you.' "

He shook his head. "She looks at me like I'm her . . ." He paused as if he couldn't bring himself to finish.

"Brother?"

"Dad."

"Seriously?" For several stunned seconds she simply stared at him, then her laughter started as a low chuckle. "That is hysterical." As if to prove the point, her chuckle turned into a full-blown laugh fest.

"It's not that funny." He shoved his hands into

the pockets of his cargo pants. "I'm only thirty-six. Hardly old enough to have a twenty-one-year-old daughter."

She clapped a hand to her chest and took a deep breath. "Technically it's possible, old man," she managed before she burst out all over again.

"You about done?"

She shook her head.

He frowned to keep from smiling and gave her his dagger stare. The one used to incite fear in the hearts and heads of hardened jihadists. It didn't work so he kissed her to shut her up. A press of his smiling lips to quiet her laughter.

"Come in and have a beer with me," he said against her mouth.

"You bored?"

"Not now."

Chapter Twelve

Sadie shoved her sunglasses to the top of her head and followed a few feet behind Vince as he moved down the hall past a lighted office, and toward the front of the Gas and Go. Her gaze slid from his wide shoulders in his brown T-shirt, down his back to the waistband of his khaki cargo pants riding low on his hips. He looked kind of sweaty. Hot and sweaty and totally doable.

"Are those brown T-shirts and cargo pants some sort of uniform?"

"Nope. Just easy to keep clean in a sandstorm."

She supposed that made sense if a guy lived in a desert prone to sandstorms. "How long are you closed?" she asked as they walked into the store. The lights were out and the space was filled with shadow and the steady hum of the refrigeration units. The shelves of perishables were mostly empty but coolers were still well stocked.

"Unless I run into some unknowables, two months. Out here I'm going to paint, retile the floors, and put in new counters." He opened the door to the big cooler. "A lot of the equipment is fairly new. He grabbed a pair of Coronas. "Except the wiener roller. That thing has to go. Luraleen calls it 'seasoned.' " He shut the door and screwed off the bottle tops. "I call it a lawsuit waiting to be filed."

The convenience store certainly needed work. It pretty much looked the same as it had for twenty years. "Who's doing your renovations?" She took the bottle he held toward her. "I can't tell you who to hire, but I can tell you who works on Miller time."

"You're looking at the guy doing the renovations."

"You?"

"Yeah, me. I'm going to hire some buddies to come down and help me lay tiles."

She was close enough to inhale the scent of him. He smelled like man and clean sweat. The grayish light in the store darkened his five o'clock shadow to at least nine-thirty.

In college she'd taken a mosaics class. "Are you good at laying tiles?"

He grinned, his teeth a white flash in the variegated light, and raised the bottle to his lips. "Among other things."

They probably shouldn't talk about the other things he was good at laying. "What's Luraleen up to these days?"

He took a drink and swallowed. "Right now she's in Vegas spending the money I paid her for this place." He lowered the beer. "One nickel slot and cheap shot of whiskey at a time."

"Not a high roller?"

"The velvet sofa in her house is from the seventies and all her music is on cassette tapes."

Sadie laughed. "Conway Twitty and Loretta Lynn?"

"Yeah." He took her hand in his, warm and hard and rough. "Right now, I'm taking care of her house for her, but I'm going to need a place to live once she gets back. If I have to hear one more 'cheatin' song' while she and Alvin get it on in her bedroom, I'm going to stab my head." He pulled her behind him down the hall and into the office. Nails and a few splinters of wood were scattered about on the floor and the paint on the walls was a different color where there had once been cabinets hanging on the walls. An olive-colored countertop, an old chipped sink, and one more cabinet still occupied the room. A pair of clear safety glasses sat on an old wooden desk; a sledgehammer rested against the leg.

"Alvin Bandy?" She stopped in the middle of the room and her hand fell from his. "I know him. Short guy with a big mustache and ears?"

"That's him."

"Oh my God. He worked at the JH for a while when I was growing up." She took a drink of beer and swallowed. "He's not that old. Probably in his forties and Luraleen is what?"

"I think she's sixty-eight."

And Lily Darlington worried that *she* was a cougar. "Holy moly. I know women can be desperate." She shook her head and thought of Sarah Louise Baynard-Conseco. "But I didn't know men were really desperate, too. Dang, that's just nasty." She stopped short. "Oh. I'm sorry. Luraleen is your aunt."

He raised one dark brow up his forehead. "He isn't her only boyfriend."

Sadie gasped.

"He's just her youngest. She has several."

Lordy. "Several?" She sat on the edge of the desk. "I haven't had a boyfriend in about a year and Luraleen has *several*. What's up with that?"

He shrugged one big shoulder. "Maybe you have standards."

She chuckled. "You probably wouldn't say that if you met my last boyfriend."

"Loser?"

"Boring." She shrugged. "So are you like your Aunt Luraleen? Several women on a string?"

"No. I don't string anyone along."

She believed him. The night of Founder's Day he'd told her he wasn't good with relationships. "Have you ever had a serious girlfriend? Ever been engaged?"

"No." He took a drink.

Subject closed. She supposed she could ask why, but he didn't look like he was in the mood to answer. "Is Luraleen your mother or father's sister?" she asked instead.

"Mother's, but they were nothing alike." He leaned his hip into the one remaining counter. "My mother was very religious. Especially after my father left."

At least her daddy hadn't abandoned her. "When did your daddy leave?"

"I was ten." He took a drink, then lowered the bottle to his side. "My sister was five."

"Do you still talk to your dad?"

He tapped the bottle against his thigh like he might not answer. His gaze moved across her face before he said, "I talked to him a few months ago. He contacted me out of the blue and wanted to suddenly see me after twenty-six years."

"Did you meet with him?"

He nodded. "He's living in northern California. I guess his latest wife left him and took the last batch of kids, so suddenly he remembered he had another son." He pointed the beer at himself. "Me."

Compared to the other night, he was suddenly a font of chattiness.

"I met with him and listened to him and his problems. At that time, I was all into thinking about forgiveness and shit, but after about an hour I'd heard enough and left."

"Just an hour?" That didn't seem very much time after so many years.

"If he'd asked about my sister or my nephew I might have given him more time." His jaw got tight and his light green eyes narrowed, and Sadie got a glimpse of the warrior in Vince Haven. The

Navy SEAL with a machine gun across his chest and a missile launcher on his shoulder. "What kind of asshole doesn't ask about his own goddamn daughter and grandson?" He raised the bottle. "Fuck him."

And she thought she had issues.

He lowered the beer and its foam bubbled up the neck. "An old buddy once told me that sometimes a person needs forgiveness so they can move on and forgive themselves. If the old man had asked about Conner, I might have given him a chance. I'm nicer than I used to be."

She bit the side of her cheek to keep from smiling.

"What?"

"Nothing. Is Conner your nephew?"

"Yeah. He just turned six. He's really funny and smart, and he sent me a picture he drew of my truck and me. He's big on drawing pictures."

And Vince missed him. He didn't have to say it. It was in the sadness in his eyes and voice. "Does your sister know about your dad contacting you?"

He shook his head. "And I'm never going to tell her." He laughed without humor. "And the ironic thing is that if my father knew who she was marrying, he'd suddenly remember he had a daughter."

"Who's she marrying?" Prince William was taken but Harry was still available.

"She's remarrying her son of a bitch ex, Sam Leclaire."

The name sounded vaguely familiar.

"He's a hockey player with Seattle."

Sadie tapped the mouth of the bottle against her chin. "Hmm." She went to a lot of Coyotes games and was an Ed Jovanovski fan. "Big guy? Even for a hockey player. Likes to instigate? Spends a lot of time in the penalty box? Blond? Hot?"

"Sounds like him. Except for the hot part."

"I saw him play the Coyotes in Phoenix a few months ago." She set the bottle next to her on the desk and, because Vince's green eyes narrowed again and she found him even more handsome when he was all irritated, she added, "He's *smokin'* hot. Or as we say in Texas, 'hotter than a goat's butt in a pepper patch.'"

"Jesus."

"And that's really hot." She turned her mouth upside down in a fake frown. "Don't be bitter."

He frowned as he raised the bottle, but she

doubted he was truly mad. She was fairly sure his ego could take the hit.

"Don't worry." She shook her head and chuckled. "You're really hot, too . . . for a guy old enough to be Becca's dad."

He lowered the bottle without taking a drink. "Are you going to laugh yourself into a fit about that again?"

"Maybe. It's just the gift that keeps giving." She stood and reached for the handle of the sledgehammer.

"What are you going to do with that?"

"Worried?" She tried to lift it with one hand. It hardly budged.

"Terrified."

"How much does this thing weigh?"

"Twenty pounds." He moved toward her and set his beer next to hers.

She used both hands and lifted it a foot off the floor. "I could get a lot of frustrations out and do a lot of damage with this thing."

With one hand, he took it easily from her grasp and tossed it behind him. It hit the floor with a hard thud. "I know a better way to get your frustrations out." His palms slid to her waist and he pulled her hips against his.

She looked up into his face, at his eyes staring down into hers. "What did you have in mind?" she asked, even though against her pelvis she felt exactly what was on the man's mind.

"Doing damage." He lowered his face and pressed his forehead into hers. "Lots of damage."

Heat warmed the pit of her stomach and spread to her thighs. She wanted to press her body against him. Skin against skin. This was why she'd stopped by the Gas and Go. She could have fueled her car in Amarillo or the Chevron across town. She pulled at his T-shirt and tugged the end from the waistband of his pants. "I've had a rough couple of days." She slid her hands beneath and touched the warm, damp skin of his hard belly. "I don't want to hurt you, Vince."

"Do your worst," he said against her lips, a whisper of breath, and she breathed him in. Breathed in his need as hot and fiery as her own. The kiss was surprisingly soft and almost sweet, while against the apex of her thighs, he pressed his ridged erection into her. Lust pooled and burned and she parted her lips beneath his. She kissed him, full-mouthed and hungry. Hungry for more of what he'd given her a few nights ago. Hungry for him to fill her body if not her heart.

She wanted to touch him and for him to touch her. She wanted him to fill up the lonely places, but even as he touched her as she wanted, she knew not to want him too much. He'd made it clear that all he wanted was sex. No dinner. No movies. No conversation. And right now, that's all she wanted, too.

He stripped her to her panties and plopped her down on his desk. He stepped between her thighs, and his hands and mouth moved to her breasts. She arched her back and planted her hands on the desk behind her. His warm, slick tongue drove her insane, and when he finally sucked her nipple into his hot, wet mouth, she moaned and her head fell back.

She didn't love him, but she loved what he did to her. She loved the way he touched and kissed, and by the time he entered her, she loved that most. She planted her feet on the desk and he looked down at her, lust narrowing his green eyes and parting his lips. His hands grabbed her knees and his fingers dug into the tops of her skin. He moved inside her, thrusting deep and stroking all the good spots. His big chest expanded as he pulled air into his powerful lungs.

A warm, tingly orgasm started at her toes and

worked its way through her body. It worked her up and down and inside out, and when it finished working its magic, it left a smile on her face.

"Hooyah."

Through the open windows, a cool evening breeze stirred the lace curtains in Sadie's bedroom. A nightstand lamp cast a nice, warm glow across the bed and Sadie's soft shoulder and the side of her smooth face. Vince slid his hand to Sadie's bare belly and pulled her back against his chest.

"Are you asleep?" he asked as his thumb fanned her stomach.

"No." She shook her head and yawned. "Tuckered out though. Geez, did I just say 'tuckered'?"

He smiled and kissed her neck. He wasn't the least bit tired. After they'd left the Gas and Go, he'd grabbed a pizza from Lovett Pizza and Pasta and met her at the ranch. They'd eaten, then had sex in the bathtub, which hadn't been easy, but they'd managed. Afterward, he'd watched as she'd dried her hair and put lotion on her elbows and feet. It smelled like lemons.

"I worked the hell out of selling those dresses," she'd told him as she sat on a white chair in the bathroom and put lotion on her heels. She'd worn a pair of pink panties and he'd sat on the edge of the tub wearing his cargos. He didn't think he'd ever just sat and watched a woman rub lotion on herself before. He'd liked the view. "I don't think I ever acted so ridiculous about a dress. I know prom is important, but sheesh."

He still wasn't real clear on how she'd come to work for Deeann Gunderson in the first place. Maybe if she wasn't talking while she was half naked, her little pink panties barely covering the pink beneath, he'd be able to focus on what she was saying.

"Those girls acted like they were at Vera Wang." She glanced up and squirted lotion into her palm. "I blame Rachel Zoe."

"Who?" He looked up and attempted to pay attention.

"Celebrity stylist Rachel Zoe? She has her own show on Bravo? Gets fabulous designer gowns and shoes? Just had a baby boy with her husband, Rodge? Any of this sound familiar?"

He shook his head and scratched his bare chest. That's what he got for trying to pay attention.

"She's like the Martha Stewart of clothes and

accessories. She has great style and taste and makes the rest of us feel like inadequate slobs." She'd looked up at him and sighed. "Don't tell me you've never heard of Martha Stewart."

"The lady who spent time in federal prison? I heard of her."

She stared across the bathroom at him. "She's more famous for her stunning cakes."

His gaze slid to her stunning breasts. At her little pink nipples that fit perfectly into his mouth. Sadie had a beautiful body. A woman's body, and she wasn't shy about walking around naked. He liked that about her. He liked that she was confident and open to sex on a desk in a destroyed office. He liked that she didn't play games. And as hypocritical as it was coming from a guy who'd hooked up with his share of random women, he liked that she didn't hang out in bars and hook up with random men. At least, not any that he knew about.

He liked a lot of things about her. No matter her difficult relationship with her father, she'd stayed in town and visited him every day. He liked that she laughed easily. Sometimes at him. Most surprising, he liked that she talked to fill up the silence, even when he wasn't paying all that much attention. Like now as she squirted lotion in her palms and rubbed it into the soft skin of her inner thighs. Holy hell. She smelled like lemon. He liked lemon. He liked inner thighs, too.

"Vince?"

"Yeah?" He returned his gaze to hers.

"I asked you a question."

He'd been trained by the finest military in the world. He could pay attention to several things at once if he chose. "What?"

She rolled her eyes. "Do you always yell 'hooyah' when you orgasm?"

How had they gone from talking about cake to orgasms? "I yell 'hooyah'?"

"Well, more like a groan."

He didn't know that. "That's embarrassing."

"No one's ever told you?"

He shook his head and rose to his feet. "Maybe I only hooyah for you." He walked across the tiled floor toward her. "Do you always ululate like an Arab woman when you orgasm?"

She laughed and looked up at him. "That's embarrassing. No one's ever mentioned it before you."

He knelt between her knees and slid his hands up her bare, smooth thighs. The tips of his fingers touched the elastic legs of her panties. "Maybe no one else has what it takes."

She sucked in a breath and held it. "Apparently you ululate me."

"Hooyah." His thumbs brushed her through the thin cotton and he took her breast into his mouth. He licked and sucked until her nipples were hard, and then he lowered his mouth and buried his face between her legs. He pushed aside the crotch of her underwear, and he'd licked and sucked her there, too.

"Vince." She hadn't ululated. No yelling nor howling. Just a soft moan of his name in the still room. The sound of her pleasure as sweet as the taste of her in his mouth. When he'd entered her tight body, he'd held her face in his hands and watched the pleasure part her lips. He'd felt it grip his dick, contract and pulse and massage his own pleasure.

He lightly bit her bare shoulder. "I'll go and let you sleep."

Her yawn whispered in the darkness. "You can stay if you want."

He never stayed. Leaving in the morning was always more awkward than leaving the night before.

"You can leave before the Parton sisters get here or stay and they'll make you breakfast."

"Wouldn't that be awkward?"

She shrugged. "Your truck has been here two nights now. So I imagine everyone on the ranch knows about you. Heck, probably everyone in Potter County knows. Besides, I'm thirty-three, Vince. I'm an adult."

Even if staying weren't awkward, waking up screaming like a girl and running into walls would be. When her soft, even breathing lifted her chest, he rose from her bed and dressed. He shut and locked her window, and glanced at her one last time before he walked from the room and down the stairs. He turned the lock on the knob of the front door and closed it behind him, making sure she was safe and secure inside. He would have felt better if she had an alarm system and a .357 in her nightstand.

Billions of stars crammed the endless Texas night as he moved to his truck and fired it up, and as he drove down the dirt road toward the highway, he thought of the Gas and Go and everything he needed to get done before he was ready for the real renovations to begin. If not for Sadie, he would have finished the demolition in the office and half the front counter tonight. But the moment she'd stepped out of the car and the sunlight had shone in her hair, he'd known he wasn't going to do anything but get naked.

Billy Idol's "White Wedding" played from the cell phone in his cup holder and he smiled. It was midnight in Texas. Ten in Seattle. He hit the answer button on his steering wheel. "Hey there."

"Hi, Vinny." His sister's voice filled the cab of his truck. She was the only person on the planet to call him Vinny. "Is it too late to call?"

Obviously not. "What's up?"

"Not a lot. How's life at the Gas and Go?"

"So far so good." They talked about his business plan and when he expected to reopen. "Luraleen is still in Vegas," he said. "I wonder if she'll get married by an Elvis impersonator."

"Funny. Ha ha."

Yeah, it was funny now. Six years ago when Autumn had married her ex in Vegas, not so funny. "How's Conner?"

"Good. School's out in a little over a month." Vince turned onto the highway and she added, "He misses you."

His heart felt like it caved in. He'd helped raise

his nephew. Seen him almost every day of his life until a few months ago, but he wasn't Conner's dad. As much as he hated Sam Leclaire, he loved Conner more. He'd left so Sam could more easily step in and be the father his nephew needed. If he'd stayed, the two would have thrown a few punches by now.

"Conner asks when you're coming home."

Home? He didn't know where that was anymore. "I don't know. I have a lot going on."

"With the store?"

She was fishing. "Yep."

"Friend?"

He laughed. His sister thought he was great and didn't understand why he wasn't good relationship material. Oh, she knew he didn't have long-term relationships. She just didn't understand why. "You know I always find friends." Although, at the moment, he had only one *friend* and he was fine with that. There was nothing boring about Sadie Hollowell. "Any big events coming up?"

"My wedding."

Oh yeah.

"It's in a few months, Vin."

He knew. He was just choosing to forget. "Still getting married in Maui?"

"And you're still going to be there."

Shit. He'd rather get kicked in the nuts. "Do I need to rent a tux?"

"No. I'll take care of everything. Just bring yourself. And Vin?"

"Yeah."

"I want you to give me away."

He looked out the window. Give his sister away? To the unworthy son of a bitch? God, he hated that guy. Perhaps with a passion that wasn't all that healthy.

"Dad hasn't been in my life for over twenty years. I want my big brother." He didn't want to. God, he hated the idea. "Please, Vin."

He closed his eyes and clenched his jaw. "Of course," he said, and looked at the road in front of his headlights. "Anything you want, Autumn." Which meant he was going to have to make peace with the son of a bitch before the wedding.

Shit.

Chapter Thirteen

Sadie found some nonskid socks with horseshoes on them at a Target in Amarillo. Her daddy still groused and grumped about not needing anything, but she noticed that he always wore the cozy socks she brought him.

She'd also stopped at the Victoria's Secret in the mall and bought a black lace bra and matching panties. Last night Vince hadn't seemed bored—yet. And she . . . she was walking a thin line between liking him and liking him too much. Between liking sex with him and mistaking it for something more. More than warm skin pressed together in all the right places. More than him knowing where to touch without asking. More than just wanting and craving his touch until neither wanted more.

Rescue Me

Last night when she'd looked at him across the bathroom, sitting on the edge of the tub, watching her, she'd almost thought about more. His eyes, hot and interested in her hands rubbing lotion on her body. They'd already had sex twice and he'd wanted more. She hadn't meant to mention that he groaned "hooyah." She'd been talking about something else entirely. She couldn't even recall what she'd been going on about, but the way he'd looked at her had made her brain go all mushy and made her want more, too. Made her go out and buy new underwear. Not that she'd get to wear the new underwear for four days. She'd started her period that morning, something that was always met with either relief or irritation, depending on her sex life, no matter how condom conscientious she was.

She wasn't positive that Vince would see her new underwear. She hoped so. She liked him, but there were no guarantees in life. Especially when her life was so up in the air. Living long-term in Lovett wasn't in her future, at least not any time soon. As far as she knew, it wasn't in his, either. They were just two people enjoying each other for as long as it lasted.

When she walked into the rehab hospital late

that morning, her father was asleep. It was only eleven A.M. and she retraced her steps to the nurse's station. She was told he had a slight fever. They were watching him but didn't seem worried. Since the accident, he'd had some fluid in his lungs, which was a concern. She asked about it and was told that there was no change in the sound of his lungs.

She sat in a chair by his bed and kicked back to watch some daytime television. Until her father's accident, she'd been fairly unaware of daytime programming, but all the court television shows pulled her in, and she vicariously watched other people's crappy lives. Lives even crappier than hers.

The cell phone in her purse chimed, and it had been so long since it rang at all, she pulled it out and stared at it for a few moments. She didn't recognize the phone number, and she hit the inbox button with her thumb. There was one text with two words: *Bored yet?*

Her brows drew together. Vince. It had to be. Who else would ask if she was bored, but how had he gotten her cell number? She hadn't given it to him and he'd certainly never asked. *Who is this?* she texted back, then set the cell on the nightstand next to the yellow daisies. She looked at her daddy. He didn't appear different, but he was usually up and grouchy by now. She thought about touching his forehead but didn't want to wake him up and have him yell at her.

She turned her attention back to *Divorce Court* and shook her head at the stupidity of some women. If the first time you meet a man, his "rig" is sitting on blocks in his front yard, he probably isn't going to be great husband material. There were just certain bona fides a man had to have. Tires on his rig was below baseline in the bona fides department.

Her cell chimed again and she opened the text and read: *How many men do you have making sure you're not bored at night?*

She laughed and glanced at her dad to make sure he didn't wake up. She ignored the squishy little feeling in her stomach at the thought of Vince and his green eyes watching her. *At the moment . . . one.* She pushed send and he texted her back. *If the guy has what it takes, you only need one.*

She smiled. She really did like him, and wrote, *Hooyah.* Her father moved in his sleep and she looked up at him. He scratched the fine gray whiskers on his cheeks as her phone beeped.

Bored right now? she read.

Sorry. Out of commission for the next few days. She hoped he got her meaning and she didn't have to go into details.

A few minutes later he texted back, *Are your jaws out of commission?*

She sucked in a breath and her thumbs flew across the tiny keyboard in a texting fury. *Seriously?* she wrote. What a jerk. *I'm not going to blow you just because I started my period.* What a horse's ass. And she'd liked him, too. Thought he might actually be an adult.

After several minutes he wrote back. *I was going to ask if you wanted to grab some lunch. What kind of men have you been hanging out with?*

Oh. Now she felt bad and texted back, *Sorry. I'm crabby and crampy.* Which wasn't true. She'd always been fortunate to have light periods with few symptoms. Her father moved again and she wrote one last time before she put her phone away. *Lunch isn't good. I'll text later.*

She reached for her father's hand on the side of the bed. It felt warmer and dry to the touch. Well, drier than normal for a man who'd lived his life in the Texas panhandle. His eyes opened. "Hey, Daddy. How're you feelin'?"

"Right as rain," he answered like always. If the man had arterial blood spurting from his throat, he'd say he was all right. "You're here," he said.

"Like every day." And like every day she asked, "Where else would I be?"

"Living your life," he answered like always. But unlike always, he added, "I never wanted this to be your life, Sadie Jo. You aren't cut out for it."

He'd finally said it. He didn't think she could cut it. Her heart pinched and she looked down at the swirly patterns on the floor tiles.

"You always wanted to do something else. Anything but herd cattle."

That was true. Maybe still was. She'd been in town for a month and a half and hadn't stepped up anywhere near her father's shoes and taken any responsibility for the JH.

"You're like me."

She looked up. "You love the JH."

"I'm a Hollowell." He coughed and it sounded a bit rattly as he grabbed his side, and she wondered if she should hit his call button. "But I hate goddamn cattle."

She forgot about the sound of his cough and calling a nurse. Everything in her stilled like he'd just told her that the Earth was flat and you fell off into nothingness somewhere around China. Like he hated Texas. Like he'd lost his mind. She gasped and clutched her chest. "What?"

"Stupid smelly animals. Not like horses. Cattle are only good for T-bones." He cleared his throat and sighed. "I do love a T-bone."

"And shoes," she managed. He looked like her daddy. Same gray hair, long nose, and blue eyes. But he was talking crazy. "And really nice handbags."

"And boots."

She held up the socks. "I got you something," she said through her fog.

"I don't need anything."

"I know." She handed him the socks.

He frowned and touched the nonskid bottoms. "I guess I can use these."

"Daddy?" She looked at him and it was as if the world was indeed suddenly flat and she was falling off. "If you hate cattle, why are you a rancher?"

"I'm a Hollowell. Like my daddy and granddaddy and great-granddaddy. Hollowell men have always been cattlemen since John Hays Hollowell bought his first Hereford."

She knew all that, and she supposed she knew the answer to her next question. She asked it anyway, "Have you ever thought of doing anything else?"

His frown turned to a deep scowl and she wouldn't have been surprised if he didn't answer or changed the subject as he always did when she tried to talk to him about anything that might make him uncomfortable. Instead he asked, "Like what, girl?"

She shrugged and pushed her hair behind her ears. "I don't know. If you hadn't been born a Hollowell, what would you have done?"

His gruff, scratchy voice turned kind of wistful. "I always dreamed of driving truck."

Her hands fell to her lap. She hadn't known what she'd expected him to answer but not that. "A truck driver?"

"King of the road," he corrected as if living out the dream in his head. "I would have traveled the country. Seen a lot of different things. Lived different lives." He turned his head and looked at her. For the first time in her life, she felt like she was making a connection with the man who'd given her life and raised her. It was just the briefest glance and then it was gone.

"I would have wandered back here though." His voice turned to his usual gruff. "I'm a Texan. This is where my roots are. And if I'd traveled the country, I wouldn't have bred so many fine paints."

And the good Lord knew he loved his horses.

"You'll understand someday."

She thought she knew what he meant, but he'd just been full of surprises today. "What?"

"That it's easy to roam if you have an anchor."

Sometimes that anchor was a heavy burden, weighing a person down.

He hit a button on his bed and raised the head a bit more. "It's the breeding season for horses and cattle and I'm stuck in here."

"Have the doctors said when you might be able to come home?" When that happened, she'd hire a home health care worker to look after him.

"They don't say. My old bones aren't healing like they would if I was younger."

Yes. She knew that. "What has your doctor said about your higher temperature? Other than you're obviously tired."

He shrugged. "I'm old, Sadie Jo."

"But you're tough as old boot leather."

One corner of his mouth turned up a little.

"Yeah, but I'm not what I used to be. Even before the accident, my bones hurt."

"Then take it easier. Once you're out of here, we should go on vacation." She couldn't recall a time they'd ever vacationed together. As a kid he'd always sent her off with her mama's relatives or to camp. She didn't think he'd ever left the JH unless it was business-related. "You said you wanted to travel the country. We could go to Hawaii." Although she could never imagine her father in a floral shirt sipping umbrella drinks on the beach with his boots on. "Or you could come stay with me in Phoenix. There are whole retirement cities in Arizona." Old people *loved* Arizona. "The JH will survive without you for a few weeks."

"The ranch will survive long after I'm gone." He looked at her, the whites of his eyes a dull beige. "It's set up that way, Sadie Jo. We've never talked about it because I thought I had more time and you'd come home on your own. I—"

"Daddy, you—" she tried to interrupt.

"—got good people runnin' everything." He wouldn't let her. "You don't have to do anything but live your life, and someday, when you're ready, it will be waitin' for you."

His words hit her in the chest. He never talked like this. Never about business or the ranch or someday when he was no longer around. "Daddy."

"But you can never sell our land."

"I wouldn't. Ever. I never even thought about it," she said, but she couldn't lie to herself. She'd thought about it. More than once, but as soon as she said the words, she knew they were true. She'd never sell her daddy's land. "I'm a Hollowell. Like my daddy and granddaddy and great-granddaddy." She was a Texan and that meant deep roots. No matter where a person lived. "All my anchors."

Clive patted her hand once. Twice. A rare three times. It was the most affectionate he got. It was like a big old hug from other fathers.

Sadie smiled. "It's a shame I didn't know Granddaddy." By the time she'd been born, both her grandparents had passed.

"He was mean as a skillet of rattlers. I'm glad you never knew him." He pulled his hand from hers. "He'd tan my hide for looking sideways."

She'd heard rumors here and there that Clive Senior had been volatile, but like most rumors involving her family, she'd mostly ignored them.

She had vague memories of her mother's opinion of her grandfather, but her father had never said a word. Of course he hadn't. Wouldn't. She looked at her daddy's profile. Closed and harsh, and she felt like a gauzy curtain was pulled aside for a moment, and the confusing love and longing and disappointment of her life became clearer. She'd always known he didn't know how to be a father, but she'd assumed it was because she was a girl. She hadn't known it was because he'd had a really shitty example. "Well, I'm glad you're my anchor, Daddy."

"Yeah." He cleared his throat, then barked, "Where's that damn Snooks? He was supposed to be here an hour ago."

Typical. When things felt a little mushy, Clive got irritable. Sadie smiled. Their relationship might always be difficult, but at least she understood her daddy just a bit more than before. He was a hard man. Raised by an even harder man.

After she left the rehabilitation hospital that afternoon, she thought about her father and their relationship. He would never be a candidate for father of the year, but maybe that was okay.

She also thought about texting Vince. She wanted to, but she didn't. She wanted to see his green eyes as he tilted his head to one side and listened to her talk. She wanted to see his smile and hear the deep timbre of his laughter, but she didn't want to want it too much.

Instead, she went home and ate dinner in the bunkhouse with the ranch hands and went to bed early. She and Vince Haven were nothing more than friends with benefits. It's what both of them wanted. She'd never had an FWB relationship before. She'd had boyfriends and a few one-night stands. And she really didn't know if she could even call Vince a friend. She liked him, but at this point, he was more a benefit than a friend, and the last thing she wanted was to fall for her benefits man.

Vince parked his truck in front of the main house and walked around the side. In the light of day, the JH was alive with activity. Like a base camp, only with more animals and slightly less dust. And like a base camp, at first glance chaotic, but it was organized and well-orchestrated chaos.

In the distance to his left, calves were herded into a metal chute one by one. The clang of heavy metal carried across the distance. He couldn't see what the men were doing or hear if the calves objected.

It was half past four, and he'd been working all day ripping up old floor tiles inside the Gas and Go. About an hour ago, Sadie had finally texted him. He hadn't seen or heard from her for four days. Not since the morning she'd accused him of expecting a blow job. He wasn't going to pretend that hadn't annoyed him. He wasn't that kind of bonehead, but neither was he the kind of bonehead who sat around waiting for a woman who said she'd contact him and didn't.

He'd spent the past few days working hard, de-molishing the store and filling up the Dumpster. At night, he'd hit a few local bars. He'd raised a Lone Star at Slim Clem's and shot back tequila at the Road Kill, and both nights he'd returned home before midnight. Alone. He could have brought someone back with him if he'd stayed long enough, but as much as he hated to admit it, he'd been tired from hours of hard physical labor. There'd been a time when he'd survived on little or no sleep for days on end. When he'd hiked or jogged or swum against the current for miles, in unbearable heat or bone-numbing cold, often packing sixty to a hundred pounds of essentials, but he wasn't in that kind of physical shape these days, and as much as he hated to admit it, years of pushing his body beyond its limit had taken a toll. These days his pain reliever of choice wasn't tequila. It was Advil.

After four days of not hearing from Sadie, she texted him and invited him to the JH. Clearly she just wanted sex. That was it. He'd never known a woman who just wanted sex and nothing more. Not after he'd been with her a few times. He didn't think he was being egotistical. He liked to excel. To be the best. There was no quit until the job was done. Women appreciated that and always wanted more. But not Sadie. She didn't want more, and he didn't know how he felt about that. He should be thrilled. It was perfect. She was beautiful. Interesting. Good in bed, and only wanted to use him for sex. Perfect.

So why did he feel mildly pissed? And if all she wanted to do was fuck, what was he doing here in the light of day? With all the ranch hands around? Why hadn't she asked him to drive out this evening after dark?

He had a lot he could be doing right now. A lot before his buddy Blake Junger finished up his own business and got his ass to Lovett. Blake was a master of many trades. Deadly sniper and licensed carpenter just two among them.

"Vince!"

He turned his attention to the right and spotted Sadie standing beside a corral attached to a big barn. She wore a pair of jeans and black T-shirt with something on the front and a pair of boots. A blond ponytail was tied at the back of her neck, and she wore the same white cowboy hat she'd worn the night of the Lovett Founder's Day. He hadn't seen her in four days. Damn, she looked good. Just standing there like a beauty queen, and for some reason, that just pissed him off a little more.

Not enough to turn on his heels and leave, though. There was something about Mercedes Jo Hallowell. Something more than her looks. Something that made him drop his pry bar when she'd texted him. He wasn't sure what it was about her. Maybe it was nothing more than that he wasn't done.

Not yet.

"Hey, Vince." Next to Sadie stood a tall, lean man wearing a blue-and-white striped shirt and a wide Stetson. He was a cowboy. A real cowboy.

Tanned from the sun and tough from the life. He looked to be in his fifties and his name was Tyrus Pratt.

"Tyrus is our horse foreman." Sadie introduced the two.

"It's a pleasure to meet you." Vince shook the man's hand. His grip and the look in his brown eyes were as tough as his hide. Vince had stared down drill sergeants and knew when he was being sized up.

"Vince is Luraleen Jinks's nephew."

The hard line around Tyrus's eyes softened. "The new owner of the Gas and Go?"

"Yes sir." He wasn't surprised that the foreman knew. He'd been in town long enough to know that news traveled fast.

"You were a Navy SEAL."

Now that surprised him. "Yes sir. Chief petty officer with Team One, Alpha Platoon."

"Thank you for your service."

He always had a hard time with that. There were a lot of men like him who served for the love of country, not for the glory. Men who didn't know the word "quit" because they felt a purpose, not so the world could thank them. "You're welcome."

Tyrus dropped his hand. "Were you in on the raid on bin Laden?"

Vince smiled. "Negative, but I would have loved to have been there."

"Tyrus just brought Maribell home," Sadie said, and pointed to a black horse standing at the fence. "She's been in Laredo breeding with Diamond Dan. The horse that kicked my daddy in the ribs."

"How is he?" Vince asked.

She shook her head, and the shadow of her hat's brim slid across her mouth. "He had a high fever that indicated possible infection, but his lungs are still the same. As a precaution, they put him on more aggressive antibiotics, and he seemed more like himself today. Back to being cranky and crabby. But I'm still worried."

"He's tough," Tyrus assured her. "He'll be right as rain." He returned his attention to Vince. "It was nice to meet you. Good luck with the Gas and Go, and tell Luraleen I said hey when she gets back from Vegas."

"I will and thank you." He turned slightly and watched Tyrus walk into the barn. "Special Forces have nothing on this town. Do you all have your own Lovett CENTCOM operating in the basement of the library?"

Sadie laughed, and he knew her well enough to know it was the kind of fake laugh she used when she didn't think something was very funny. "I think there's something in the water, but we have our own well out here, so Daddy and I miss out on the gossip. Not that we like it anyway." She looked out across the flat Texas plains and Vince lowered his gaze to the front of the "Cowboy Butts Drive Me Nuts" print on her T-shirt. "It's weird being back. In some ways, it feels like I never left, and at the same time, I feel like I've been gone forever. I don't know a lot that goes on around here these days."

He pointed to the herd of calves. "What's going on over there?"

"Just one of the hundred or so things that has to be done on a routine basis." She adjusted the brim of her hat. "The hands herd each calf into the squeeze chute, tag their ear and weigh each one. Then they enter the information into their computers so they can keep track of them and make sure they're healthy."

"You just said you don't know what goes on around here."

She shrugged. "I lived on the JH for eighteen years. I've picked up a thing or two." Her brows lowered as she looked out over the property. "Now I'm back, and I don't know when my daddy will be well enough for me to leave again. I'd fooled myself into thinking it would be just a few weeks. Maybe a month and I'd be back to my real life. Selling houses, going out with friends, watering my plants and flowers. Now I don't have a job. All my plants are dead and I'll be stuck here through June. At least. June is castration season." The corners of her mouth turned down and she shuddered. "God, I hate castration."

"Good to know."

She laughed as the horse hung her head over the top rail. A real laugh this time. The kind that slid across his skin and made him want to kiss her throat. Right there in front of half a dozen cowboys. In the light of day. When he was still half pissed for no reason.

"You have nothing to worry about, sailor. I like your balls."

He looked into her face. At the corners of her tilted pink lips and smooth cheeks. He couldn't recall if he'd every really noticed a woman's smooth cheeks before. At least not the cheeks on her face. Nor did he remember why he'd been even mildly annoyed with her. "I like a couple things about you, too."

One blond brow rose up her forehead and she turned toward the corral. "Which two?"

The two that filled his hands and bounced nicely when she rode his lap. He smiled. "Your blue eyes."

"Uh-huh." Sadie raised her hand and scratched the side of Maribell's head beneath the blue halter. "Tyrus says you're gonna be a mama again. You doing okay, Maribell?"

The horse nodded as if answering.

"Diamond Dan is a rude asshole. We hate him, don't we?" The horse didn't nod and Sadie patted her nose.

Vince leaned a hip into the fence and crossed his arms over the T-shirt covering his chest. "I don't know anything about breeding horses, but shouldn't there be some sort of precaution. Why was your dad close enough to get kicked?"

"'Cause he's set in his ways." Sadie pulled off her sunglasses and set them atop the brim of her hat. "Have you ever seen horses breed—old school?"

"Not in person. Maybe on a nature show when I was a kid."

"It's violent. The mare is tethered and lead ropes hold the stallion. He mounts her from behind, and there's a lot of screaming and thrashing about."

Sounded like a few women he'd known. He looked into the horse's big black eyes set in her shiny black head. She didn't appear to have suffered. "Maybe she likes it a little rough." Horses mated in the wild. It couldn't be too horrible for the mares or they'd run away. No way a stallion could mount a moving target.

Sadie shook her head and her ponytail brushed the backs of her shoulders. "She hated it."

"Bet I could make you scream if I tied you up." He lifted a brow. "You wouldn't hate it, either."

She looked up at him from within the shadow of her hat. "Does that line usually work for you?"

He shrugged. "It did the last time I used it."

She turned her head to one side and bit her lip to keep from smiling. "I assume that since you are a military man, you can shoot straight."

"Are you talking about weapons?" His expertise with weaponry was wide and varied with the situation, but his own weapon of choice was an automatic Colt pistol. The ACP was accurate to one inch at twenty-five yards and held eight deadly full metal jackets.

"Shotguns. I thought we could shoot trap."

He tilted his head just to make sure he heard her clearly and dropped his gaze to her mouth. "You shoot?" The last shotgun he'd held had been the short version with a pistol grip.

"Is a frog's butt waterproof?" She rolled her eyes. "I'm a Texan and I grew up on a ranch." She shoved the glasses onto her face. "Traps and skeet are two things that Daddy and I did together."

A beautiful woman who was good in bed and wanted nothing from him but sex? A woman who could lock and load and was wrapped up in one soft package? Had he died and gone to heaven?

"I thought that since the benefits part of our friends-with-benefits situation is good . . ." She put a hand on the letters on her T-shirt. "At least I think it's good. I thought we might try the friends part."

Is that what they were? Friends with benefits. "You wanna be friends?"

"Sure. Why not?"

"Ever have male friends?"

"Yes." She raised her eyes to the heavens as if counting. "Well, no. Not really." She returned her gaze to him. "Have you? Had a female friend, I mean."

"No." He slid his hand to her waist and pulled her closer. He didn't believe it was really possible, but he liked spending time with her more than anyone else in town. So, what the hell? "Maybe I could give you a try."

Chapter Fourteen

Sadie stumbled out of bed and stepped over her black lace panties, which lay on the floor. A smile tilted her lips as she reached for her robe and remembered Vince shoving her underwear down her thighs the night before. "You didn't notice my underwear," she'd complained as she'd reached for his belt buckle.

"I noticed," he'd answered, his voice rough with lust as he'd pushed her onto the bed. "I'm just more interested in what's beneath your underwear."

The fact that they'd lasted until after traps before they'd torn at each other's clothes had been a miracle. A frustrating, sexually charged miracle.

She threaded her arms through the purple satin sleeves and tied the belt around her waist. She was competitive, but Vince was super competitive. She supposed she should have guessed that about him. He'd missed the first two clay targets, but once he got the hang of the long barrel and adjusted his shots for accuracy, the guy was deadly. He'd hit forty-one out of fifty pigeons.

Sadie had been shooting clay pigeons for as long as she could recall. She was rusty, which accounted for her score of thirty-three.

She moved into the bathroom and looked at herself in the mirror above the sink. Her hair was a tangled mess from Vince's hands and she looked like crap. Once again, she'd fallen asleep before he'd left, and she was glad he wasn't around to see her so scary.

Eyes still a little bleary, she walked down the hall and back stairs to the kitchen. The ends of her robe flapped about her calves and she came to a dead stop on the last step.

"More coffee, Vince?"

"No thank you, ma'am."

"Oh you. I told you to call me Clara Anne."

Sadie slid her bare feet to the hardwood floor and squinted across the kitchen to the cheery breakfast nook. Bathed in golden morning light, Vince sat at the table, the remnants of a feast in front of him.

Well, this was awkward and embarrassing. "Good morning," she said, and tucked her robe more securely.

Vince glanced up and didn't appear the least bit embarrassed. "Hello."

"Look who I caught sneaking out," Clara Anne said as she reached into a cupboard and pulled out a coffee mug.

She supposed that was a rhetorical question since he was sitting at the table. She took the mug from Clara Anne and poured coffee into it. She'd woken with men in the past, but seeing Vince threw her. Maybe because he was a benefits man. Maybe because now everyone at the JH knew he'd spent the night. Or maybe because he looked so damn good and she looked a mess. If she'd known, she would have at least brushed her hair.

"You cooked for Vince?" she asked as she poured a generous amount of hazelnut creamer into the mug. Clara Anne never cooked.

"Goodness no. Carolynn brought him over a plate from the cookhouse."

Great. No doubt they'd already started to plan her wedding. She raised the mug to her lips and blew into it. Her gaze met Vince's as she took a big drink. She recognized the look in his eyes, reminding her that she was naked beneath the silk robe.

"I have to get going," he said as he tossed his napkin on the table and stood. "It was nice to meet you, Clara Anne. Tell Carolynn I enjoyed her breakfast very much."

"I will and don't be a stranger." Clara Anne gave him a hug and he patted her twice on the back. "You're as big as hell and half of Texas."

He looked over at Sadie, who shrugged and took a sip of her coffee. Hey, he was in Texas. Around natives. Natives were huggers.

Clara Anne let him go and he moved toward Sadie and took her free hand. She was careful not to spill her coffee as they walked to the front door. "I sacked out. Sorry, I don't know how that happened. It never happens," he said in the entry. "Then I got caught sneaking out like a felon."

"And Clara Anne forced you to eat breakfast?"

"She offered and I was hungry." He smiled. "I worked up an appetite last night."

"And wore yourself out?"

"Yeah. Sorry."

"Don't be sorry. It's fine." Although she would have liked a little warning so she could have brushed her hair. "Except you look good and I look like shit."

He kissed the messy part in her hair. "That's the thing about you, Sadie. You can look like shit and I still want to get you naked." He lifted his head and reached for the knob behind him. "See you later."

She nodded and took a step back. "Maybe I'll swing by the Gas and Go."

"Do, and maybe I'll let you swing my sledge-hammer." He opened the door and stepped outside. "Or put you to work prying up old vinyl floor tiles from the fifties."

"Yuck. I'll text first to make sure you're done with that." She said good-bye and closed the door behind him. She let out a breath as she leaned her back against it. She took a sip and figured she had two choices. Head upstairs and take a shower or retrace her steps to the kitchen and convince Clara Anne that a wedding was not in the cards. She took the easy way out and headed up the stairs. She jumped in the shower and washed her hair. She exfoliated with a loofah, then brushed her teeth in the sink. For the past few days, her daddy had talked more and more about the ranch and the day he wouldn't be around much longer. She wished he wouldn't talk like that. It gave her a panicky tightness in her chest. Not just because she wasn't ready for the responsibility of the JH, but because she didn't want to think of her daddy not being here. On the ranch. Breeding his paints. Being a cranky pain in the ass.

Her anchor.

She dried her hair and pulled on a blue sundress over her white bra and panties. Maybe she'd swing into the store and buy him some flowers to cheer up his room. Not that it ever seemed to make a difference.

The phone rang as she swiped her lashes with mascara, top and bottom until they were long and lush. She wasn't much of a beauty queen like her mama, but she did give special attention to her hair and lashes.

"Sadie Jo," Clara Anne called from the bottom of the stairs. "The phone is for you. It's the rehab hospital in Amarillo."

She set down the mascara and moved down the hall to her bedroom. It wasn't all that unusual for one of her father's doctors to contact her after his morning calls. "Hello." She sat on the side of her unmade bed. "This is Sadie."

"It's Dr. Morgan," the geriatric specialist said.

"Hi, Doctor. How's Daddy this morning?"

"When the morning shift nurse checked in on him, she found him unresponsive."

Unresponsive? "Is he just really tired again?"

"I'm sorry. He's no longer with us."

"He left? Where'd he go?"

"He passed away."

Passed away? "What?"

"He died in his sleep between three A.M. when the night nurse checked on him and six this morning."

"What?" She blinked and swallowed hard. "He felt better yesterday."

"I'm sorry. Are you alone? Do you have someone who can drive you to the facility today?"

"My daddy died? Alone?"

"I'm sorry. We won't know the cause of death until after autopsy, but it was peaceful."

"Peaceful." Her face felt tingly. Her hands were numb and her heart felt tight and on fire in her chest. "I . . . I don't know what to do now." What was she going to do without her father?

"Have you made arrangements?"

"For what?"

"Come in and talk to someone in the administration office."

"Okay." She stood. "Bye." She hung up the phone on the bedside table and stared at it. *Thump-thump-thump,* her heart pounded in her chest and head and ears. She grabbed her flip-flops and purse and headed down the hall. Past the wall of Hollowells. The doctor was wrong. Her dad had been himself yesterday. Cranky and cantankerous. Fine.

She moved out the front door to her car. She thought maybe she should tell Clara Anne. Clara Anne would cry. Carolynn would cry. Everyone would cry and the news would beat her to Amarillo. She wanted to hold it in. Hold it inside herself for a while. Until she talked to the doctors. Until she knew . . . she didn't know what.

Miranda Lambert blared from the car speakers as she turned over the engine. She turned down the volume and headed toward Amarillo. Her daddy couldn't be dead. Wouldn't she have known it? Wouldn't she have somehow felt it? Wouldn't the world be different? Look different?

Her mouth was dry and she took a drink from an old fountain Diet Coke in her cup holder. Her ears had a strange, high-pitched buzzing. Like cicadas were in her head. Her fingers tingled and she wondered how it could be that the wildflowers on the side of the road weren't wilting and dying like she was inside.

She drove through Lovett and past the Gas and Go. Vince's truck was parked by the Dumpster in back. Had she just seen him a little over an hour ago? In her kitchen? Eating breakfast? It seemed like more time had passed. Like a week. Like a lifetime. Like when her life had been whole.

Before.

Before her world came apart.

Vince plugged the coffeemaker into the socket in the office and pushed the on button. Most of the demolition was done and the remodeling would begin soon.

A soft rustle drew his attention to the doorway. Sadie stood there. Keys in one hand and a pair of flip-flops in the other.

"Change your mind about ripping up those floor tiles?" he asked.

She looked at him and licked her lips. "I need a fountain Diet Coke."

He slid his gaze over her, from the top of her blond hair to the toes of her bare feet. There was something off about her. "I threw the fountain machine away and ordered new."

"I'll take a can."

Something wasn't right. "I emptied the refrigerators and pulled them out. All that stuff's stacked in a corner of the storage room."

"That's okay. I'll take one anyway."

"You want a hot Diet Coke?"

She nodded and licked her lips again. "My daddy died last night." She shook her head. "This morning, I mean." The keys rattled in her hand and her brows lowered. "The hospital called. I have to go make arrangements." Her brows lowered as if nothing made sense. "I guess."

He dipped his head and looked into her eyes. "Did you drive here, Sadie?"

She nodded. "My mouth is dry." Her eyes were wide, glassy, with the thousand-yard stare of someone in deep shock. He recognized that look. He'd seen it in the eyes of hardened warriors. "Do you have water?"

He grabbed his coffee mug and filled it with water from the sink. He took the keys and shoes from her and handed her the water. "I'm sorry about your daddy." He put her things on the old desk and walked back toward her. "I didn't know him, but everyone who mentioned him had good things to say."

She nodded and drained the mug. "I need to go."

"Hang tight." He took her wrist and placed his fingers over her pulse. "Not yet." He looked at his watch and counted her heartbeats. "Do you feel light-headed?"

"What?"

"Is someone in your family driving you to Amarillo?" Her pulse was fast but not dangerously high. "One of your aunts or cousins or uncles?"

"My daddy was an only child. My aunts and uncles are on my mama's side."

"Can one of them drive you?"

"Why?"

Because she shouldn't be driving around in shock. He let go of her wrist, then grabbed her shoes and keys from the desk. "I'll drive you."

"You don't have to."

He dropped to one knee and put her flip-flops on her feet. "I know I don't." He rose and placed his hand on the small of her back.

She shook her head. "I'm okay."

She wasn't hysterical, but probably not anywhere near okay. They moved down the hall, her shoes softly slapping the soles of her feet. "Will Clara Anne contact everyone for you?"

"I don't know." They stopped and he pulled

a set of keys out of his pants pocket. "I should probably tell her."

Vince looked across his shoulder into Sadie's face as he locked the back door of the Gas and Go. "You didn't tell her before you left?"

Sadie shook her head. "She would have asked questions and I don't know anything yet." Together they moved to his truck and he helped her into the passenger seat. "I'll call her from the hospital when I know something."

Vince grabbed a bottle of water out of the cooler in the bed, then moved around to the other side and climbed inside. As he started the car, he handed her the water and studied Sadie's face. She looked a bit pale, that certain shade of shock white. Her blue eyes were dry, and for that he was grateful. He hated to see women or children cry. It was a cliché, he knew, but he'd rather face a tribe of Taliban insurgents. He knew what to do with terrorists, but crying women and children made him feel helpless.

He pulled out of the parking lot and asked for the address of the hospital. She gave it to him and he plugged it into his GPS. Silence filled the truck as she unscrewed the bottle. He didn't know what to say, and he waited for her to talk so he could take his cue from her. He drove a few blocks and turned onto the highway. When she finally did say something, it was not what he expected.

"Am I the only woman you're sleeping with at the moment?"

He glanced at her, then back at the road. "What?"

"It's okay if I'm not." She took a drink. "I'm just wondering."

Okay his ass. No matter what a woman said, she was never "okay" with that shit. "*That's* what you want to talk about?"

She nodded. "It's half an hour to Amarillo, Vince. I can't talk about my daddy right now." She placed a hand on her chest as if she could keep everything inside. She took a deep breath and slowly blew it out. "I can't do it. Not yet. Not until after I know everything." Her voice wavered and almost broke. "If I start to cry, I won't stop. Talk to me please. Talk to me so I won't think about my daddy dying all alone without me there. Talk about anything."

Shit. "Well," he said as he looked back at the highway, "you are the only woman I've *slept* with for a long time." He still couldn't believe he'd fallen asleep in her bed. He hadn't allowed that to happen since he'd left the teams. If that hadn't been bad enough, he got busted like a kid sneaking out. "And 'at the moment' you are the only woman I'm having sex with."

"Oh." She looked out the passenger window and screwed the cap back on the bottle. "At the moment you are the only man I'm having sex with." She paused for a few seconds, then added, "In case you were wondering."

"I wasn't. No offense, darlin', but I've met some of the single men Lovett has to offer."

She looked down and almost smiled. "There are some really good guys here. Not that I want to date any of them. Mostly because I've known most of them since grade school and remember when they used to pick their noses." The corner of her lip quivered as if for a few seconds she'd forgotten where they were going and why, then suddenly remembered. "Thank God I didn't sleep with any of them."

That surprised him a little. Probably because he'd grown up in several small towns and there hadn't been a lot to do but roll around in hay fields. "None?"

She shook her head. "I didn't lose my virginity until I went away to college."

"What was his name?"

"Frosty Bassinger." Her voice wavered.

"*Frosty?*" He chuckled. "You gave it up for a guy named Frosty?"

"Well, his real name was Frank." She unscrewed the cap and took a drink from the bottle. "How old were you?"

"Sixteen. She was eighteen and her name was Heather."

Sadie choked. "Sixteen? And your girlfriend was eighteen? That's illegal."

"It was my idea and she wasn't my girlfriend."

"You weren't even a relationship guy at sixteen?"

He glanced at her and smiled. "I had a few girlfriends in high school."

"What about since?"

He glanced across at her. At the flat Texas plains, the green and brown grasses passing in the window framing her head. At the desperation in her blue eyes, pleading with him to talk. Just to keep talking so she didn't have to think about her daddy and the reality of what waited for her in Amarillo. "Nothing really since I joined the teams." He'd never been good at small talk or talking just to talk. He'd give it a try if it distracted her. "I don't know anyone on his first marriage, but I know a lot of guys on their third. Good guys. Solid." He pulled to the left lane and passed a Nissan. "The divorce rate in the teams is around ninety percent."

"But you're not in the military now. It's been five years."

"Almost six."

"And you've never fallen in love?"

"Sure." He hung his wrist over the steering wheel. "For a few hours."

"That's not called love."

"No?" He looked over at her and turned the tables. "Have you ever had a real serious relationship? Ever been engaged?"

She shook her head and set the bottle in the cup holder. "I've had relationships, but no one's ever put a ring on it." Her anxiety leaked out her fingers and she drummed the console. "I date emotionally unavailable men, like my dad, and try and make them love me."

"Did a shrink tell you that?"

"*Loveline* with Mike and Dr. Drew."

He'd never heard of *Loveline*, but he'd certainly had a shrink tell him why he ran from relationships. "Apparently I have a disconnect with deep emotions." He glanced at her, then back at the road. "Or so I've been told."

"By a woman?"

"Yep. A Navy psychiatrist." He could feel her gaze on him. "A damn smart woman."

"Why are you emotionally disconnected?"

He was willing to distract her . . . to a point. That point did not include digging into his head or his past. "It's easier."

"Than what?"

Than living with guilt. "Did Mark and Dr. Drew give you tips on avoiding emotionally available men?"

"They gave me warning signs."

"Did you heed their advice?"

Sadie studied Vince's profile from the passenger side of his big truck. His strong jaw and cheeks were covered in dark stubble. He hadn't shaved since she'd seen him earlier, but he looked like he'd showered, and he'd changed his clothes. "The fact that I am in any way involved with you points out the glaringly obvious fact that I didn't listen." Just below the surface of her skin, she could feel her pain and grief aching. It was so close. So close to leaking out if she let it.

"Clearly."

She looked out the window at the dusty Texas plains. Her daddy was dead. Dead. It couldn't be possible. He was too cantankerous to die.

For the next half hour, Vince kept up her plea for him to talk. He didn't run on and on, just a few observations about Texas and Lovett. Every time the silence pushed her close to the edge, his voice drew her back. She didn't really know why she'd pulled into the Gas and Go. She could have driven to Amarillo, but she was glad for his strong, solid presence.

At the hospital, he placed his hand on the small of her back and they moved through the automatic doors. He waited outside her father's room with the nurse while she moved inside. The daisies she'd left the other day sat on the bedside table next to his nonskid socks she'd left out for him. Someone had pulled the sheet up to the chest of his pajama shirt. His old hands lay at his sides and his eyes were closed.

"Daddy," she whispered. Her heart pounded in her chest and throat. "Daddy," she said louder as if she could wake him. Yet even as she said it, she knew he wasn't asleep. She took a step closer to the side of his bed. He did not look asleep. He looked sunken . . . gone. She placed her fingers in his cool hand.

He was gone just as she was beginning to understand him.

One tear and then another slid down her cheek. She closed her eyes and shoved it all down until her chest ached. "Sorry, Daddy. Two got out," she said. He'd been her anchor when she hadn't even known she needed one.

She slid her hand from her father's and dried her cheeks with a tissue on the nightstand. Even in her raw grief, she couldn't lie to herself. He hadn't been a perfect dad, but neither had she been a perfect daughter. Their relationship had often been difficult, but she loved him. Loved him with a deep, soul-devastating ache. She took a breath past the pain in her chest and blew it out. "You did the best you could." She understood that now. Understood it, given his own difficult past. "I'm sorry I wasn't here when you passed. I'm sorry you were alone. I'm sorry about a lot of things."

She kissed his cool cheek. There was no reason to stay by his bedside. He wasn't there. "I love you, Daddy." Emotion clogged her throat and she managed a weak "Good-bye."

She moved out into the hall and made the difficult call to the JH. Vince stood beside her, his hand on her back as he spoke in a low tone to the nurses. Predictably, the Parton sisters fell apart, while Snooks and Tyrus were deeply saddened but not surprised. They were tough old cowboys like Clive and would make sure the JH ran smoothly like always.

She didn't know how she was going to live without her anchor, and over the next five days, she just went through the motions. She ate little and slept less. Her life was a blur. A numb, hazy blur of people stopping by the JH to talk and remember her father. A constant stream of casseroles and Clive stories. A fog of picking out a casket and burial clothes. Of signing documents and writing the obituary. Of discovering that her father had died of heart failure due to deep vein thrombosis. Meeting with the estate lawyer, Mr. Koonz, and the executor of Clive's will.

She'd sat within the lawyer's office, the scent of leather and wood polish filling her blurry head. She sat with five of her father's loyal employees and listened as each was bequeathed fifty thousand dollars and guaranteed employment at JH Ranch for as long as they chose. The lawyer mentioned a trust to an unnamed beneficiary that Sadie assumed was set up for children she might have.

Everything else in his estate was left to Sadie. Everything from his old Ford truck and unexpired insurance policies to the JH.

There was a time, a few short weeks ago, when the weight of responsibility would have overwhelmed her. It overwhelmed her now, only maybe not as much. Now the JH felt a bit more like an anchor than a noose.

He left a letter for Sadie. One that was short and to the point:

"Talking never came easy to me. I loved your mama and I loved you. I wasn't the best daddy and I regret that. Don't let the folks at the funeral home put makeup on me, and keep the lid to my casket closed. You know how I hate people gawking and gossiping."

And through the worst of it, Vince was there. His strong, solid presence just when she seemed to need him. He'd helped her gather her father's things, then driven her to the funeral home the next day. Mostly he'd been with her at night. When everyone was gone. When the house was too quiet. When she was alone with her own thoughts and the numbing grief threatened to swamp her. He came and pressed his body into hers. His solid warmth chasing the chill from her bones. It wasn't about sex. It was more like he came to see how she was holding up and stayed for a few hours.

He never made the mistake of falling asleep in her bed again, and when she woke from a restless sleep in the darkness, he was always gone.

Chapter Fifteen

It seemed the entire population of the Texas panhandle turned out for the funeral of Clive Hollowell. Mourners from as far away as Denver and
Tulsa and Laredo packed the pews of the largest
Baptist church in Lovett. Like a lot of Southern
Baptists, Clive had been baptized at the age of
four after his profession of faith. Other than at his
wife's funeral, no one could actually recall ever
seeing Clive's tall frame sitting in the pews of the
First Baptist Church on the corner of Third and
Houston. But through the years, a lot of Hollowell
money had flowed into the church coffers. Money
that had paid for additions and renovations and
the new forty-five-foot steeple and carillon bells.

Senior Pastor Grover Tinsdale delivered the
sermon, hitting all the high points about sin and

souls and God welcoming His son Clive back. After the pastor took his seat, Sadie moved to the pulpit and gave the eulogy. There was no question about whether she would give it. She was a Hollowell. The last Hollowell. She stood on the dais in her black sleeveless sheath, her hair pulled back, her eyes dry.

Below her sat her father's casket, made of simple pine with the JH brand burned into it, as was due an old cowboy. And like all old cowboys, he'd been buried with his boots on. As was his wish, Sadie insisted the casket be closed, and an arrangement of sunflowers and asters, daisies and blue bonnets, which grew wild on the JH, covered the top.

In contrast to the simple casket, the front of the church was crammed with elaborate floral tributes. Crosses and wreaths and sprays crowded around big photos of Clive and his horses. Sadie stood above all that splendor, her voice clear as she spoke about her father. The Parton sisters loudly wept in the front pew, and she knew that there were those in the congregation who would judge her. They would hear her clear voice and see her dry eyes and whisper that she was an unfeeling and cold person. An ungrateful daughter who'd closed his casket so people couldn't say their good-byes as was proper.

She talked about her father's love of the land and the people who'd worked for him. She spoke of his love for his paint horses. Grown men and women cried openly, but she didn't shed a tear.

Her daddy would be proud.

Following the funeral, the graveside service was held at Holy Cross Cemetery. Clive was laid to rest with generations of Hollowells and beside his wife. Afterward, the JH was opened up for mourners. The Parton sisters and dozens of other members of the First Baptist Church made cucumber and chicken salad sandwiches. They'd set up banquet tables beneath tents on the lawn, and the women of Lovett arrived with funeral food in hand. Recipes handed down through the generations loaded the tables with fried chicken and every conceivable casserole. Salads and five different kinds of deviled eggs, vegetables and breads, and a whole table filled with desserts. It was washed down with sweet tea and lemonade.

Everyone agreed that the service was lovely, and a fine tribute to someone of Clive's stature and reputation. And it just went without saying that no funeral would be considered a success without a few scandals. The first was of course Sadie Jo's emotional distance while real mourners fell on each other's necks. She was no doubt much too busy counting her inheritance to really grieve. The second happened when B.J. Henderson declared that Tamara Perdue's homemade pickled relish was better than his wife, Margie's. Everyone knew that Tamara wasn't above poaching another woman's man. B.J.'s declaration sent Margie into a tailspin, and Tamara's relish ended up on the losing end of an accidental dose of Tabasco.

"Where's your young man?" Aunt Nelma yelled across the parlor at Sadie, who stood near the fireplace sipping her iced tea and just trying to get through the day.

First, Vince wasn't her young man. He was her friend with benefits. He'd been a great friend the past five days, but he was still just an FWB. If she let herself forget that, if she ever let herself crave his solid presence in her life, even for one second, she'd be in deep, deep trouble. And second, Sadie knew for a fact that Nelma was "wearing her ears" and there was no reason to yell. "Vince is at the Gas and Go. I believe he is painting today."

"Your man is handy," she said loud enough to

be heard in the next county. "It's always nice to have a man who is handy to fix stuff and such. Does he have a good dental plan?"

Sadie had absolutely no idea about Vince's "dental plan" nor was she likely to ever know, and there was absolutely no reason for him to attend her father's service. Vince hadn't known Clive, and while Sadie might have found comfort in the weight of his hand on the small of her back, it was best that he didn't attend. His being here would have added another, juicier layer of gossip that she didn't need.

Vince had been real sweet to take her to Amarillo the day her daddy died and the funeral home after, but he wasn't her boyfriend. No matter how much she liked him, she could never forget their relationship was temporary, and as she'd discovered since she'd blown into town two short months ago, life turned on a dime and everything changed in the blink of an eye.

Her life was certainly changed. She had a lot to think about. A lot to figure out. But not today. Today was her daddy's funeral. She just had to get through today, one minute, one hour at a time.

"You poor orphaned child." Aunt Ivella wrapped her arms around Sadie's neck. She smelled like hairspray and powder. "How are you holding up?"

Honestly, she didn't know. "I'm okay."

"Well, nothin' dries as quick as a tear." Ivella pulled back. "It was a lovely service and so many people. Lord, they had to find a second book."

Sadie didn't understand the whole guest book thing at funerals. Perhaps some people found it a comfort, but she didn't ever foresee a day when she would look at it.

"You better get yourself somethin' to eat. There's plenty. Charlotte made her cherry pie. The kind she makes every Christmas."

"I will." She took a sip of her tea. "Thanks for coming, Aunt Ivella."

"Of course I came. You're family, Sadie Jo."

Dozens of relatives from her mother's side had shown up to pay their respects. Most of them had dropped off a casserole or pound cake and left after an hour. The elderly aunts had dug in and were there for the long haul.

"And even though Clive could be difficult," Ivella continued, "he was family, too."

Which was one of the nicest things Ivella had ever said about her late sister's husband. Sadie had made a point of thanking everyone who attended the service and who'd come to the house, but she was sure she'd missed someone. Someone who would talk about the snub for the next decade.

She excused herself from the parlor and ran into Uncle Frasier and Aunt Pansy Jean. It was past four in the afternoon, and Frasier was white-knuckling it until the cocktail hour. Frasier told a slightly off-color joke and Pansy Jean gossiped about Margie and Tamara's pickled relish throwdown. "Tamara Perdue is just naturally horizontal," she said.

After a few moments, Sadie slid into the kitchen and filled her glass with tea. She added a little ice to the glass and rolled her head from side to side. She was getting a crick from so many hugs, and her feet were starting to ache from her three-inch pumps. She wondered if anyone would notice if she sneaked upstairs to change her shoes.

"I hear you're spending time with Vincent."

Sadie recognized that tobacco-rough voice before she turned. "Hello, Mrs. Jinks." Luraleen wore a pink prairie shirt and long bead earrings hanging to the bony shoulders of her "Fabulous Las Vegas" T-shirt. The older woman held a covered dish in her hands. "I didn't know that you were back."

"I got home this mornin'. I came to pay my respects and bring you a Frito pie, is all." She shoved it at Sadie. "I always liked your daddy. He was respectful to everyone."

Sadie took the dish. "Thank you." She was right. Clive had been respectful and had taught her to be respectful, too. "We have a full buffet if you're hungry."

"So are you stayin' in town now?"

"I'm not sure of my plans." And even if she was sure, Luraleen Jinks would be the last person she would tell anything. "I have a while yet to figure it out."

"Don't take too long. Girls can't wait as long as boys," she said, her voice a raspy wheeze. "You've gone back on your raisin', but now your daddy is gone." She held up one bony finger. "You need to remember your place around here."

Sadie just smiled and handed the dish to Carolynn as she moved past. "Thank you again for coming out and paying your respects." She turned and said next to the cook's ear, "I'm going to my room to lie down."

"Of course, sugar. Clara Anne and I will make

sure everything is taken care of down here. You go rest."

Without a backward glance, she moved up the back stairs and down the hall lined with photos of her ancestors. She slipped into her room and out of her shoes. She wanted a few moments of peace and sat on the edge of her bed. Just a little quiet, but voices drifted through the window and up the stairs. Laughter mixed with hushed, respectful tones. She was exhausted but didn't bother to lie down. She knew sleep would just be an exercise in frustration.

She rose and moved down the hall to the closed doors of her father's bedroom. She stood with her hand on the tarnished brass knob for several seconds before she took a deep breath and opened the door. She'd been in here only once since her father's death. The day she'd had to grab his one and only suit, shirt, and string tie. Her daddy had been a man of few words and fewer personal belongings. An old ring quilt lay at the foot of the wrought-iron bed. Three portraits sat on the old wooden dresser: Johanna's Miss Texas picture, the couple's wedding portrait, and Sadie's graduation picture. On the mantel above the rock fireplace hung a painting of Captain Church Hill, one of his favorite and most successful Tovero stallions. Captain Church Hill had died ten years ago.

Tears slid from the corners of her eyes and she bit the edge of her trembling lip as she remembered her daddy talking to her about the history and bloodlines of his paint horses. He'd never really talked to her about growing up on the JH. She'd always just thought it was because he was grouchy and uncommunicative. And both those things were true, but she now knew that he had been raised by a volatile father and he'd had his own unfulfilled dreams of becoming a "king of the road."

A crash from below made Sadie jump. Her heart pounded and she took a step back out of the room. She brushed the tears from her cheeks.

She felt like a cup that was about to overflow. She couldn't stand in the hall staring at her father's things and she couldn't return downstairs. The thought of sipping more tea and smiling politely felt like one drop too many.

She moved into her bedroom and shoved her feet into her old boots. She slapped her Stetson on her head and grabbed her little black clutch from the bedside table. The heels of her boots made a soft thud on the hardwood floor of the hall and down the stairs. She passed several people on her way out the front door, but she didn't stop to say hello. She just kept walking. Past the line of parked cars, down the dusty road. The hat shaded her eyes from the late afternoon sun and she kept going. Anxiety and grief gripped her heart. What was she going to do now that her daddy was gone? What was she going to do about the JH? She didn't have to live on the ranch. She had several options. Get involved in the day-to-day management of the ranch, let the current ranch manager and foremen take over completely, or something in between. She had a meeting with Dickie Briscoe, Snooks Perry, and Tyrus Pratt Monday morning. The ranch manager and two foremen wanted to talk to her about her plans and options. She was now the sole owner of ten thousand acres, several thousand head of cattle, and a dozen registered American paint horses. She was fairly certain she owned a few cattle dogs and a slew of barn cats, too.

A part of her wanted to run, like always. To jump in her car and leave it all behind. Yet there was also a part, a new and intriguing part, that wanted to stick around and see what she could do.

A slight breeze blew the wild grasses and dust. She stopped in the middle of the road and looked back at the house. She figured she'd walked about a mile. She should go back.

"Everyone says Sadie is leaving town as soon as she gets her daddy's money."

Vince glanced up at Becca. He hadn't seen her for about a week. Thought maybe she'd forgotten about him. No such luck. "Is that what everyone is saying?"

"Yep."

He tossed her a cold Dr Pepper out of a Coleman cooler on the floor of the office at the Gas and Go. Today her hair was a short bubble. A little strange but not as strange as the lopsided do she'd had a few days ago. "I don't know her plans." She hadn't discussed them with him.

"Aren't you dating Sadie Jo?"

He knelt and rummaged through the deepest part of his toolbox sitting in the middle of the room. The renovations were taking longer than he'd planned. Instead of working, he'd spent the day looking at apartments, and now he was going to have to stop everything and take a trip to Seattle sooner than he'd expected.

"Aren't you?"

"Aren't I what?"

"Dating Sadie Jo?"

His sex life wasn't Becca's business. "I don't know that I'd call it dating."

"What do you call it?"

He glanced up at the annoying little twenty-one-year-old. "I call it none of your business."

Becca frowned and popped open the can. "I saw the way you looked at her, Vince."

"When?"

"Last week when I was here and she drove up." She leaned a shoulder in the doorway where the jamb had been a few days prior. He hadn't planned to remove the wood doors and moldings, but decades of Luraleen's cigarette stench had seeped into the wood and made it smell like a bar in old Vegas. "You had sparks in your eyes for her."

That was fucking ridiculous. If there had been anything in his eyes, it had been pure lust. "I don't spark," he told the girl who wore glitter on her eyelids. He continued to rummage for his level and added, "I've never sparked."

"Oh, you sparked."

His face felt hot, and if he didn't know better,

he'd think he was embarrassed. Which was just damn ridiculous. He didn't get embarrassed.

"Remember when we met at Tally's wedding?"

He wasn't likely to forget. He rose and grabbed his tool belt off the desk.

"I didn't think I'd ever find someone again after Slade."

He wrapped the soft leather belt around his waist. Lord, she was dramatic.

"But I did. His name is Jeremiah."

He looked up and wondered why she thought he'd care. Oh yeah, she thought he was her dad.

"So I won't be around as much."

Praise Jesus.

"So is Sadie gonna stick around?"

Even if he wanted her to stick around, she'd always said she was going to get the hell out of Lovett as soon as she had the chance. *Back to her real life.* When they'd first met, it was one of the reasons he'd found her so appealing. Now there were a lot of things about her that appealed to him. Besides the obvious, she was smart and tough. These past few days, she'd been strong in the face of her loss. Unlike his own mother who had always fallen to her knees when she fell apart, Sadie stood and faced what came at her with calm dignity. He liked that about her. Sadie's leaving was no longer one of the things he liked about her though. He wouldn't mind if she stuck around. When he'd first driven into town, he'd thought he was going to be around for only a week or maybe two. Shit happened, or to paraphrase Donald Rumsfeld, there were known knowns, known unknowns, and unknown unknowns. The press had made fun of the former defense secretary for that statement, but it made perfect sense to guys like Vince who'd gone into known unknowns only to land in a shit storm of unknown unknowns. He loved a well-executed plan of known knowns. He liked to anticipate complications. Liked to see trouble coming before a known known became a known unknown. Or worse. An unknown unknown where there was nothing left but to blow shit up and shoot anything that moved. Just burn the fucker down.

"You're a nice man and deserve a nice woman."

Which showed how much she knew. He wasn't a nice man. He'd seen and done things he would never talk about with anyone outside the teams. Things civilians would never understand. Horrific things that left a mark on his soul, yet things he wasn't sorry about and would do again if his country asked it of him. Things he would do to protect his family. Only his family didn't need him to protect them anymore.

"I think you're really great, Vince." Her big brown eyes looked across at him.

His phone beeped and he pulled it out of his pocket. He opened the text and read: *Rescue me*. There was a lot to do at the Gas and Go. He'd spent all day looking at apartments, and the last four days he'd spent with Sadie. He was behind on his renovations. He could get in a few good hours yet today. He *needed* to get in a few more hours today before he left for Seattle in a few days. The unexpected trip was going to set him back even further, which could cost him money.

Vince hated losing money almost as much as he hated the unknown unknowns and owing people.

He slid the phone into the side pocket of his cargo pants. "It's late," he said. "Time to go home." He ushered Becca out the back door and jumped into his truck. On the drive out to the JH, he didn't bother to ask himself why he was dropping everything to rescue Sadie. It made no sense, and he preferred things to make sense. A well-executed plan. A clarity of purpose. A known known.

He turned off the highway and drove beneath the entrance of the JH Ranch. He'd like to tell himself that it wasn't anything more than a sex thing. That was the simple answer. Straightforward. Clear. But walking toward him, tiny plumes of dust coming off the heels of her boots, looking sexy as hell, was one smoking hot complication. What old Don Rumsfeld called the known unknowns.

The smart thing to do would be to turn around before the unknown part of that equation blew up into a shit storm. He hated shit storms. Hated the feeling creeping up on him like he was in unfamiliar territory. Every good warrior knew when to abort. To get the fuck out. For half a second he thought of flipping a U. Then she smiled and her hand lifted in a little wave and it felt like someone shoved a fist to his diaphragm. He had to remind himself to breathe. He hit the button on the door and the window slid down.

"Hey there, sailor," Sadie said as a cloud of pale dust rose from the dirt road. She looked through the open window and her gaze met black hair and green eyes set in a face that just seemed to get better-looking every time she saw him.

"Where ya headed?" he asked.

"Anywhere." She waved the dust away. "Interested?"

"Depends." He grinned. "What do you have in mind?"

She smiled, a real smile, for the first time that day. "Poor decisions we'll probably regret later."

He motioned to the empty seat beside him. "Hop in."

She didn't have to be told twice. Several cars filled with mourners had passed her on her walk down the road. They'd been kind and well-intentioned, but she was all talked out. She slid into the seat and pulled the belt around her. "Lord, what a day." She took off her hat and leaned her head back.

"Tired?"

"Mmm."

"How'd it go?" He turned the truck around and headed back toward town.

She turned her head on the rest and looked across the cab at him. This from the guy who said he didn't want conversation? "The service was nice. Tons of flowers, and a lot of people turned out. Enough food to feed a village. Which in Texas is a big deal." Sitting in the comfort of his truck, she let herself relax for the first time all day. Perhaps in the past week. "What did you do all day?" Wow, they alarmingly sounded like a couple. Which was a little scary.

"Looked for an apartment and bought an air mattress and sleeping bag in Amarillo."

"I didn't know you were looking." He wore his usual uniform of brown T-shirt and beige cargo pants. He was the only guy she knew who could wear such bland colors and make them look anything but dull.

He pulled onto the highway. "Luraleen came home last night."

"I know. She was at the funeral and brought a Frito pie afterward."

He glanced at her, then back at the road. "Which is just one of many reasons I moved out."

Her brows lifted up her forehead as she studied his profile, his big neck and shoulders in his tight T-shirt. "You found something already? That was fast."

"I move fast."

"I remember. The second time I met you, you had your hand up my dress."

He chuckled and glanced over at her. "You weren't complaining."

"True."

He reached around the back of his seat and handed her a cold bottle of Diet Coke and a bag of Chee-tos.

She looked at the orange bag in her lap. Felt the cold bottle in her hand, and her chest suddenly got heavy. The bottom of her heart pinched a little. In the past, men had given her flowers and jewelry and lingerie, and her heart was getting all achy about Chee-tos and Diet Coke? "Dinner?" It had to be the emotions of the day. "Careful. Next you'll be asking me to a movie."

"I have an ulterior motive."

She opened the bottle, took a drink, and blamed the funny little feeling in her stomach on carbonation. "I'm pretty much a sure thing. You don't need to ply me with Chee-tos and Diet Coke to get lucky."

"I never rely on luck." He glanced over at her and the corner of his mouth lifted up. "I rely on a well-executed plan. It's called full-circle readiness."

"Is that in the SEALs handbook?"

"Somewhere." He laughed, a soft, amused sound that tickled her pulse. "Somewhere between 'on time, on target, never quit,' and 'grab your sack and jump.'"

She smiled. "Your rucksack?"

"That, too."

"Do you miss jumping out of airplanes?"

He looked out the driver's side window. "Not as much as I used to, but yeah."

"Why'd you get out?"

Several moments passed before he answered, "Mostly because of family obligations."

She thought there was probably more to the story but didn't want to pry. Okay, she *wanted* to pry but felt she couldn't. "What do you miss most?"

"My teammates." He cleared his throat and returned his attention to the road in front of him. "Being part of something with a noble purpose." He paused a moment, then added, "Swimming in the ocean. Attack vehicles tricked out with M–2 machine guns and 40mm grenade launchers. Shooting shit up."

She chuckled and opened her Chee-tos as they pulled into Lovett. "Sounds like my kind of job. I'm a pretty good shot."

He looked at her out of the corners of his eyes. "For a girl you're all right."

"I can outshoot most men. If we have a re-match, I can probably outshoot you, too."

"That would never happen."

True. She'd seen his deadly accuracy, courtesy of his government training. "What else do you miss about the military?"

"I miss finning up and hitting the waves."

"Lake Meredith is about sixty miles west of Lovett." She took a crunchy bite and added, "My uncle Frasier has a pool a few blocks from here, but it's past cocktail hour and Uncle Frasier is probably swimming around drunk and naked by now. I could ask though."

"For the past sixteen years I've lived near the ocean. I prefer it to a pool." He turned onto Desert Canyon Street, then hooked a left on Butte. "Especially a pool with a drunk guy floating around in it like a naked cork."

Which pretty much described Uncle Frasier.

Chapter Sixteen

The Casa Bella Apartment Complex was new and was made of terracotta-colored stucco and Spanish tile roof. There looked to be around twenty units, and Vince pulled the truck beneath a covered parking spot. He led her to an apartment on the second story. It was a basic eight-hundred-square-foot, two-bedroom, one-and-a-half-bath unit. The carpet was clean and it smelled of new paint, perfect for a guy who didn't know how long he'd be living in the small town. "If I'd known," she said as she moved into the kitchen and looked around at the mid-priced appliances, "I'd have brought you a housewarming plant." She opened the refrigerator and set her Diet Coke next to a case of Lone Star and a six-pack of bottled water.

"I don't want a plant." He grabbed her hat and

tossed it on top of a box sitting on the counter. Then he slid his hands to her waist. He pulled her back against his chest and kissed the side of her neck. "I didn't work much at the Gas and Go today. So I shouldn't stink."

She smiled and tilted her head to one side to give him better access. "Does that line work for you?"

"Does it work for you?"

"Apparently."

He unzipped the back of her dress and slipped it from her shoulders. "Your bra's black."

"It matches my panties."

"I noticed." The crepe dress fell to the floor, and he said against her bare shoulder, "I wanta fuck you with your boots on." His fingers moved to the back of her bra. "Does that work for you?"

Oh yeah. She turned, and her bra joined her dress. "Yes, Vince." She pulled his shirt over his head and ran her hands up and down his hard muscles. She kissed the side of his throat and her hand dived down the front of his pants. "You work for me," she said, and wrapped her hand around his thick, corded erection. "You're on time, on target, and never quit." He sucked in a breath and she smiled against the warm skin of his neck. "I believe you called it your 'full-circle readiness.' I like a guy who is fully ready with a really nice, big, hard"—she slid her hand up and down his shaft and over the plump head—"body." She bit the lobe of his ear and whispered, "Fuck me with my boots on, Vince."

And he did. Right there against the refrigerator with her legs wrapped around his waist. It was fast and furious and so hot their skin slid and stuck and she felt burned up from the inside out.

"You're good. So good," he groaned as internal combustion raged through her and she gasped, unable to catch her breath. Her heart pounded and her whole world blew apart. When it was over, when every cell in her body reassembled, she felt different. Not *in love* different. More like *not so alone* different. She'd been surrounded by a crowd of people all day. Hardly alone, but with Vince she felt alive.

"Are you okay?" he asked against the side of her throat, his warm breath tickling her still sensitive skin.

"I am. Are you? You did all the work."

"I like this kind of work." He sucked in a breath and let it out. "Especially with you."

For how much longer? she wondered for the first time since that first night he'd come to her house. She'd known he would fill her nights. She just hadn't counted on him to fill up her life so completely. And it was scary as hell. And letting her mind wander down that scary path meant she cared. Caring wasn't necessarily bad, but caring *too much* would really be bad. Something that at the moment she probably shouldn't think about. She'd think about it later when she had to think about every other screwed-up thing in her life.

Afterward, she sat cross-legged on his back patio, drinking Lone Star. The hard concrete chilled her backside as she watched the setting sun.

"I booked a flight Monday afternoon for Seattle."

Sadie wore her panties and his brown shirt that hit her just above the knees. "Why?"

"Now that I know I'm going to be here for a while yet, I need to get some of my stuff out of storage." He sat beside her with his back against the wall. His bare feet rested on the bottom rung of the wrought-iron railing. He wore his cargo pants and nothing else. "I'm renting a van and driving back." He took a drink. "I'll stick around for a few days and see my sister and hang out with Conner."

"Your nephew?"

"Yeah. And I'm sure I'll have to see the son of a bitch."

"Sam Leclaire?"

"Yep. God, I hate that guy. Especially now, since the rules of engagement have changed."

She took a drink and squinted her gaze at the orange sun sliding below the trees. "Since he's engaged to your sister, you mean?"

"No. Since the SOB bailed me out, I can't hit him now."

Sadie choked. "Out?" she sputtered. "Out of what?"

"Jail." He looked at her out of the corners of his eyes. "I got into it with some guys at a bar last December."

"Some? How many guys?"

"Probably ten." He shrugged like it was no big deal. "They thought they were big bad-ass bikers."

"You fought ten bad-ass bikers?"

"They *thought* they were bad-ass." He shook his head. "They weren't."

Still . . . "Ten?"

"Started with only two or three. The others just piled on until it was a full-on brawl and everyone was swinging at anything that moved."

"What started the brawl?"

"A few guys wanted to run their mouths off and I wasn't in the mood to listen."

"What?" Her mouth fell open then snapped shut. "You got into a fight with bikers because they *said* something you didn't like?" That was crazy. It didn't even make sense. "Couldn't you have just left?"

He looked at her out of the corners of his eyes like she was the crazy one. "I'm all for freedom of speech and shit. But with that freedom comes the responsibility to know what you're talking about. And if you're going to accuse the military of being uneducated rapists, then I have the freedom to shut you the fuck up. No. The *obligation*."

"A biker said that?" She would have thought bikers would defend military guys.

"It was Seattle," he said as if that explained it. "Washington is filled with some crazy liberals."

Now might not be a good time to tell him she'd voted for Obama.

He reached into the side pocket of his pants and pulled out his cell phone. "You drained my energy and I'm starving. Chee-tos aren't going to cut it." He ordered a pizza, then helped Sadie to her feet. "If I keep eating junk and hanging out with you instead of working, I'm gonna get fat."

She stood in front of him and put her hand on his flat belly. "I don't think you have to worry about it."

"I'm out of shape."

"Compared to who?"

He moved into the apartment and she followed him to the kitchen. "Compared to when I trained every day." He tossed her hat from the top of a box on the kitchen counter. "My sister sent me old photos and crap when she sent me my tax information for the past five years." He reached inside the box and pulled out a handful of photos. He tossed several onto the counter, then handed her one.

She looked at the young man with the clearly defined chest muscles and wet shorts. "Goodness." She hadn't thought the guy could get any more buff. She looked from his wet pecs in the photo to his face. "You look so young."

"I was twenty. That was taken the day I passed drown proofing."

She was afraid to ask what that meant and

picked up a photo of Vince on one knee in front of a bullet-ridden wall, a machine gun by his side and decked out in full camo and black scruffy beard. In another he was clean-shaven and doing push-ups with two scuba tanks on his back. "How much do those weigh?"

He turned his head and glanced at the pictures. "About eighty pounds. I didn't mind pushing out reps. I hated 'get wet and sandy.'"

They'd already established that he loved the water but hated the sand. She reached for a different photo of the younger version of Vince with his arms around a woman and a red-haired teenage girl. He wore a white sailor suit with a black neckerchief, white hat, and a huge smile.

"That's my mom and sister at BUD/S graduation." She could see the resemblance to his mother somewhat. To his sister, not at all. "What exactly does BUD/S mean?"

"Basic Underwater Demolition/SEAL."

She could also see the pride in his mother's eyes. If her daddy had a son like Vince, he would have been proud. May have even given him three pats on the back. "Was your father there?"

"No. I'm sure he had something more important to do."

From the little bit he'd said about his father, she wasn't surprised by his answer. But what could be more important than your son graduating from SEALs training? "Like what?"

He shook his head. "Don't know."

"My father didn't attend my high school graduation." But at least she knew what had been more important. "He was branding cattle." She thought of the events of the day and all the Clive stories. Good and not so good. The last time she'd seen him, they'd made more of a connection than they had in years. She got a glimpse into her father that she'd never seen before, but it had no way been the big emotional connection she'd always longed for. "Your father is still alive, maybe he'll change."

"I don't care." He looked into the box and pushed stuff around. "I don't think people change unless they really want to. No one changes just because someone else wants it. And even if he does, it's probably too late."

She didn't think that was true, but who was she to argue? She'd never made true peace with her father. Not the kind of big, satisfactory Hollywood ending that would have tied things up in a nice bow for her. If he'd lived another ten years, she probably never would have gotten that from him. She looked in the box and pulled out a blue helmet with "Haven" written in white on the front and "228" on the sides. "What's this?"

"Second phase BUD/S helmet." He took it from her hands and set it on her head. It fell to her brows. "It matches your eyes."

She pushed it up. "It covers my eyes."

He took out a gold medal from a velvet box and pinned it to the T-shirt. "You look really hot in my helmet and Trident."

"Really?" She chuckled. "How many women have you let wear your helmet?"

"That particular helmet, none." He lowered his mouth to the side of her throat and said against her skin, "You're the first woman to touch my Trident."

She didn't know if that made her special or not, but his warm mouth against her skin did special things to her insides. "I don't have anything for you to touch."

"You have lots of things for me to touch." He slid his mouth to just below her ear. "Soft things. Things that feel good."

"You've already touched those things."

"I want to touch them a lot more." She tilted

her head back, and his helmet fell onto the counter. "I like touching you," he said between kisses across her jaw. "I love going deep."

He loved going deep, but that didn't mean he loved her. In the past, she might have gotten that twisted around in her head to mean that this emotionally unavailable man loved her. He didn't, and she could never let herself have any deep feeling for him.

The doorbell rang and Vince lifted his head. His brows lowered, his eyes a little glassy. "Who could that be? No one but you knows where I live."

"Pizza guy."

"Oh yeah." He blinked. "I forgot."

Together they sat in the middle of Vince's empty living room and chowed down on double pepperoni and drank Lone Star. Sadie was surprised by how much she ate, given her own house was filled with funeral casseroles.

"I don't think pizza is energy food. I feel like a slug now," she said as she leaned back on her elbows and stretched out her full stomach. "If I keep hanging out with you, I'm the one who's going to get fat." At the moment, there was no place she'd rather be. There was, however, someplace she needed to be. "I should probably get home."

"I should probably show you my air mattress first." Vince washed down his last bite with Lone Star and set the bottle on the empty box.

"Why?" She'd seen the air mattress and double sleeping bag when he'd shown her around the apartment. "Does it do something extra special that other mattresses don't?"

"It will once I get you on it."

"Are we gonna spoon nekkid?"

He nodded. "Nuts to butts."

Her soft laugh turned into a yawn. "You're so romantic."

Something was wrong. Sadie sensed it before her lids fluttered open. For several disorienting seconds, she couldn't remember where she was. She heard a thump and looked about the dark room. She was at Vince's. In his sleeping bag on an air mattress. She didn't know how long she'd been asleep, but it was full dark now. She turned her head and looked across at the empty pillow next to her.

"Roger that!"

Sadie rose and grabbed Vince's brown T-shirt

off the floor. Another thud and she threaded her arms through the shirt and moved toward the hall. It sounded like he was fighting an intruder.

"Fuck it!"

"Vince!" She had a fleeting thought of grabbing something to help, but she knew there was nothing.

"Kill all those goat-herding fuckers!"

Light from the kitchen stove worked its way into the hall. One darker shadow moved within variegated light. "Vince?"

"Oh God." He panted hard, like he'd been running for ten miles in the blazing heat. "Oh fuck! . . . Wilson." He moved a few steps back. "Hang on, buddy . . . Shit. I'll fix you up."

Wilson? Who was Wilson?

He knelt; the dim light shone on his naked thigh and waist. Tension made the air thick. "Don't do this, Pete."

"Vince?"

His breathing got worse. More rapid. He coughed and gasped. Light caught on his hard arm, the veins bulging like he was lifting weights. He was huge, crouching in the narrow hall. "Stay with me."

"Vince!" She didn't touch him. Didn't go any closer. She wasn't afraid of him. She was afraid for him. Afraid he was going to hyperventilate or hurt himself. "Are you okay?" she asked, although he clearly wasn't.

He jerked his head up and she thought he might have heard her. "The helo's coming. Hang on."

She turned on the bedroom light and knelt on one knee in the doorway. "Vince!" His wide eyes stared into hers, staring at something that only he could see. Her heart broke for him. Cracked all apart. She didn't mean for it to happen. She had no control.

He jerked his head up and back like he was watching something in the sky. His mouth opened as he pulled air into his lungs, and his hands moved in front of his chest like he was grabbing at some invisible something.

He was usually big and powerful and in total control of everything around him. "Vince!" she yelled.

He blinked and turned his unseeing gaze toward her. "What?"

"Are you okay?"

His mouth snapped shut and his nostrils flared as he breathed through his nose. His brows lowered and he looked around him. "What?"

"Are you okay?"

"Where am I?"

Her heart heaved and cracked a little more. "In your apartment."

The sound of his heavy breathing filled the hall and he returned his wide gaze to hers. "Sadie?"

"Yeah." It felt like she was falling through the cracks in her heart. Right there in the hall of his unfurnished apartment. On the worst possible day of her life. She tried hard. Tried hard not to fall in love with Vince Haven, the most unavailable man on the planet, but she did.

"Jesus."

Yeah. Jesus. She moved toward him and placed her hand on his shoulder. His skin was hot and dry. "Can I get you something?"

"No." He swallowed hard and leaned his back against the wall behind him.

She rose anyway and moved through the living room to the small kitchen. She grabbed a bottle of water out of the refrigerator. She tried hard not to cry for him and for her, but her tears slid down her cheeks and she wiped them away on the hem of Vince's T-shirt. When she returned, he still sat with his back against the wall, his forearms resting on his bent knees. His gaze staring up at the ceiling.

"Here." She knelt beside him and unscrewed the bottle cap.

He reached for the water but his hand shook and he made a fist instead.

"Are you going to be okay?"

He licked his dry lips. "I'm fine."

He wasn't fine. "Does that happen often?"

He shrugged. "Sometimes."

He obviously wasn't up to talking about it. She kissed his hot, dry shoulder. "I love the way you smell," she said. He didn't say anything and she sat next to him and wrapped her arm around his bare waist. She loved him and it scared the hell out of her. "Who's Wilson?"

He looked down at her, his brows drawn. "Where did you hear that name?"

"You called it out."

He turned his gaze away. "Pete Wilson. He's dead."

"Was he a buddy?" She grabbed his fist and forced the plastic bottle into his hand.

"Yeah." Water leaked out the corners of his

mouth as he took several big gulps. "He was the finest officer I ever met." He wiped the water away with the back of his hand. "The best man I've ever known."

"How'd he die?"

"Killed in the Hindu Kush Mountains in central Afghanistan."

Anger rolled off him and tension turned his muscles even harder. "What can I do to help you?" she asked. He'd been so good to her the past week. Just when she'd needed him, he'd been there. Driving her and walking beside her with his hand on the small of her back. Talking to her and sometimes not saying anything at all. Rescuing her even when she didn't ask. Working his way into her heart when that was the last place he wanted to be.

"I don't need help." He stood, and her hand slid down his bare leg. "I'm not a little girl."

She stood up and looked into his green gaze. "Neither am I, Vince." Right before her eyes she watched him draw inward. She didn't know where he went, other than he was gone. "Vince." His name caught in her chest, clogged with emotion, and she wrapped her arms around his neck. She pressed herself against his hard, hot chest and rambled, "I'm sorry. It must be horrible. I wish there was something I could do."

"Why?"

"Because you helped me when I needed you. Because I'm not lonely when you're around. Because you rescue me even when I don't ask you to." She choked back her tears, and opened her mouth to tell him that he was big and strong and wonderful. That he was the best man she'd ever known. Instead something raw and new and really horrible tumbled out, "Because I love you."

Awkward silence stretched between them until he finally said, "Thank you."

Oh God. Had he just *thanked* her?

"Let's get you home."

His hands stayed at his sides, but his words felt like a physical push. She'd just told him she loved him and he reacted with a thank-you and an offer for a ride home.

"It's late."

She dressed quickly in her black dress and shoved her feet into her cowboy boots. Neither spoke much as she grabbed her hat and clutch purse on the way out the door. An uncomfortable silence filled the cab of the truck as Vince drove toward the JH. An uncomfortable silence that had never existed before. Not even the first time she'd seen him standing by the side of the road, the hood of his truck raised.

She didn't ask if he would call or text. She didn't ask when she would see him again. No more declarations of love. She had more dignity than that when the last thing he wanted was her love. He'd always been clear about that, and as she watched the taillights of his truck fade, she knew it was over.

What had she expected? He'd been upfront with what he wanted. It was what she'd wanted too, but somewhere within the past few weeks she'd started to have feelings for him. Started to feel something more than just lust.

She'd buried her father, fallen in love, and been dumped all in the same day.

Chapter Seventeen

The cool, humid wind brushed Vince's knuckles and cheeks and ears. The bad dog pipes of his Harley rumbled the air on Morning Glory Drive in Kirkland, Washington, a suburb of Seattle. The back of Conner's helmet hit Vince's chin for about the tenth time as the two of them slowly rode up and down the street in front of Conner's house. They wore matching leather bomber jackets, but Conner's was tighter on him than the last time the two had driven up and down the street.

It had been five months since he'd left Washington. Five months that somehow seemed like years.

The bike slowed as they rolled toward the split-level house with the rental truck in the driveway.

"One more time, Uncle Vince!" Conner hollered over the reverberations.

"You got it." He flipped a U and headed back down the tree-lined street. Vince lost count of how many times they rode up and down the street. When he did finally pull into the drive behind the truck, Conner protested.

"I don't wanna stop."

He shut off the bike and helped his nephew to the ground. "Next time I'm in town, we'll have to get you a new jacket." He hooked the kickstand with the heel of his boot and lowered it. "Maybe your mom will let us ride to the park." Autumn hated the Harley, but Conner loved it so much she'd always let them ride in front of the house. No faster than fifteen miles an hour.

Conner reached for the strap beneath his chin. "Maybe I can drive."

"When your feet touch the ground, we'll talk about it." He rose off the seat of the bike and swung his leg over. "Don't tell your mom."

"Or Dad."

"What? Your dad doesn't like bikes?" Figured.

Conner shrugged and handed Vince the helmet. "I don't know. He doesn't got one."

That's because the guy was a pussy. "Go tell your mom I'm leaving."

"I don't want you to go."

Vince set the helmet on the seat. "I don't want to go." He knelt on one knee. "I'll miss you." The seams of his jacket popped as he hugged Conner. God, he smelled the same. Like the laundry detergent his mom used and like little kid.

"When are you coming home?"

Good question. He wasn't quite sure. "When I sell the Gas and Go and make a ton of money." Only this didn't feel much like home these days. He didn't know what felt like home anymore.

"Can I have tons of money?"

"Sure." Who was he going to give it to?

"And the Harley?"

He rose and hefted Conner over one shoulder. "Unless I find another little boy to give it to one day." His nephew screeched as Vince swatted him twice on the behind. Then he set him back on his feet. "Now run and get your mom."

"Okay." Conner turned on the heels of his Spider-Man sneakers and headed toward the front door. "Mom!" he hollered as he ran up the steps.

Vince opened the back of the moving van and pulled out a ramp. He wheeled the Harley inside between an outer wall and a leather sofa and tied it down. He'd been in Washington for three days.

Drinking beer with old friends, hanging out with his sister and Conner, and packing up the truck with essentials like his bed, leather couch, and sixty-four-inch HDTV.

"Conner says you want a little boy? I know that I am not one to talk, but you really should have a wife before you have the kid."

Vince looked behind him at the open door of the big truck. The misty morning sun caught in his sister's red hair. "Wife?"

"You need someone in your life."

"You're forgetting Luraleen," he joked.

She made a face. "Someone without a smoker's hack and pickled liver. I just hate to think of you lonely and living with Luraleen."

"I moved out of her house." He thought of Sadie. He hadn't been lonely since the day his truck broke down on the side of the highway. "I was never lonely."

"Never?" Lord, he'd forgotten that he had to watch what he said around her. She knew him so well and pounced on every word. "Did you meet someone?"

"Of course." He rose and moved to the open door. "I always meet someone."

Autumn crossed her arms over her chest, unamused, and stared him down—even when he towered over her—the way she'd always stared him down. Even as kids. "Have you been seeing someone for more than just a night or two?"

He jumped down, grabbed the overhead door, and pulled it closed. He locked the door and shrugged. Autumn knew him better than anyone on the planet, but there were things even she didn't know. Things no one knew.

Except Sadie. She knew. She'd seen him at his absolute lowest. Helpless and locked in his nightmares. God, he hated that she'd seen him that way.

"Vinny!" She grabbed his arm.

She'd taken his silence as some sort of admission. "It's over," he said, hoping she'd drop it even as he knew she wouldn't.

"How long did you date her?"

He didn't bother to explain that he and Sadie never really *dated*. "I met her the night I arrived in Lovett." He looked down into her green eyes. "It ended a few nights ago." When she'd seen him naked and pathetic. She said she loved him. He didn't know how that was even possible.

She gasped. "Two months. That's long for you. Really long. Like fourteen months in dog years."

Vince couldn't even get mad because she was serious and it was more or less true. It hadn't seemed like two months though. It seemed like he'd known her forever, yet not nearly long enough. He turned and sat on the edge of the truck.

"Why did you break up with her?" Autumn sat next to him, and he should have known she wouldn't let it go.

She knew him too well. Knew that he was the one who usually broke things off. "She said she loved me." That wasn't the real reason, but his sister didn't know about the nightmares and he wasn't about to tell her now.

A grin pressed across her lips. "What did you say?"

"Thank you."

Autumn gasped.

"What?" Thank you wasn't bad. It wasn't good, but it was better than not saying anything.

"Then what?"

"Then I took her home."

"You said thank you and took her home? Do you hate her or something?"

Hate Sadie? He didn't hate Sadie. He wasn't real sure what he felt, other than some strange sort of confusion. Both gut-level panic and bone-deep relief churned and burned in his head and chest at the same time. How could he feel both panic and relief that it had ended? It didn't make sense. "I don't hate her."

"Did she yell it out during"—Autumn looked around for prying ears—"sex? 'Cause it probably doesn't count if someone yells it during sex."

He almost laughed. "She didn't say it during sex."

"Is she really ugly?"

"No." He thought of her blond hair and big smile. Her clear blue eyes and pink mouth. "She's beautiful."

"Stupid?"

He shook his head. "Smart and funny, and you'll be happy to know, I didn't pick her up in a bar. She wasn't a one-night stand." Although she'd started out that way.

"That's progress, I guess, but it's sad." Genuine sorrow turned down the corner of Autumn's mouth. "When you lock everything down tight so that the pain can't get out, you also keep good stuff from getting in."

He looked down into her eyes, a few shades darker than his, and a bemused smile lifted his lips. "What? Are you the new white Oprah?"

"Don't make fun, Vin. You're so good at taking care of everyone else. So good at fighting for everyone else, but not yourself."

"I can take care of myself."

"I'm not talking about bar fights. They don't count."

He chuckled and stood. "Depends on if you're on the losing end."

She stood, and he wrapped his arms around her. "Now when is this wedding you're hell bent on having?"

"You know it's in July so Sam's face isn't all messed up for the wedding pictures. All you have to do is show up and walk me down the aisle. I've taken care of everything." She hugged him. "Will you still be in Texas?"

"Yeah. I think for at least the next year." He dropped his hands and thought of Sadie. He wondered if she was going to be sticking around Lovett or if she'd already left town.

A red truck rolled up the street and pulled into the driveway. Autumn looked up at Vince and warned, "Be nice, and I mean it."

Vince smiled as Sam Leclaire, hotshot hockey player, Conner's father, Autumn's fiancé, his future brother-in-law, and all-around son of a bitch, got out of the Chevy and moved toward him. Sam was a few inches taller than Vince and as tough as a bare-knuckled street fighter. Vince would have dearly loved to beat his ass, but he knew Sam would never go down easy. At the moment, the guy had a purple bruised cheek. It was April. Still early in the playoffs. Another game or two, the guy would have an eye to match.

"You look better than the last time I saw you." Sam offered his hand, and Vince reluctantly shook it.

The last time Vince had seen Sam, they'd both been beat up. Sam from his job and Vince from a bar fight. "You look worse."

Sam laughed. A satisfied man living a good life. Vince couldn't recall the last time he'd felt like that. Before he'd left the teams, for sure. Maybe a few glimmers of it in Texas.

Sam wrapped his arm around Autumn's shoulders. "I need to talk to your brother."

"Alone?"

"Yeah."

She looked from one to the other. "Behave," she ordered. Then she gave Vince one last hug good-bye. "Call me when you get to Texas so I don't worry."

He kissed the top of her head. "You got it."

Both men watched Autumn move up the steps to the house, then go inside.

"I love her," Sam said. "You don't ever have to worry about her and Conner."

"She's my sister and Conner is my nephew." Vince crossed his arms over his chest and stared into the hockey player's blue eyes.

Sam nodded. "I never did thank you."

"For what?"

"Taking care of my family when I ran from the responsibility. When I didn't know that everything I wanted, everything that mattered, was here in this forty-year-old house in Kirkland. Not a high-rise condo downtown."

A high-rise condo that had been filled with supermodels and Playboy playmates until last fall.

"It's not where you live," Sam added. "It's who you live with. I'll live anywhere your sister and Conner want to live." He grinned. "I admit though, I'd rather have a bigger spa tub."

Even though it killed him, Vince said, "You're welcome." And even though it killed him, he reminded himself that this was why he'd left Seattle five months ago. "But this doesn't mean I like you."

Sam laughed. "Of course not." He slapped Vince's shoulder. "You're an asshole frog squat."

Vince tried not to smile but lost the battle. "Good to know we're on the same page, dickless." He moved to the driver's side door of the rental truck. He waved good-bye to his sister and nephew watching him from the window, then he headed the U-Haul toward Texas. Home. Toward gossipy little Lovett and the Gas and Go.

Home. When had that happened? When had Lovett, Texas, started to feel like home? And would it still feel like home now? Now that Sadie wasn't a part of his life? He thought of never seeing her again, never seeing her walk into the Gas and Go, never seeing her face looking back at him or her body pressed into his, never feeling her hand on his face or her soft voice in his ear or on the side of his neck, and he got that panicky relieved feeling in his gut again.

His sister had asked about a *breakup*. There had been no breakup. What had happened in that dark corner of his apartment had been more like a destruction. He'd awakened from a nightmare, disoriented and confused and scared shitless.

And humiliated. Sadie was the last person on the planet he'd ever want to see him in that state.

He'd looked into her worried blue eyes and felt like he'd landed ass-deep in the unknown unknowns and he'd done what he'd been trained to do. Blow shit up and kill everything in sight.

He thought of her face. The way she'd looked at him as they'd hurriedly dressed. Waiting for him to say something he hadn't been able to say. Something he'd never told anyone outside his family.

She'd said she loved him, and he'd hurt her. He hadn't even had to look into her eyes as he'd dropped her off at the JH to know how deeply he'd hurt her, and hurting Sadie was the last thing he wanted. For the first time in his dealings with women, he did give a shit about what that said about him. He just didn't know what he was going to do about it. If anything. It was probably best if he did nothing at all.

Sadie hit the button on the door panel of her Saab and the window slid down an inch. Cool air whistled through the crack and across her cheek. The breeze caught several strands of her straight blond hair, blowing them about her face as she headed toward Lovett and home.

Home. Unlike that day several months ago

when she'd driven toward Lovett, she didn't feel anxious and antsy to leave again. She felt at peace with her past. She didn't feel trapped or tied down. Okay, maybe a little, but her future was wide open and that allowed her to breathe when her chest got tight.

For the past week, she'd been in Arizona throwing away dead plants and packing up. She'd tied up a few loose ends, put her little house on the market, and hired a moving company.

The Monday after her father's funeral, she'd met with Dickie and the rest of the managers and foremen as well as various lawyers in Amarillo. She'd had meetings with them in the following days before her trip to Arizona, and she'd learned a lot about the business of running the ranch. She knew she had a ton more to learn, but she had to admit, she liked the business end. All those years of never earning a degree in anything was kind of paying off. Well, except for that Zombies in Popular Media class. She didn't know how the study of zombie movies and their impact on society would be helpful, but who knew what apocalyptic event might happen in the future? She'd never thought there'd be a day when she'd actually want to live at the JH. Never saw that one coming, but she was looking forward to schmoozing lenders as she had as a real estate agent. Working with hard and soft deadlines, and keeping everything organized. She could be involved in as much or as little of the day-to-day running of the JH as she chose. She hadn't really decided how much she would take on yet, but she had come to the conclusion that she was a lot like her daddy. She loved the JH, but hated cattle. Stupid, smelly animals only good for T-bones, shoes, and really good handbags.

She turned off the highway through the gates of the JH. Unlike the last time two months ago, there was no black truck broken down on the side of the road. No big, strong man who needed a ride into town.

She couldn't help but wonder if Vince had returned from Seattle. Not that it mattered. Their friends-with-benefits relationship was over. Done. Dead. Buried. He hadn't tried to call or even text her since that night in his apartment, and she wished she could take back the words she'd said that night. She wished she hadn't blurted that she loved him. Mostly, she wished it wasn't true.

Still.

Rescue Me

The late afternoon sun blazed through the front windshield, and she lowered the visor against the piercing rays. She'd fallen in love with an emotionally unavailable man. A man who couldn't love her back. A man who'd pulled her in, only to push her away. After she said she loved him. On the worst day of her life. Which pretty much made him the biggest jerk on the planet.

Other than her daddy, she'd shed more tears for him than any man on the planet, too. Certainly more than he deserved. She was heartbroken and sick and she didn't have anyone to blame but herself. He'd told her up front he wasn't a relationship kind of guy. He'd told her he got bored and moved on. She wished she could hate Vince, but she couldn't. Each time she worked up to a full head of anger at him, and it wasn't hard for her to do, the image of him naked, pulling air into his lungs, and staring at things only he could see, entered her head, and her heart broke all over again. For her and for him.

Once again she'd fallen for an emotionally stunted man. This time she'd fallen harder and deeper, but as with all the other stunted men who had ever taken up space in her life, she'd get over him.

She pulled the Saab to a stop in front of the main house and grabbed her overnight bag and purse from the backseat. The Parton sisters were still around someplace, but the house was silent when she entered. A copy of her daddy's will sat on top of a stack of mail and other documents on the table in the entry. She dropped her bags and carried the stack into the kitchen. She grabbed a Diet Coke from the refrigerator and moved to the breakfast nook where Vince had once sat, chowing down on Carolynn's ranch hand special.

She flipped through the will that included the letter her daddy had written to her and smiled. Unlike the Hollowells of the past, she would be modernizing the house. She would have all her father's bedroom furniture stored and her own things moved in. The cowhide couch and all the portraits of her father's horses were going into storage also. If she was going to live at the JH, she wanted to make it her own. She was also giving serious thought to taking down the numerous portraits in the hall upstairs. If and when she ever did have children, she didn't want all those ancestors scaring the crap out of her kid as they had her.

She flipped to the part of her daddy's will

that had provided for any unnamed beneficiary, which she'd assumed meant any child or children she might have. She raised the bottle of Coke to her lips and frowned. She didn't know if she'd misheard the clause or if it hadn't been read right, but the clause talked about a trust fund set up for an unnamed beneficiary. An unnamed beneficiary born June tenth of 1985 in Las Cruces, New Mexico.

June tenth of 1985? What the hell did that mean? *Las Cruces, New Mexico?* The trust fund couldn't be about her. She'd been born in Amarillo. And it couldn't have anything to do with any *future* children she might have. What did this mean?

The back door screen slammed shut and Sadie jumped.

"I saw you drive up," Clara Anne said as she entered the kitchen. "If you're hungry, I can get you something from the cookhouse."

She shook her head. "Clara Anne, you were there when my daddy's will was read."

"Sure was. Such a sad day."

"Do you remember this?"

"What, honey?" Clara Anne bent over the document and her hair dipped a little to one side. She shook her head. "What is that?"

"I'm not sure, but why would my daddy set up a trust fund for an unnamed beneficiary born in New Mexico, June tenth of 1985?"

She scrunched up her nose and brow. "Is that what that says?"

"I think so. Did you hear this read in the lawyer's office that day?"

"No, but you can't go by me. I fell apart like a flour-sack dress that day." She straightened. "June tenth of 1985," she pondered, and clicked her teeth with her tongue. "I wonder if this has to do with Marisol? She left in such a hurry."

Sadie lowered the Coke to the table. "Who?"

"Ask Mr. Koonz," Clara Anne suggested, then bit her lips together.

"I will. Who's Marisol?"

"It's not my place to say."

"You already did. Who's Marisol?"

"The nanny your daddy hired right after your mama died."

"I had a nanny?"

"For a few months and then she left. She was here one day and gone the next." Clara Anne folded her arms beneath her breasts. "She came back about a year later with a baby. We never believed that baby was your daddy's."

"What?" Sadie stood before she realized she'd jumped to her feet. "What baby?"

"A girl. At least the blanket was pink. If I remember right."

"I have a sister?" This was crazy. "And I'm just now hearing about it?"

"If you had a sister your daddy would have told you."

She scrubbed her face with her hands. Maybe. Maybe not.

"And don't you think everyone in town would have talked about it?" Clara Anne shook her head and dropped her arms. "They'd still be dinin' out on it at the Wild Coyote Diner."

Now that was true enough. If Clive Hollowell had an illegitimate child, it would be the topic of the century at every dinner table in town. She would have certainly heard something by now.

"Then again, me and Carolynn were the only two here when Marisol showed up that day. And we never spoke about it."

Chapter Eighteen

The Road Kill bar hadn't changed much in ten years. Country music poured from the same Wurlitzer jukebox. Old road signs and stuffed critters still decorated the walls, and fashion-minded patrons could purchase rattler skin belts and tanned armadillo handbags from a display case behind the mahogany bar. The owner of the Road Kill was a taxidermist on the side. And it was said that Velma Patterson, bless her heart, had hired him to stuff her poor yappy dog, Hector, the unfortunate victim of some maniac hit and run driver.

Sadie sat at a table near the back corner beneath a stuffed coyote, its head lifted and howling at the ceiling. Across from her, dim bar lights reflected off Deeann's red pouf as the two of them threw back a couple of margaritas. Deeann had called earlier and talked Sadie into meeting her at the bar. Not that she'd had to twist Sadie's arm. Sadie hadn't had anything else going on and a lot on her mind. She'd met with Mr. Koonz that morning and discovered that her daddy had been supporting "the unnamed beneficiary" for the past twenty-eight years. There was no acknowledgment of any paternity. Or even any name on the Wells Fargo bank account in Las Cruces. At least that's what her father's lawyer told her, but Sadie didn't believe him.

"I always try and get out on the weekends that the ex has the boys," Deeann said as she sipped her blended drink.

Sadie preferred hers served over rocks. Less chance of brain freeze. For her outing at the Road Kill, she'd worn a simple white sundress, a blue cardigan, and her boots. The more she wore the boots, the more she remembered why she'd liked them so much. They were so worn in; they fit her feet like the caress of a glove.

"The house is too quiet without the boys."

Sadie knew a thing or two about quiet houses. Once the Parton twins left for the night, the house was too quiet. So quiet she could hear her daddy's horses in the corral. So quiet she listened for a phone that never rang, a beep from a text message that was never sent, and the sound of a truck that never rolled up to her front door.

"We haven't really had a chance to chat since before your daddy died." Deeann took a sip. "How are you doin'?"

"Busy." Which was how she liked it. Busy so she didn't have time to sit around and think about losing her daddy. And Vince. Although she supposed Vince had never really been hers to lose.

"I drove past the Gas and Go the other day, and noticed the new signs. When is Vince opening again?"

Sadie had seen the new signage and Vince's truck parked on the side of the building on her way through town that morning when she drove to the lawyer's in Amarillo. Her heart had sped up and stopped all at the same time. A painful pound and dull thud. A pain that stung the backs of her eyes, and she'd tried really really hard to hate him. "I don't know when he'll open the Gas and Go."

"Aren't you two dating?"

Dating? "No. We're not together. He's free to

see whomever he wants." She took a drink and swallowed past the hurt in her chest. "You can date him." Although she should probably warn Deeann that Vince would get bored and move on. Possibly on the worst day of her life. The day she buried her daddy and had to put up with his aunt's Frito pie. Asshole.

Deeann shook her head, and her brows lowered over her brown eyes. "I'd never date a friend's ex. Vince is a good-lookin' guy and all, but that's just wrong. It's against the rules. The girl code."

Sadie knew there was a reason she liked Deeann.

"Although . . ." Deeann stirred her drink. "I did date Jane Young's former boyfriend." She lifted one hand to the side of her mouth. "But she casts a wide net, if you know what I mean."

Sadie leaned forward. It had been so long since she'd sat around with girlfriends, she'd forgotten how much she missed it. And, yes . . . gossip. As long as it was about someone she didn't like. "Jane gets around?" Which she normally wouldn't hold against a girl. But Jane had a bad soul.

"Well, as my grandmama used to say, 'She lets her hair down and everything else.'" She dropped her hand to the table. "And she took up with my ex Ricky for a time."

Sadie gasped. Deeann had been friends with the Young girls since charm school. "That's against the rules."

"She thinks I don't know." Deeann shrugged and toyed with her silver necklace. "If she didn't buy jewelry from me, I'd freeze her out."

Ah, Deeann didn't let the friend code get in the way of her mercenary heart. Good for her.

"Her old boyfriend was way better in the sack than Ricky. It's a miracle I got two boys out of that man."

Sadie laughed and the two ordered another round. She sipped it as the Road Kill filled with people she'd known most of her life. She played pool in the back room against Cain Stokes and Cordell Parton and managed to lose to both. She had a good time, but by eleven she was ready to leave. The veterinarian was coming out to the JH in the morning to check out Maribell and give her a Pneumabort shot. Tyrus was capable of taking care of the mare, but Maribell was getting older and this would be her last foal. The last of her daddy's foals, and Sadie just wanted a second opinion that everything was progressing as it should.

She put her cue away and headed out of the back room to find Deeann.

"I was just coming to find you," Deeann said from the middle of the bar. "Vince is here."

Sadie lifted her gaze above the pouf in Deeann's hair to the defined pecs in a T-shirt several feet behind her. He wore his customary brown T-shirt and cargo pants, and the sight of him made her heart squeeze. She lifted her gaze up his wide neck and chin to his green eyes looking back at her.

"Do you want to go?" Deeann asked.

"No." She shook her head even though she'd been planning on leaving. In a town the size of Lovett, she was bound to run into him. Best to get it over with. He moved toward her and she forced herself to stand perfectly still. Not run away or swing at him or wrap her arms around his big chest.

He tilted his head to one side and looked into her face. "How are you, Sadie?" he said above the noisy bar.

The sound of his voice brushed against her and tugged at her insides. "Getting by."

He crossed his arms over his chest. "Are you staying in Lovett?"

"For now." Small talk. With Vince? She couldn't do it. Not without falling apart.

"This is my buddy Blake," he said, and motioned to the man standing beside him. "He's helping me with the counters at the Gas and Go."

Sadie turned to the man she hadn't noticed before and wondered how she could have missed him. He was big and blond and obviously military. She stuck out her hand. "It's a pleasure to meet you, Blake."

Blake grinned and took her hand. "Pleasure's mine, sweetheart."

Vince stuck his arm out and placed a palm on his friend's chest. They exchanged looks, and Blake turned his attention to Deeann. "I love redheads. What's your name, beautiful?"

Sadie fought not to roll her eyes but Deeann ate it up like a peanut patty. The two had hardly exchanged names before they were off to the back room to play pool.

"You need a drink?"

Standing so close, her heart pounded in her chest and throat. "I was just on my way out."

His gaze lowered to her lips. In that way he had of watching her talk. "I'll walk you."

"No need."

He placed his hand on the small of her back and she let him. Like it was no big deal. Like he hadn't shattered her heart. Like his touch didn't make her want to curl into his chest. Like she didn't hurt so badly she wondered why she didn't die from it.

"How are things at the JH?"

Like the touch of his hand and the smell of his skin didn't muddle her head and confuse her senses. "I might have a sister," she blurted as they stepped out into the cool May night. She hadn't meant to confess that to anyone. Especially not Vince. They weren't friends anymore. He didn't need to know her business, but she knew him well enough to know that he wouldn't mention it to anyone. She didn't have to ask him not to.

"What?"

"Nothing. Forget it. Never mind." Once outside, she stepped away and his hand fell to his side. "It might not even be true, and I wouldn't even know how to find her if it is true."

They moved beneath the stars cramming the dark Texas sky, but Vince found no calm on this night. Peace did not soothe him. He hadn't known Sadie would be at the Road Kill. Hadn't known how he would feel the first time he saw her again. Hadn't known it would feel like the world was falling apart beneath his feet even as it stood absolutely still. Hadn't known his lungs would burn with each breath he tried to catch.

"There's my car." She pointed to the left, and the crunch of gravel beneath the heels of her boots filled the space between them. The last time she'd worn those boots, he'd been deep inside her, up against his refrigerator. Lost in her and not thinking about the end. Not thinking about anything but how good being with her felt. "You can go back in now," she added.

He couldn't go back. Not now. They stopped by her driver's side door and he reached for her. She stepped back, and once again his hand fell to his side. "I never wanted to hurt you, Sadie," he said.

She looked down at the toes of her boots. "I knew you'd get bored and move on."

"I wasn't bored." He didn't make the mistake of reaching for her again and curled his hands into fists. "Never bored."

She shook her head, and the moon shone in her pale hair and the side of her face. "It doesn't matter."

"It does."

"Then why did you treat me like I didn't matter?" She looked up and placed a hand on her chest. "Like I was nothing."

Because she'd seen him at his worst. Because he hated that he had nightmares like a little girl and now she knew about them. Because he'd felt lower than nothing. "*You* were never nothing."

"I always knew you'd move on. I always knew it would end, but did you really have to break my heart on the same day I buried my daddy?"

"I'm sorry."

"Couldn't you have waited? At least one day?"

He hadn't meant to end things at all. He'd give anything to take back that night. To have stayed awake all night and not allowed himself to fall asleep. To have stayed awake and watched her while she slept. "I'm sorry, Sadie."

Moonlight bounced off her forehead as she lowered her brows. "Sorry. People who step on my foot say they're sorry. You stomped on my heart and that's all you can say? You're sorry?"

"Yeah." Mostly he was sorry that he was standing next to her and couldn't touch her. He couldn't talk to her about all the stuff he'd done at the Gas and Go and listen to her talk about everything happening in her life.

She moved before he saw her coming at him. She placed her hands on his chest and pushed hard. "Sorry?" She was so angry she actually shoved him back on his heels. "You probably think that makes everything okay."

"No." He placed his hand over hers. "Nothing is okay anymore." He slid his palm to the side of her head and lowered his face to hers. "I want you," he whispered. "I've never wanted anything like I want you."

"Vince." His name on her lips brushed his and blew him apart. He came undone. He kissed her. Devouring her with a hot hunger he didn't even know rested in his soul. It burned him up in a raging inferno of primal need and longing. Bursting and unrestrained. Wild and out of control. His hands moved over her. Touching, pulling her against him as his mouth ate her up. He wanted to pull her in, eat her up, and never let her go again.

"Vince!" She pushed him and took several steps back. "Stop it." She raised the back of her hand to her mouth. "I won't let you hurt me anymore."

His lungs ached as he pulled air deep, trying to catch his breath. "I don't want to hurt you."

"But you will." She opened the door to her Saab, but she wasn't going anywhere. She was his. He could change her mind.

He grabbed the top of the doorframe. "You said you love me." He wanted her to love him. Wanted it more than he could recall ever wanting anything in his life.

"I'll get over it." Beneath the light of the moon, a tear ran down her pale cheek. It punched him in the gut and he dropped his hand to his side. "Stay away from me so I don't love you anymore. Stay away so I don't feel anything for you anymore."

Sadie didn't cry. Not on the day her daddy had died or the day she'd buried him. Vince watched her drive away, feeling numb and gutted at the same time. Helpless. Like when he'd tried to save Pete.

The primal inferno raging through him turned outward. Real rage. The kind of rage he'd felt during the days after Pete had died. During the days he'd fought to get his hearing back and later after leaving the teams he'd loved. And the rage he'd felt the night he'd taken on a bar of bikers.

Chapter Nineteen

Sadie arranged the pillows on her bed and stood back to study her handiwork. Perhaps a splash of purple was needed. The next time she drove to Amarillo, she'd look for something at a bed and bath store.

She looked around the master bedroom with a mix of sadness and peace. She'd made the room her own, with her white bedroom furniture and big white area rug, and she felt at home. Comfortable. Captain Church Hill still hung above the stone fireplace and her mama and daddy's wedding photo sat on the mantel, but everything else had been taken out and stored in the attic. Everything but the silver brush and comb set she knew her father had given her mother on their wedding night. She'd found the set in her father's sock drawer with an old string tie and had decided to leave both on her own dresser.

The veterinarian had stopped by earlier and checked on Maribell. He and Tyrus had done an ultrasound on the fetus and learned that the mare would deliver a little stallion next fall. Somewhere in heaven, her daddy was doing a happy jig. Probably with her mama.

Sadie moved from the room and down the hall filled with portraits, still unsure what she wanted to do with all those old pictures. She walked down the stairs to her daddy's office and sat behind the old wood and hide desk that would definitely have to go. The old leather and Navajo chair was comfy and might stay though. She opened up her laptop and wrote "finding lost relatives" in the search engine. She had to find something interesting to fill her days. Fill the lonely void. She couldn't call Vince to rescue her anymore, and finding a long-lost sister—if she had a long-lost sister—seemed like the right thing to do. If Sadie had been kept in the dark her entire life, what did her sister know? And if she really did have a sister, what was she like?

Finding her was like flying blind. She didn't know how to go about finding a long-lost person.

She had a mother's name, birth date, and hospital. The information of her daddy's trust he'd set up and a bank account number, but she didn't know what to do with the information. She didn't know whom to trust with the information, either. It wasn't something she wanted to get out. At least not yet. The only person she'd told was Vince, and that had been a total accident.

She glanced up from the computer screen. Seeing Vince had been hard. Just looking at him made her battered heart ache all over for him. Then he'd kissed her with more passion and lust than she'd ever felt from him before. He'd packed more need in that kiss than all kisses combined. Probably because he hadn't found a replacement for her yet, and it would have been so easy to kiss him back. To let him touch her and go home with him and make love. He wanted her. He'd said it himself, but he didn't love her. And she was through loving men who couldn't love her as she deserved to be loved. If nothing else, her daddy's death had taught her not to wait around and hold her breath for a big declaration that some men just weren't capable of giving or feeling.

The doorbell rang and she waited for Clara Anne to answer it. When it rang again, she rose and moved to the entry. She swung open one side of the big doors and Vince stood on the JH's big welcome rug. Gone was his usual uniform of T-shirt and cargos, today he wore a white dress shirt and khaki pants like the night of Tally's wedding. All that was missing was a tie. He was big and strong and looked so good it tied her stomach in a knot.

He stared at her through those green eyes of his, seeming to take her in all at once. Touching her here and there with his gaze. "Sadie" was all he said.

After a few long moments she asked, "Why are you here?"

"I brought you a name."

"Of?"

"Someone who can find out if you have a sister." He handed her a slip of paper he'd folded in half. "He'll do as little or as much as you need."

"Thank you." She took it from him and slipped it into the back pocket of her jeans. "You didn't have to drive all the way out here to give this to me. You could have texted me the information."

"There's more."

"What?"

"Invite me in." He cleared his throat. "Please."

More? How could he know more? She hadn't given him any information. She stepped aside and he moved past her in the entry. She turned and leaned her back against the closed door.

"Last night after you left the bar, I wanted to kick some ass. I felt like shit and I wanted to make someone feel as bad as I was feeling. I would have done that in the past."

Sadie glanced at his hands then up to his clear face. "But you didn't."

He shook his head, and a lopsided smile twisted his lips. "If I show up with a black eye at my sister's wedding, she'll kick *my* ass." He paused and his smile fell. "Mostly I didn't because I don't want you to think I'm the kind of guy who can't control himself. For the first time in my life I care what a woman thinks of me. I care what you think."

The bottom of her heart squeezed a little and she tried not to make his words mean something they didn't. Caring what someone thought wasn't love.

"Last night when I saw you, I thought we could just go back to the way things were. That we'd just pick up where we left off."

"That's not possible."

"I know. I never meant for you to be anything other than a one-night stand."

"I know." She looked down at the floor beneath her feet. She'd never meant for him to be anything but a friend with benefits. But the friend part had turned to love.

"But one night turned into two and two into three and three into a week and a week into two weeks. Two weeks into two months. I've never been with a woman as long as I was with you."

She looked up. "I guess I should be flattered that it took you longer to get bored."

"I told you last night I wasn't bored. I wasn't ready for it to end."

"Then why did it?"

He folded his arms across his chest. "Because you saw me that night. I never wanted you to see me like that. No one besides a Navy doc knows about the dreams and I never wanted anyone to know. Especially you." He shook his head. "Never you."

She pushed away from the door. "Why?"

"Because I'm a man." He shrugged and dropped his hands to his sides. "Because I'm supposed to handle everything. Because I'm a Navy SEAL. Because I'm a warrior and don't have

PTSD. Because I'm not supposed to be afraid of a little dream."

"It's not a little dream."

He looked over her shoulder at a vase filled with yellow roses Clara Anne had cut from the garden. He opened his mouth and closed it again.

"How long have you been having them?"

"Since Pete died. On and off for about six years."

"Your buddy, Pete Wilson?"

"Yes."

"What happened to Pete?"

He looked at her, but once again, she thought he was seeing beyond her to something she couldn't see. And like the last time, it broke her already broken heart. "It should have been me. Not him. We were pinned down, taking heavy fire, bullets slamming into trees and rocks, coming from every side. Pete blasted away, shooting at everything with one hand as he radioed for air support with the other. We were boxed in, with the Marines below us firing straight up at the Taliban. But there were so many of them. Hundreds. No way to fall back off that fucking mountain. Too many terrorists. Nothing to do but slam new magazines in the breech and hope to hell the airstrike happened in time to save our asses."

She felt an urge to place her hand on the side of his face and look into his eyes. But she didn't. She loved him but she couldn't touch him. "I'm glad you didn't die that day."

He looked to his left again. "Pete took three bullets. One to his left leg and two to the chest. I didn't get hit. At least not by Taliban bullets. The fighter-bombers and attack choppers screamed in and blasted the living hell out of the crevasses until all those Taliban fighters were obliterated. When the rescue helos finally rocketed in from the south, Pete was gone. I was deaf and puking my guts out, but I was alive."

Sadie held up one hand. "Wait. You were deaf?"

"From the concussion of the airstrike." He shrugged like it was no big deal. "I got it all back but about sixty percent in my left ear."

So that's why he watched her talk sometimes. She'd thought he liked watching her lips.

"I've never told anyone about Pete, but you saw me at my worst, I thought you should know that. I came out here today to tell you why I acted the way I did after you saw me pathetic and . . . Well, saw me in the corner of the hall."

He didn't owe her an explanation. "You weren't pathetic."

"A woman should feel safe around a man. Not find him shaking in a corner, yelling at shadows."

"I always felt safe around you. Even that night."

He shook his head. "A man should take care of a woman. Not the other way around. You saw me at my worst and I'm sorry about that. I'm sorry for a lot of things, especially that I just dropped you off that night. I was kind of hoping you could forget that whole night ever happened."

"Is that why you drove all the way out here?" He should know she didn't gossip. Well, about anything other than Jane's promiscuity. "I would never talk about it to anyone." And as far as being dumped on her doorstep, she wasn't likely to ever tell anyone about that, either.

"I'm not worried about you telling anyone. And that isn't the only reason I'm here. There's more."

More? She didn't know how much more she could take before she fell apart again. Like last night when she'd bawled all the way home. She was just grateful no one had seen her.

"I'm sorry I made you cry last night."

Crap. It had been dark and a single tear had leaked out. She wished he hadn't seen that. Wished she'd been able to suck it up better.

"I don't ever want to be the reason you cry again."

The only way that could happen was if he left and gave her time to heal her shattered heart. She took a step back and reached for the doorknob behind her. The backs of her eyes stung and if he didn't hurry and leave, she was afraid he might see her cry again. "Is that all?"

"There's one more thing I came out here to tell you."

She lowered her gaze to the third button on his shirt. "What?" She didn't know what there was possibly left to say. Just goodbye.

He took a deep breath and let it out. "I love you."

Her gaze rose to his and a single "What?" whispered from her lips.

"I'm thirty-six, and I'm in love for the first time. I don't know what that says about me. Maybe that I've waited for you all my life."

Her mouth fell open and she sucked in a breath. She was feeling kind of light-headed, like she might pass out. "Vince. Did you just say you love me?"

"Yes, and it scares the hell out of me." He swallowed hard. "Please don't say thank you."

She bit the side of her lip to keep from smiling or trembling or both.

"Did you mean it when you said you love me?"

She nodded. "I love you, Vince. I thought you'd be just a friend with benefits. Then you became a real friend and brought me Chee-tos and Diet Coke. I fell in love with you."

"Chee-tos?" He frowned. "That's all it took?"

No, there'd been a lot more. "You rescued me, Vince Haven." She took a step toward him and tipped her head back to look up into his eyes. Whenever she'd needed him, he'd been there.

"I'll always rescue you."

"And I'll rescue you, too."

One corner of his mouth turned up. "From?"

"From yourself. From turning thirty-seven without me."

He placed his hands on the side of her face. "I love you, Mercedes Jo Hollowell. I don't want to live without you for another day." He brushed his thumb across her cheek and bottom lip. "That son of a bitch Sam Leclaire said something. Something about it not mattering where a person lives. It's who you live with." He kissed her and added against her lips, "God, I hate when that guy is right."

Sadie chuckled and reached for Vince's hand. Sometimes an anchor wasn't just a place, it was a person. The JH was her home. Vince was her anchor. "Let's go."

"Where?"

"Someplace more private. Someplace where you'll rescue me from these tight jeans and I'll rescue you from those non-issue pants."

"Hooyah."

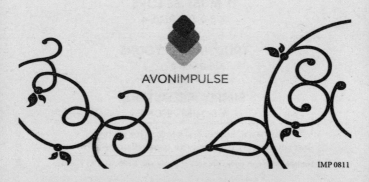